LO♥E,
IN THEORY

FLANNERY
O'CONNOR
AWARD
FOR
SHORT
FICTION

Nancy Zafris,
Series Editor

LO♥E,
IN THEORY

TEN STORIES BY E. J. LEVY

The University of Georgia Press

ATHENS & LONDON

Published by the University of Georgia Press
Athens, Georgia 30602
www.ugapress.org
© 2012 by E. J. Levy
All rights reserved
Designed by Kaelin Chappell Broaddus
Set in 11/15 Arno Pro
Manufactured by Sheridan Books
The paper in this book meets the guidelines for
permanence and durability of the Committee on
Production Guidelines for Book Longevity of the
Council on Library Resources.

Printed in the United States of America
12 13 14 15 16 C 5 4 3 2 1

Library of Congress Cataloging-in-Publication Data
Levy, E. J. (Ellen J.)
Love, in theory : ten stories / by E.J. Levy. — 1st ed.
p. cm. — (The Flannery O'Connor Award for Short Fiction)
ISBN-13: 978-0-8203-4349-5 (alk. paper)
ISBN-10: 0-8203-4349-8 (alk. paper)
1. Lesbians—Fiction. I. Title.
PS3612.E93685L68 2012
813'.6—dc23   2012006675

British Library Cataloging-in-Publication Data available

"Theory of the Leisure Class" was first published in the *Paris Review* (166, 2003).

For my beloved

An ounce of practice is better than tons of theory.

—*Sadhana Tatwa*, H.H. SRI SWAMI SIVANANDA

La théorie, c'est bon, mais ça n'empêche pas d'exister.
(Theory is good, but it doesn't prevent things from existing.)

—CHARCOT

CONTENTS

ACKNOWLEDGMENTS

GRATEFUL ACKNOWLEDGMENT IS MADE TO THE FOLLOW-
ing publications, where these stories first appeared: "Theory of the
Leisure Class" in the *Paris Review*; "The Best Way Not to Freeze"
in the *Gettysburg Review*; "Theory of Enlightenment" (as "Supernatural Powers") in *Mid-American Review*; "My Life in Theory" in
Bloom; "Rat Choice" in the *Missouri Review*; "Small Bright Thing"
in the *North American Review*; "Theory of Transportation" in *Ever-
green Chronicles*; "The Three Christs of Moose Lake, Minnesota" in
the *Chicago Tribune*; "Gravity" in *PRISM International*; and "Theory
of Dramatic Action" in *Another Chicago Magazine*.

I wish to extend my deep appreciation to Nancy Zafris, series editor and wonderful writer, for selecting my collection for this award
and for guiding me through the process of publishing my first book; I
am grateful to the terrific staff of the University of Georgia Press, especially Regan Huff, Jane Kobres, Melissa Buchanan, Kaelin Broaddus,
and Sydney DuPre, and to freelance copyeditor Courtney Denney.

Finally, I am indebted to the teachers Lee K. Abbott, Nicholas Delbanco, Donald Faulkner, Michelle Herman, Maureen Howard, Michael Martone, Melanie Rae Thon; inspiring friends Maureen Aitken, Jennifer Cognard-Black, Lauren Fox, Stephanie Grant, Wendy Leavens, Gretchen Legler, Glenda Morgan, Sawnie Morris, Mei Ng, Linda Lightsey Rice, C. W. Riley, Lisa Schamess, Cheryl Strayed, Marly Swick, Amy Weil, Suzi Winson, Betsy Wolf, and the wonderful D.C. writers group (Carolyn, Amy, Leslie, Kitty, and Ann); the editors, judges, and agents whose recognition and guidance supported and spurred: Bob and Peg Boyers, Charles Buice, Elyse Cheney, Alan Cheuse, David Lynn, Maria Massie, Speer Morgan, Richard Peabody, George Plimpton, Christina Shideler, Evelyn Somers, Debra Spark, Peter Stitt, Elizabeth Taylor; and especially Howard Levy, who ordered the chaos, and Maureen Stanton, who showed me the way and kept faith.

LO♥E,
IN THEORY

THE BEST WAY
NOT TO FREEZE

THEY MET IN A CAMPING EQUIPMENT STORE, WHERE HE was working as a clerk and she had come to rent a pair of climbing shoes. The store was a block from the university where she taught composition in the Department of English. She was adjunct faculty there, though she referred to her status as abject. She made less than the graduate students, after all: $2,700 for each ten-week class. No health insurance, no benefits. On her salary she could not afford therapy, not even sliding scale; she could not scale it at all, she'd told the receptionist who'd quoted her prices by phone the week before, $80 to $100 an hour—"That's a scale I'd slide right off," she said; the receptionist asked if she'd like to make an appointment; "No, thanks," she said. "Maybe next crisis."

Instead, she signed up for a women's rappelling class, part of the low-cost stress-management program they were promoting at the campus health clinic. They offered yoga, they offered meditation, they offered people the chance to throw themselves off cliffs. She opted for this last, though she could not see the sense of sending

1

anxious people to the brink of a bluff to cure them, but it was something she could afford and of all the options on offer only it had the cast of a vacation. According to the promotional flyer, they would travel on three consecutive Saturday mornings by bus to Taylors Falls, an hour north of the Twin Cities, a state park known for its waterfalls and scenic rock formations, hidden caves and high cliffs. The lemon-yellow flyer was optimistic, urging its readers to "confront your fears and practice techniques for self-esteem and stress management through this fun, recreational, noncompetitive sport."

She was standing in the aisle across from the cash register looking at camping equipment—at the water bottle holders made of colorful nylon and netting, at the shapely stainless steel objects (espresso makers, pots and pans), at all the many things she could not, for the most part, identify or afford but which she picked up and inspected anyway, knowing all along that she was wrong to admire them for their color and shape, ignorant of and indifferent to their uses but liking nonetheless the fleece, the nylon in neon orange and teal and violet. She pondered the nature lover's ironic predilection for wildly unnatural colors and synthetics, trying all the while to get up the nerve to ask where they kept the shoes (store clerks terrified her; she preferred to shop from catalogs, whose models did not watch her as if she might be pilfering the goods)—when she heard his voice beside her.

"Can I help you find something?"

She looked up into the sort of face that, as a general rule, scared her—huge and German. He possessed an unnatural breadth and height, as if he were another species. She was embarrassed to be caught fingering the goods, as though she'd been found inspecting dildos in a sex shop, though a dildo she could've justified perusing as a cultural critic. Here there was no excuse.

"I need to rent some shoes," she said, "for climbing."

He was not handsome, but he held her interest the way beauty did, or ugliness, though he was neither. His eyes were pale as a wolf's, and he had a large square head that seemed carved from balsa. He looked too old for her, she thought, though this was a casual unconsidered thought, the way, as casually, she would undress an attractive stranger walking toward her on the street or unthinkingly catch the scents of things—exhaust, burning rubber, baking bread, coffee. Deep grooves bracketed his mouth. A slight muscular pouch bulged at the curve of his jaw; he had a cleft chin. He looked like he should be advertising stew.

"For rappelling?" His voice was soft, in contrast to his size.

"Yes," she said. His name tag said Ben. *Big Ben,* she thought. *Gentle Ben. A clock, a bear.* He was huge as a wall; she wondered idly what size shirt he'd wear.

"Size?" he asked.

"Excuse me?"

"Shoe size?"

"Five."

Delicate, she thought she heard him say, as he turned away.

"Excuse me?" she said again.

He turned to her. "I said, 'It'll be a minute.' That okay?"

While she waited, she perused a bulletin board that hung on the wall beside the wrap desk. There were notices for climbing clubs and hiking clubs and even archery; there were ads for adventure tours in Costa Rica and Belize; there were posters exhorting students to row crew and drive a Subaru. There were hand-written index cards printed with neat inked lettering, offering a kayak, a canoe, a six-person tent, a backpack with internal frame. Wanted and unwanted things.

And then she saw the warning signs. Tacked to the board in neat sheaves were Xeroxed flyers warning campers how to protect themselves from bears, how to treat poison ivy and oak, how not to freeze. Her life was full of information that had no practical application, so she liked that all this did. There were never postings like this in libraries; they did not offer warnings and survival tips to their habitués, though perhaps, she thought, they should. But the flyers reminded her too that venturing out into the world was a risk and that she could get hurt out there.

The flyer on how not to freeze described hypothermia and listed its signs and steps to take. Among the Warning Signs were *Racing thoughts and/or mental confusion. Lack of coordination. Mood swings. Unrealistic expectations. Marked indifference to physical circumstances.* By such standards, most of the people in her department were in imminent danger of dying of hypothermia. The Danger Signs were more precise: *chills, disorientation, drowsiness, loss of appetite.* Under the heading How Not to Freeze were four simple steps.

"You said size five, right?" he said.

"That's right," she said.

She tore the flyer from the bulletin board, figuring she'd read the four steps later. You never knew what you might need to know, especially in Minnesota in winter, and lately, despite all her education, she felt clueless. She folded the flyer in half and went to pay at the register.

"Don't I need to try them on?" she asked, as he rang up the shoes.

"One size fits all," he winked. "Don't worry. The leather's soft. They'll stretch."

She wondered if he meant anything by the wink, but decided he probably didn't. She hated to get her hopes up. Pessimists, a Harvard study had found, had a far more realistic view of life.

While he bagged her shoes she rambled irrelevantly, nervously confiding: She told him that she was teaching English at the university, that she didn't know squat about rocks.

He handed her the bag. "You'll learn," he said. "Doing's the best way to learn."

"You know what they say," she said. "Those who can't do—"

"And those that want to learn need teachers." He had a nice smile.
She stuffed the colored flyer into the bag with her receipt and
shoes.

"Have a safe trip," he said.

She said, "You, too." Then hated herself for sounding dumb, all the
way out of the store.

In her apartment, she tried on the rented shoes. They were like ballet slippers made for hoboes, a patchwork of red and green and beige
suede panels. Tight and unshapely, like foot condoms. She was very
particular about shoes. She was very particular. This much she knew
about herself. In the mirror, inspecting the shoes, she saw how she
must look to others, to all the people who were not her.

She could see that she was pretty, rail thin and frail as china, austere, and slightly awkward; she liked order in her appearance and
in her place. She kept her cuticles trimmed, her eyebrows plucked,
her Oriental carpets (inherited from her grandmother) vacuumed;
ivory lace curtains hung in front of her windows. She could never live
with anyone; it was too late for that. Her half brother had a family, a
brood; she was the smart one, the one with the PhD (which she insisted meant Perfectly Hopeless Degree), a shoe collection, tea pots
and plates in bone-colored glaze; on weekends she refurbished furniture, collected cheap antiques; her one-bedroom apartment was elegant and orderly, color-coordinated in sea foam and bone. She had
a four-poster bed she'd bought secondhand and a down comforter
she'd gotten on sale; flannel and linen sheets with a ruffle draped
over the box spring.

She had made a beautiful life, a comfortable life she shared with
no one. Her hair was straight and chestnut brown, blunt cut at her
shoulders like a young girl's, the same hair cut she'd had since fourth
grade. She had good bones and no breasts to speak of. She joked that
she was the only person she knew who had to go to a tailor to have

darts put into her bra. She had the hungry lines fashionable in Kate Moss, the ethereal frame of the heroin addict, the fair translucent skin of the English, which she just might be.

Truth was, she didn't know whose kin she was, and she thought about it only at such moments as this when she faced herself in a mirror and wondered who it was she might resemble. She looked nothing like her mom or dad or half brother. Of her biological parents, she knew only this: that her mother had been a graduate student and unmarried, Caucasian, Protestant, when she'd given her daughter up for adoption at a hospital in 1968. She had no real interest in knowing more. But sometimes, at conferences, when distinguished lady lecturers took to the podium, their graying hair pulled up in a chignon or cut neat and short, she sometimes wondered, *Is that she?*

When she went to stuff the shoe bag under the sink, in the bag of bags she kept there beside the recycling, she heard the crunch of paper and remembered the warning signs. She took out the flyer. She considered throwing it out but instead clipped it with a magnet to the fridge, beside a picture of herself holding a snowball in one hand, like a trophy.

She liked the ironic juxtaposition—a flyer on hypothermia tacked to her freezer door. As a scholar, it was her job to see things in relationship to other things; the only thing she couldn't see in a relationship was herself. In her mind's eye—as in the photo on the fridge and the birth certificate that bore her name and no one else's—she was always and forever alone.

On Saturday morning, she got up early to drive to campus and catch the charter bus that would take her with the others to Taylors Falls. The October air looked thin and blue, and she wondered if she was making a terrible mistake. The program was called Wild Women, a title that seemed to underscore just how tame they really were. As she merged onto 94, heading east to campus, she imagined what the others would be like. Because it was sponsored by university health services, they would be students mostly. The undergraduates would be shy, ungainly girls with unhealthy interests in medieval lit and crushes on their bald and aging mentors; they would dress badly, in tight turtlenecks that hugged the shelves of their large breasts and ample waists; they would tack up posters of Virginia Woolf in their apartments and name their cats Tristan and Cassandra; they would subscribe to the *New York Review of Books* and use the word *vexed* when they meant *pissed off*. These girls would have long hair and fragile glasses. They would be named Eden and Astoria by parents who'd raised them in communes and later become real estate agents; the girls' impractical abstraction would be their understated revenge. Then again, they might be anorectic grad students with a nicotine pallor and breakable bones; disdainful of conversation, they would remain miserable and silent at the back of the bus, staring longingly out the window. The grad students would study Gramsci and Walter Benjamin and feel a kinship with suffering genius; they too suffered for scholarship. The faculty—assistant, associate, tenured, and abject—would be merely out of shape and embarrassed to be here. Prozac would seem like a good option to them after this. That or a quart of Scotch.

When she arrived at Coffman Union, a sporty twenty-year-old handed her a waiver to sign, with which she promised to hold no one but herself responsible for her injury or death. It asked for her next of kin, a question that depressed her. It was humiliating to write her mother's or her father's name. She would have to admit they were her parents after all, since the adjacent blank requested Relationship to You. Instead she named her brother, whose phone number she could not now recall. She made one up. It broke her heart. She was thirty-three and her closest kin were just that, kin.

In thirty-three years on this earth, she had found no one to love, no one love made hers. She was not involved with anyone and hadn't been for longer than she cared to consider. (The last time she'd heard from a beau on Valentine's, it was an ex- who called to ask if she was seeing anyone. She told him no. "Perhaps you should seek professional help," he said.) Truth was, she had dated boys in high school, men in college, grad school, here, but it never took. She seemed vaccinated against passion. The men she dated were friendly, good companions; they discussed the subaltern and structuralism; they went to movies; they went to bed, but somehow nothing ever grew from this. No feeling blossomed in the thin soil of the mind; though they talked endlessly about sex as a performative category, the performance was only so-so. Love somehow got left behind, defied their reasoning. These relationships ended as they began, cordially, in corridors and seminar rooms, on e-mail, collegially. Without hard feelings, or soft.

She had an MLA, an APA, a *Chicago Manual of Style*. She had tomes on rhetoric and comp, on modernism, postmodernism, feminist essentialism, the structuralists, post-structuralists, and post-coloniality, but none of them could tell her the first thing about love. And where could you get instruction in that?

Ben was not working on Monday, when she returned the climbing shoes to the camping store, but the following week she seemed to see him everywhere—getting off a bus at Nicolett and Fourth, drinking frothy cappuccino in a café on Lake. But it was never him she saw when she looked closer. She decided that it was simply Minnesota, land of ten thousand blondes, and that a lot of guys here wore jeans like his, work boots, red-and-black wool hunting jackets; a lot of guys were huge and blond with giant freckled heads and pony tails (in Minnesota it was still and forever 1975). She was crossing the pedestrian bridge over the Mississippi, connecting the East Bank of the campus to the West, on her way to teach her Friday class, and thinking this, when she realized that, shit, it was him, walking toward her. He seemed as surprised as she, and as delighted.

"I'm just heading to lunch," he said. "You wanna grab some Vietnamese? You have time?"

"Sure," she lied and cut her own class. Her students did it all the time, after all.

Later he would tell her that he'd walked that bridge every day that week—sometimes two, three times a day—hoping to run into her. He'd been ready to give up when they finally met.

"I'm glad you didn't give up," she said.

"So am I."

For the first two weeks, he was an anecdote she told to friends. A punchline. A subject heading in her e-mail. She called the time they spent together "weird dates." There was the boat show at the Convention Center. There was the polka fest in New Ulm. Miniature golf. The Laurel and Hardy film festival. A canoe trip by moonlight. Bowling, without irony. They saw each other almost every night. He was eager to get involved and made no bones about it. His divorce, he told her, had been finalized a month ago, though it had been in the hands of lawyers for a year. He was tired of being alone. He was forty-two. He had no children and no pets. He wanted some.

"Which?" she asked.

"Both," he said.

"Do you have a breed in mind?"

On her third and final Saturday among the Wild Women, she threw out her back and had an intimation of what it would be like to be old. She called her friends from bed and told them that she wanted to die young. "Too late," they said and laughed. "Ha ha," she said. She lay in bed, too uncomfortable to read, too awake to sleep. She hadn't had a chance to clean the apartment, and it hurt when she sneezed. To pee, she rolled to the edge of the bed, bent her legs over the side, and let the painful weight of gravity pull her upright, pinching a nerve as she made her way to the bathroom. To catch the phone when it rang, she charged the kitchen wall bent over.

If he hadn't called her that Saturday night to ask how the climbing trip went, if he hadn't come and nursed her when she told him that she'd pulled a muscle in her back, if he hadn't been there that whole weekend, it would have been a misery. But he was. He came over straight away. He brought a brown paper sack with a bottle of Jim Beam, three fat lemons, and a jar of honey in it.

He made himself at home. He put on music ("What the heck is this?" he asked, coming on her Suicide Commandos CD and the Sex Pistols. He opted for Bach pieces played by Yo Yo Ma) and settled into the kitchen. She could hear him among her pots and pans. When he came back into her room, he had a steaming mug in one hand and a tumbler of whiskey and ice in the other.

"What's this?" she asked, accepting the mug.

"Hot toddy," he said.

"I strained my back," she said. "I didn't catch a cold."

"An ounce of prevention," he said, and sipped his drink.

He helped her to turn over, face down, then rubbed her neck. He massaged Tiger Balm into the muscles of her ass, working his thumbs down the knots that ran the length of her spine. He sat cross-legged at the end of the bed and took her left foot in his lap and began to massage the arch, working to the toes, then back to the heel and the ankle. Then he did the other foot. Growing old, she realized, would not be half bad if she had someone to grow old with—if she had him.

At the end of their first month together, he cooked her dinner at his place in St. Paul—a one-bedroom with a redwood deck and a garden share out back. He served her things he'd killed himself: wild duck in morel sauce; lettuce from his garden with pansies and tomatoes and dandelion greens mixed in; pumpkin soup from pumpkins he'd grown here. He took her into the bathroom so that she could see out the one window that overlooked the backyard. He pointed out the pumpkin patch below where green vines snaked across black soil. Proud as a papa.

Sometimes their dates seemed like a send-up of romance, but she knew that he was not being ironic. She liked him for this, and it gave her the creeps, his earnestness. And then, sometimes, just as she was about to write him off, he would surprise her with what he knew—star constellations and opera plots, a passion for Haydn, a fluency in French—things, it turned out, he'd learned from his ex-wife, who, it turned out, was a concert pianist and an associate professor of music at Augsburg College in town.

He didn't talk about his ex-wife much, but he said enough.

They spent the deepest part of winter together, then together headed into spring. For the first time in ten years she had a Valentine in February. He stopped by her office hours with a hokey card (a heart framed by white lace) and a small rectangular box, maybe four inches long, an inch wide, too large to be a ring, thank God. Still, the box was weighty, and she worried that she'd be obliged by this somehow.

They'd reached that unnerving stage in romance when gifts become significant. To circumvent this, she had bought him a heart-shaped tin of chocolates with a photo of Elvis printed on the lid, each foil-wrapped chocolate shaped like a tiny guitar, and a card, which she signed *Yours*. He laughed at the gift and kissed her.

She shook the box he gave her, afraid to look.

"Open it," he said.

"What's in it?" she asked.

"You have to open it and see."

When she unwrapped the red foil paper, she found a Swiss Army knife inside.

"It's red, isn't it?" he said, obviously pleased with himself. "More use than flowers."

It was still early in their relationship and his practicality charmed her. It did not yet grate; it did not yet seem tasteless and desiccated, like freeze-dried beef. She opened each spidery arm of the knife—blade, blade, toothpick, scissors, corkscrew, blade, fork—lovingly touching each stainless steel arm.

Then he wrapped her in his arms; beneath his soap and shampoo smell, he smelled faintly of kerosene and moth balls and wet wool and sweat. She loved the way he smelled.

In the course of their relationship thus far, he'd taught her many useful things. He'd taught her how to snowshoe and ice fish, how to orienteer and winter camp. He'd taught her to stay upright on cross-country skis and how to gut a walleye. He had useful information to impart, and he was generous with it. He told her these were things to know, things that came in handy—a word he used a lot and without irony—so that you didn't have to stay indoors all winter, not knowing that she was someone who preferred to stay indoors all summer too. He taught her how to gather morels in oak forests in spring. He taught her how to tie a fly and unzip his with her teeth.

She was grateful to him and told herself that gratitude approximated love. She craved useful information, and he had it. His hands were large and calloused; he looked wrong in anything other than flannel or cotton tees and jeans. He had to shave twice a day or his cheeks abraded her.

By June they were talking about moving in together, although she had not lived with anyone since her freshman year of college at U Mass, and he was—she knew—a slob. Moving in together was his idea, not hers. They compromised and decided to go camping instead, as a sort of trial run, a ten-day trip into the Boundary Waters

Canoe Area, a vast chain of lakes that stretched along the border between Canada and the United States, the largest water wilderness preserve in the world, he said.

He was a slob, but he was also a control freak, so she knew it was a sign of nearly matrimonial faith that he offered to let her plan and pack the food. It was an act of trust and love. He'd pull together the equipment, he said, check the tent for holes and patch them, get packs and maps and compasses, arrange the permits, take down the canoe from the shed. They were a team after all, he said. They could depend on one another.

She thought hard about what to bring, spent hours perusing the little foil-packaged, freeze-dried meals, as if she were doing textual analysis. She visited various camping stores to check out their offerings; she read the labels, considered ingredients, weighed protein against carbs. She chose carefully. She chose snacks for them to eat on moonlight canoe trips; she designed the menus for three-course candlelight dinners (complete with candles, matches, tiny linen tablecloth, and two very carefully packed china plates). "My ex-wife was always surprising me," he'd said. She wanted to surprise him too, and to impress him. So she asked him for the army packs, and he brought them by. And then she half filled one with her sleeping roll and clothes, as he'd instructed, and the other one she filled entirely with food. Freeze-dried fettuccine Alfredo; freeze-dried chicken and dried tomato sauce and herbs; freeze-dried stroganoff; powdered milk and half-and-half; gorp and couscous and pilaf and raisins and pumpkins seeds and dried apples and beef jerky and oatmeal and margarine in a tub. A corkscrew. Pancake mix and pasta.

He picked her up before dawn, a little after five in the morning, when the sky was still a deep and sleepy midnight blue, and Jupiter and Mars glowed in the city sky alongside the Pleiades. She carried the food pack on her shoulder to the car, and he carried the other, after adding his sleeping roll and clothes. He cinched the army packs' belts tight. They loaded the two packs into the trunk, slammed it shut in the quiet chilly air.

The drive up was lovely, the roads nearly empty, and they made good time, reaching Cloquet before nine. They had agreed to stop there to see the world's only Frank Lloyd Wright–designed gas station, which she had read about in the guidebook to northern Minnesota and wanted to see. They took the exit west to Cloquet and drove along a wide boulevard toward town. When they saw it on the right—unmistakable—they pulled in and parked beside the pumps. No one seemed to be working, so they got out to look from different angles. The station was two stories tall and looked like one quarter of a pyramid turned upside down, so that the pyramid balanced on its apex, a single pointy corner thrust out like an arrow pointing west. The ground floor was of poured concrete, in austere angles; the second story was a sort of waiting room observation deck composed of glass that thrust out over the gas pumps like a giant beak. The whole structure looked unstable, as if it might tip into the parking lot and shatter.

"It looks like the Guggenheim with pumps," she said.

He smiled at her vaguely, and she realized the name Guggenheim meant nothing to him; for all he knew, it could be a brand of beer.

"It's a museum in New York City," she said, "that Wright designed."

He squinted at her like she'd gone blurry and he was having to fight to see her there. "I know what the Guggenheim is," he said. "I lived in New York, after college. That's where I met my wife."

"Your ex-wife," she said. "I never knew that."

He shrugged. "I never told you."

They had a permit to put in at a lake on the Gunflint Trail, but they drove on past the turnoff and up to Grand Portage, near the border with Canada, so that they could have breakfast at a place he loved, a log cabin restaurant that overlooked Lake Superior and served, he guaranteed, the best hot cakes she would ever eat. The pancakes were flecked with wild rice and came with thick salty pads of butter and real maple syrup, corky and sweet, and he was right. Watching the gulls arc above the lake outside the window, she thought about how close they were to the border; if they kept going, they could cross into another country. She recognized the thought as childish, but it thrilled her nevertheless to know they were that close, to know that they could leave this territory behind and together find some new and foreign ground, even if it was only Canada.

He'd told her that the Gunflint Trail would be scenic, but it was torn up and mostly mud, overrun with logging trucks carrying out huge limbless trees. There was a traffic jam and long delays, even though they could count fewer than ten cars on the road. Still the construction crews stopped them with the rest of the incoming traffic and made them wait behind handheld stop signs, flagged them on, with palms raised, meaning *slow*. It took them an hour to travel fifteen miles, and he was monosyllabic by the time they pulled into the gravel lot, where they would leave the car. They unloaded the gear from the trunk, and she helped him lift the canoe down from its rack on the roof. Then they each took a pack and walked down to the dock, which was run by an outfitter who charged a modest fee to let equipment and to allow people to park and put in here.

"Been a while," the outfitter said.

"It has," Ben said, and then he put a credit card down on the counter and said he'd leave that till they got back.

She carried the army packs down to the dock while he went back for the canoe. She could see him from the dock, heading across the grassy lawn toward the lake, the aluminum canoe worn like a long silver hat, pulled down past his ears, obscuring his head.

The lake where they put in was small and round and weedy and edged by summer cottages, more like a suburban pond than wilderness; she felt disappointment settle over her like a private fog, but she tried not to show it. As they canoed across it, they dodged motor boat waves and he told her that there wouldn't be any motorized vehicles once they reached the Boundary Waters. She nodded, like she'd known this all along, and paddled on, relieved.

Some things, she realized, it was better not to know. It was better that she hadn't known that—before they reached the Boundary Waters wilderness—they would have to paddle through three boggy ponds, short uninspired crossings that ended in muddy banks and mosquito-infested forests through which they'd have to trek, bearing on their backs all that they'd need to sustain them for ten days. It was better that she hadn't heard of portaging. Portages—in which you carried the canoe from lake to lake—were, in theory, a pleasant change from sitting and paddling. But this was true in theory more than in fact. In truth, in fact, the novelty wore off fast.

By the third portage they were no longer speaking. They trudged with mute determination from one end of the trail, where they beached and left the canoe, to the other with their packs. Then they trudged back to retrieve the canoe, which he then carried through the woods on his head. She followed behind him, helping him up steep embankments, holding the tip up when the trail required climbing up a six-foot wall of rock or down steep stairs.

Halfway through the third portage, he asked her if she wanted to give it a try.

"Sure," she said.

He tilted the canoe against a tree and ducked out from under it.

"It's easier than it looks," he said. "You'll be surprised."

She was small and not very strong and thought that maybe he would be the one who'd be surprised. But she walked under the overturned canoe as he'd instructed her to, and let him settle the yoke onto her shoulders, delicately, like a shawl, before she unhooked the bow from the tree and stood up so that the boat lifted, its weight rest-ing solely on her. She was scared at first, and then she was amazed. The burden was surprisingly easy to bear, eighty pounds on your neck seemed light, if balanced properly. She took a few giddy steps, amazed by what he could teach her and by what she had it in her to carry. She did a little Irish jig, touching her left toe over her right foot, then right over left. She smiled at him, full of what she knew was love.

"Be careful," he said, smiling back. "Don't turn your ankle, Bud." No one in the history of the world had ever called her Bud. She felt like a six-pack at the MLA. She felt great.

And then they were in wilderness. She knew they were because they passed a sign that said so, posted to the right of the trail three-quarters of the way along the portage. She hadn't noticed it when they'd come this way before, carrying the army packs. But she saw it now, from under the brim of the canoe. *Welcome to the Boundary Waters Canoe Area Wilderness.* If there were warnings against bears or other dangers on that sign, she didn't notice them. She noticed the hollow resonant gong as the stern knocked birches along the trail; she noticed the fingernail scrape of twigs along the metal belly of the boat. Each root and stone she had to step around. It was slow going, but she didn't mind it. She could hear him whistling behind her on the trail. It was nice to walk through the woods with him. It was a nice change from paddling, and the woods were lovely—patches of blue sky overhead, a tunnel of green, swamp and forest, moss and wintergreen, dense and leafy along the trail. It was midday, but in here the air was cool and sweet.

They were paddling for the last portage of the day, the fourth and final one that would bring them to the lake at which—he promised—they'd set up camp and rest, when she noticed that he'd stopped whistling sometime back. She heard only the sound of water rushing off the bow, the slow steady dip of the paddles, the haunting song of a white-throated sparrow, high and eerie. They beached the canoe, just the sound of sand against the belly of the boat. She stepped out and grabbed the rope and pulled the bow onto shore as he had shown her, scraping the canoe on rocks a little as she hauled. He grimaced. "Careful," he said—before tying the rope to a branch. Then he got out and began to hand her things. He hefted the food pack onto his shoulder and said, "What the hell's in here. Rocks?" He pretended he was joking, but she knew better. She knew that he was thinking that she was the burden. Dead weight.

A hundred yards up the path, he stumbled on a root and swore, "Jesus H.," and dropped the army pack into the muddy path where it fell over into a bed of wintergreen and sumac. There was a tinselly sound of glass striking glass, a fragile, breakable chiming.

"What in the fuck is in there?" he said.

"Food," she said. "It's the food pack."

"I know it's the food pack. What the hell did you bring?"

Without waiting for her to answer, he crouched by the side of the trail and undid the belts that cinched it closed and began to pull out things. At first he pulled out the usual items: freeze-dried this and freeze-dried that and gorp. And then, deeper down, he found the special things, the ones she'd wanted to be a surprise. He pulled out the bottle of chardonnay that she'd stowed for the romantic candle-light dinner she'd planned; he pulled out a plastic bottle of half-and-half for coffee; maple syrup; cranberry juice (in case she got a bladder infection); Jim Beam; candles and two china plates wrapped in a linen cloth, buffered from breaking by individual packets of Quaker Oats.

"For Christ's sake," he said, shaking his head slowly, like this was for the record books. He stood up and looked at the stuff he'd hauled out, the stuff scattered now by the side of the trail. She was afraid he'd abandon it there, all that she had planned for them to share.

"I gotta take a leak," he said and walked into the woods, breaking twigs as he went. A cloud of gnats encircled her; she waved them off, feeling water rise in her eyes. If she could, she'd have walked away and left him there, but she knew it was too late, they'd come too far. When he got back he crouched by the trail and began to jam the containers back into the pack any which way.

"I don't believe this," he said, holding up the wine. "How could you *be* so—?" and then maybe because he turned and saw her face and saw that it was red and scrunched like an old Kleenex, he said, gently, "It's just not practical, Buddy. Stuff like this is too heavy. It won't last out here."

She nodded, but she couldn't say a thing without the risk of tears.

They didn't talk much after that. She had a lot of time to think about what he'd said as they walked through the mosquito-infested woods, as each glistening green branch thwacked her face and made her think of ticks. The radiant red leaves at her ankles, which she'd thought were early turning sumac, she realized were probably poison ivy. *It's just not practical, Buddy.* Love was impractical, she thought. It was a heavy thing to carry, like the army pack on her back, which would flip her like a turtle and leave her flailing were she to fall.

The only sounds were the scratch of aluminum on rocks as they eased the Grumman into the shallow water; the splash of water against the gunnels as they loaded in the packs and then stepped into the boat; the slap of her paddle as it entered the water; the draw of it; the rain of drops onto the boat as she lifted the paddle free of the water and brought it forward, to begin again.

The camping site on the far side of the big blue lake was beautiful, on a smooth granite shelf overlooking the water. He docked from the stern and got out first to secure the boat; then he took her hand and helped her up onto the rock. It was marvelously quiet. Even if she strained she couldn't hear the stutter of an outboard motor or a prop plane, the rush of traffic that seemed to be a part of the breeze everywhere but here.

"I want to show you something," he said, and folded her hand into the crook of his arm. He took her to the edge of the woods that surrounded the campsite and pointed to a ring of bushes studded with raspberries and blueberries tight and small as buds.

"Are they edible?" she asked.

"Better than Lunds," he said, naming her favorite grocery store, known for gourmet food.

While he set up the tent, she walked the woods gathering dry twigs and snapping them into bundles for kindling, separating these from the larger branches they'd burn. When they finished, they ate lunch—cheese sandwiches she'd packed for each of them, cheddar with arugula and English chutney. ("This is great," he said, "what's in here?" But she was ashamed to tell him, afraid that he'd laugh at her expensive tastes, the imported and impractical foods she loved.) Then he proposed they take a swim.

They had the lake to themselves, so they left their clothes on the rocks and dived right in. The water was cold but clear, and she could hear loons calling and see cormorants gathered on a little stone island two hundred yards out into the lake. They swam farther and farther out. And then she noticed something dark swimming toward her, popping up out of the water, then going down, then coming up again. She started to swim toward shore.

"Hold still," he called, in stage whisper.

"What is it?" she said.

"A loon."

"That's a loon?"

"Stay still," he said. "See how close it will come."

"I don't want to see how close it will come," she said.

"I do."

"I don't."

"I think it thinks your head's a potential mate. It thinks your head's a loon."

The bird approached her, swimming on the surface now, bobbing in the slight waves, tacking back and forth on its approach. It had a haunting cry, that quaver. How could it *be* so dumb, so ignorant of its own kind, so easily tricked into thinking it had found a mate when they weren't even the same species? Cormorants. Coots. Loons. Her. Him.

"Those birds are stupid," she said, when they were back on land.

"They're friendly," he said.

"No wonder there's a duck season," she said.

"People don't hunt loons."

"They should."

They gathered raspberries and blueberries, then together they built a fire, and then he started dinner. He was quiet as he pulled foods from the army pack. There hadn't been much to say since their fight on the trail, though they both were trying, she knew. He put a pan of water on to boil for pasta and sat on a log facing the fire. The first faint stars were just beginning to come out, and she felt sorry for them both, lonely in all this beauty. She walked up behind him and began to massage his neck. The cords of muscle were thick and tense.

"You okay?" she asked. She didn't expect an answer, but it seemed like the right question.

"This is where we spent our honeymoon," he said.

Her hands froze. She felt a weird tingling on her palms, the sudden sickening sense of vertigo she'd felt on the cliff that day months ago and hoped never to feel again.

"Why didn't you tell me?" she said. She let her hands fall from his neck, palms tingling.

He shrugged. "Didn't seem important."

"Which part?" she said. "Telling me or your honeymoon?"

"I'm sorry," he said. "This was probably a bad idea. I didn't think it would get to me. All that."

When the water boiled, making a plunking sound of bubbles against the thin tin pot, he tore open a cellophane bag of corkscrew noodles (they were noodles, he insisted, *not* pasta; before the 1980s no one had heard of pasta, let alone eaten it; they ate noodles, he said, and they liked them) and poured them in and covered the pot.

She took a seat across the fire from him on a thick log set there for that purpose. At night they would have to haul the food pack into midair, suspend it by a rope from a tree limb to avoid attracting bears, but right now it was beside her, behind the log, and she dug among the contents and pulled out the bottle of Jim Beam.

"We ought to drink this," she said, "if we don't want to carry it."

"Probably," he said.

He patted the pocket of his shirt and drew out a crumpled pack of cigarettes and offered her one. She took it and then took a swig from the bottle and then passed the bottle to him. She had two glass tumblers stowed somewhere in the pack, but she didn't bother get them; they'd been meant to be a happy surprise, part of a celebration she'd imagined they'd be having out here together and now knew they would not. Instead they drank straight from the bottle, handing it back and forth.

They watched the fire and ate the pasta when it was done. And drank some more. The sky emptied of light. The loons called and quieted. The moon rose. They tossed resinous twigs on the flames to watch them crackle; she watched him across the flames, his face orange lit, distorted by shadow, until the wind changed, and he coughed from the smoke and batted his arms as if to clear the ashy plumes and then gave up and came over to her side and put his hand on her thigh.

The front of her jeans was scalding hot where she faced the fire, and her shins hurt, but she left them there, did not draw back, and when he asked her if she knew any songs, she said she wasn't sure, maybe, and after a moment, she began to sing, her voice wavering and reedy. "Amazing grace, How sweet the sound, That saved a wretch like me." On the second verse he joined her with an off-key harmony and they sang like that for awhile, their shoulders leaned into one another, close enough that she smelled beneath the wood smoke the flinty scent of moth balls from his coat and the cologne she'd given him for his birthday last month and whiskey and the pond smell off the lake. They sang there together, starting new songs as they remembered them, joining in where they could, harmonizing until the moon was risen high overhead and the fire died down and he buried it in sand and took her hand and led her to the tent, where he undressed her snap by snap, Velcro strip by Velcro strip.

In the morning, she woke alone and looked up at leaf shadows shifting on the blue nylon roof of the tent; the tent smelled of sweat and pine needles, and the door flap was unzipped and peeled back, revealing through the mosquito netting a white blur of sky. A cardinal cried out, and a white-throated sparrow called tee-doe-tee-tee-tee-tee-tee-tee. When she sat up, she saw Ben through the netting.

"Hey," she called.

"Hey," he said.

She let the sleeping bag fall from her breasts; the day was warm and delicious. It would be a scorcher. Rare here, he'd said. He was crouched by the fire grate, but he stood up and brought over a cup of coffee in a blue, white-speckled tin cup.

"Breakfast is ready," he said, handing her the cup. "You want to eat in bed?"

She nodded.

"Be right back," he said.

He'd made pancakes with fresh blueberries and raspberries in the batter, and he kissed her gently on the mouth before he handed her her plate. He brushed the hair back from her forehead with his huge freckled hand. He sat outside the tent, cross-legged on the sun-warmed dirt. He was cheerful and gentle and talked about places they could go today, day trips they might take, and as she listened to him and chewed, she thought it possible that she loved him more than she'd loved anyone before, but she knew too it would be over between them when they got home. Though her body still turned heliotropically toward him, she knew that what they had was done; it had ended here.

This had been a test of sorts, a proving ground, to see if new love could assuage old pain, and they had failed it, that test. She felt as she imagined her students must, those who each term protested their Bs as if an A weren't earned but an entitlement, as if she'd gypped them somehow, gypped them as she felt he had her, though there was no logic to it, she knew. He owed her nothing. No one did. You found love or you didn't. There were no guarantees. Not ever. Not with anyone.

He tapped his fork against his plate and cleared his throat like he was preparing to make an announcement, and when she looked over, he looked down at her plate. She looked too. He'd served their breakfast on the china she had brought, the real china, blue willow pattern, inherited from the grandmother who was not really kin to her by blood. Seeing the pattern beneath the glossy syrup, she remembered how her mother had kept a giant serving platter from this same set atop the mantle when she was growing up. "It's the pride of the collection and worth a lot," her mother said. They'd used the thing for holidays, for Thanksgiving and Christmas dinner, when they used the set. And then one afternoon, when her mother was dusting, the platter had fallen from the wooden rack where her mother kept it on display. They'd gathered the pieces and chips from the floor and kept them, and later they sat at the table and glued them back together with ceramic glue, as their words this morning were trying to do. But she felt now as she did then the futility of the effort, that once something had been shattered, it could never be restored. They'd put the platter back up, but the cracks still showed, and it couldn't be used. It became another pretty, useless thing, as perhaps he would think of her now, after this.

She was wrong, but only partly. They stayed together for another four months after that, before his ex-wife called him up at Halloween to tell him that she missed his pumpkin soup and ask if he missed her and for a second chance, and he gave it to her. He hadn't moved in, so he didn't need to move out, but over the months he had left a lot of his things at her place, and so he'd called last week to say that he'd be coming by on Saturday, if that was okay, to get his things, and so, because it was Saturday today, she was gathering them into the bag at her side for him.

She had not been a pack rat before she met him, but now she was amazed by all the junk of his she had, all that had accumulated between them. There were stubs from movies they had seen and photographs of them she did not want to see again and a Xeroxed article on distinguishing morels from false morels, which were poisonous. She wondered about giving back the Swiss Army knife, but she knew that if she did, she would regret it. She wanted the knife, with all its weird appendages, as she still wanted him. She found the cards he'd given her and the notes he'd left on her office door, and she found the flyer she'd picked up the day that they first met, folded and faded but legible still. She was amazed that such things last, how such things stuck to a life when little else did; when she died, she knew, they'd find among her books and socks and earrings a host of such scraps—ATM receipts and credit card carbons, flyers she'd picked up somewhere and departmental memos announcing gatherings long past—the residue of living that accumulated in her rooms as love had not, that clung more surely than people ever did.

She read again the four steps for how not to freeze. After Warning

Signs and Danger Signs, she read the Steps to Take. *Keep the victim awake. Keep the person warm. Administer hot liquids.* She knew the last and final step by heart; it had been a joke between them months ago, when she'd kept the flyer on her fridge, before she took it down and put it here. The best hope for saving a person from freezing was to do the opposite of what logic taught. The best way not to freeze was to strip—to get naked with another naked body, lie there skin to skin inside a sleeping bag or under blankets. Body to body contact could save your life, they used to joke. It was the only hope for survival, the best way not to freeze.

When she heard him knock at the door, it occurred to her to pretend she was not home. But she realized that was impractical. He'd only come back later, call again, or come on in (he still had a key). So she ran into the bathroom, stopped up the tub, and turned the hot water tap on full, leaving him to find his own way in. She heard him open the door and call her name.

"I'm in the tub," she yelled. "Come on in. Your stuff's in the hall. Feel free to look around, make sure you haven't left anything behind." She heard him opening closet doors, checking drawers for things he wouldn't want to leave. She heard him in the hall outside. She heard him knocking quietly on the bathroom door. She heard him call her name.

"I wanted to say good-bye," he said. "Can I come in?"

She heard him try the doorknob, was glad she'd thought to lock it.

"I can't hear you," she yelled above the water. "Did you find your stuff?"

"I'm sorry," he said, to the door. "I'm going."

"Call me, sometime," she yelled. "Let me know how you are."

When she heard the front door close, she shut off the water. She heard him turn the lock and shove the key under the door, and then she stripped and stepped into the scalding tub, amazed that she could feel so much pain. Her skin was red beneath the water and felt like it might peel off, the way a green chili's shiny skin will when you roast it over an open fire as he had shown her how to do. But she was shivering, too, there in the tub; her legs and arms were shaking and would not stop. She tried to hold her hands over her face, but she couldn't get them to rise from the water to her cheeks, and she remembered having felt this once before, this quaking fear, her limbs heavy and rubbery, as if exhausted from a long exertion, and then she realized when it was she'd felt this: it was when she'd climbed the cliff at Taylors Falls.

She had been among the first to climb the cliff face above the river. They had spent the day clambering over boulders and learning knots, and she'd felt a confidence she hadn't felt since she was a kid, a faith that her body would back her up, do her bidding. She had felt agile and young. She had started up the cliff, taking the harder route to the left, and then, half way up, out of nowhere, she'd frozen with fear. The fear was less a feeling that a physical force, a weight, like a sandbag suddenly dropped into her arms. It pressed her chest, made her breath shallow. Her legs shivered. She stopped dead and hung on, clinging by her fingertips to the cliff, not far from the top, too far from the bottom, unable to move. "Are you all right?" someone yelled up to her. "I'm not sure," she said. "I can't seem to locate my arms and legs." There was friendly laughter from below. "It happens," someone said. They told her where her body was—"You're about twenty feet from the top, to the left of the big crack"—but she could not feel her limbs. Or rather, she could not seem to connect her thoughts to her muscles. Somewhere a connection had been severed. Her mind said, *Move.* Her muscles would have none of it. Her arms ached. Her left leg—the leg she was balanced on—began to quiver and shake. They tried to cheer her up with jokes: "Hey Elvis, what's with the leg?" A few of them sang, "You ain't nothing but a hound dog." Someone yelled, "Breathe." Someone yelled, "Relax." She yelled, "Help me," pleading now. "I'm scared." "What did she say?" "She's scared." She knew she was humiliating herself, but what choice did she have? She was not equipped for this. She was unprepared. This was not where she'd expected to be at thirty-three, alone, clinging to a sheer rock face where nothing grew, with nothing to hold on to, just shallow handholds, cold and dark, just narrow ledges. "Make a move," the instructor yelled. "Just make a move." "I can't," she said into the rock. "You *can*." She didn't know what to reach for. They told her: "There's an outcropping of rock just to your right, about a foot over from your right foot. Slide your leg over to it." But she couldn't. Information could not help her now. She lacked more than knowledge. Her mind and body were not on speaking terms. "I can't feel my hands," she yelled. "I don't think I can hold on much longer." "Hold on," they said. "We'll help you." "What's going on?" she heard someone ask. "She needs help," someone said. "She freaked." "She's frozen." "Can we lower her down on belay?" "She could flip, hit her head." "Look where she is." "Besides, the rope could snap if we ran it on the rocks." She listened to them deliberate on whether to climb up or rappel down. She had come too far to go back now. Her eyes were blurry with tears when someone overhead yelled, "I'm coming, hold on," and so she did. She flashed on the waiver she had signed, the one acknowledging that her injury, her death would be on her own hands. Her fingertips prickled with numbness, stinging as if from cold; her legs shook uncontrollably, but she held on to the rock face and to the idea that someone was coming, keeping her mind occupied, free of the fear that could make you fall, concentrating on the knowledge that someone was coming, would arrive soon, any minute now, confident then, as she could not be now, that help was on its way, that someone would show up any minute to show her—if she could hold on just a little while longer—how to move again.

THEORY OF
ENLIGHTENMENT

Sadhana Tattwa. *The Science of Seven Cultures for Quick
Evolution of the Human Soul. These thirty-two instructions
give the essence of the Eternal Religion in its purest
form. Suitable for modern busy householders . . .*
11. . . . Adapt yourself to men and events.

H.H. SRI SWAMI SIVANANDA

EVER SINCE HER LOVER LEFT HER FOR AN ASHRAM IN THE
Catskills, Renee Kirschbaum has been picking fights with strangers.
Yesterday, in a Brooklyn Laundromat, she came to fisticuffs with a
twenty-year-old boy who tried to take the laundry cart she'd parked
in front of her dryer. The kid was tall and lanky, with a cowlick that
wobbled like a lewd tongue from the crown of his head. He strode up
to the Renee's dryer, yanked away the cart she'd parked in front of it,
and was heading off across the linoleum, when she collared him. No
doubt it was reflex that made him swing at her, just as it was reflex

that made her duck, leaving him to drive his delicate knuckles into the yellow enameled machine.

This morning, as she was crossing Park Avenue on her way to work, a car skidded to a halt in the crosswalk, missing her by inches.

"Where did you get your license? A raffle?" she shrieked, banging her attaché case on the hood of the car. The man behind the wheel wore the bland cheap suit of a Jersey commuter and stared at her in disbelief, his mouth slightly ajar.

"Sorry," she said, recovering herself and patting the snout of the car. "I'm a little premenstrual."

As she rides the elevator up to the ninth floor, where her office is, Renee thinks about the day Gil left her two days ago. Renee had stood in the kitchen of the Brooklyn brownstone, looking out at the garden squashed between their building and the next, and said, "Don't go."

"I need something to believe in, Ren."

"Believe in yourself."

"That's not enough," Gil said.

"Then believe in us," she said.

"That's not enough," he said gently. "I'm sorry."

"You can't just give up on the world."

"I can't save the world."

"You're afraid of trying."

"I know my limits." Gil stretched out a hand to touch her shoulder but she shrugged it away. "The best I can hope for is not to do any harm," Gil said.

"Everyone has blood on their hands."

"I don't want to hurt anyone."

"Too late."

As the elevator approaches Renee's floor, the guy beside her ruffles a *New York Times* in her face and she elbows him in the kidney. When he stares at her, she smiles. Steps off on nine.

This is not a thing they feature in women's magazines: How to Steal Your Boyfriend Back from God. So Renee has to turn to relatives, to friends, to strangers who lurk in adjacent cubicles. That morning, she confides in her coworker Alice, hoping against hope for good advice.

"He's certain. He's at peace. And he left me on Saturday when our lease ran out," Renee tells Alice, a fellow researcher at the midtown environmental consulting firm where Renee works in air quality. Alice is in toxic wastes. Together they stand in the narrow kitchenette having the first cup of coffee of the day.

"It's tough to be two-timed with God," Alice says, clutching her mug in both hands like it might escape. Alice grew up in Alabama and is well acquainted with conversion. Her great-great-grandmother on her mother's side, Ida Lee, ran off with a revival meeting just after the Civil War. More recently her father converted to Catholicism and enrolled in divinity school in Connecticut.

"It wasn't till my father left my mother for the church that she began to drink," Alice explains. "God has put asunder more marriages than any mortal man."

"He's devout?" Renee asks.

"Oh, no, he's not a believer," Alice says. "He just doesn't want to miss out in case they're on to something."

Renee does not know Alice well, but adversity builds allegiances, and in the space of a day they are friends. Over lunch, they talk sex, they talk self-esteem. They share rape stories and religious denominations. By that afternoon, Renee has agreed to help Alice find an apartment in Brooklyn. Alice lives on 72nd Street, but she is looking for a cheaper place now that her roommate abruptly moved out, so Renee volunteers to show her around Park Slope. After work, they catch the subway home together.

As they ride, Alice talks about her therapist, the drugs she takes for depression, her adolescent obsession with Salman Rushdie. In junior high, she had wanted to send him a box of homemade fudge but she was pretty sure it wouldn't get through.

"I just felt so sorry for him, all alone. I mean, the people he wrote the book for wanted to kill him."

"The man's life was threatened," Renee says. "I don't think he'd have wanted to eat something from a perfect stranger."

"I know, I know," Alice says. "I just wished there was something I could do."

Last week, when a parade of Greenpeace activists stormed up Park Avenue under their office windows, waving banners with dead whales and dolphins and chanting "Stop the Slaughter," Alice had broken down weeping. Her therapist—Alice tells Renee—has told her to cool it.

"Repeat after me," the therapist has said. "I"

"I"

"Alice Riley"

"Alice Riley"

"Am not responsible"

"Am not responsible"

"For the entire fucking Western Hemisphere."

"Now," Alice tells Renee, "I just want a place to sleep."

As the D train clatters over the Manhattan Bridge headed for Brooklyn, Renee thinks that maybe this is all that her lover Gil has wanted too: a place to sleep, perpetual naptime. Escape from the messy struggles of the living. Maybe it's the rattle of the tracks, repetitive as obsession, or Alice's example, but that is when she decides to go and visit him at the ashram, come what may. If Orpheus can go to hell for Eurydice, the least she can do is go to the Catskills for Gil.

"I'm going to bring him back alive," she tells Alice, as they emerge from the subway at Grand Army Plaza. "Alive or alive." Truth is, she simply wants him back. This man she has loved as she has loved, will love, no other.

That night Renee calls her mother in Arizona and cries. Her mother listens. Speaks calmly. Says it has to feel really bad to separate from someone you've spent a lot of time with over the last several years.

"Spent a lot of time with? We were married for all intents and purposes. We bought Revere Ware. An OED."

"You're young. You have your whole life ahead of you. Maybe you'll go back to graduate school, finish that law degree, who knows?"

"But that wouldn't make me happy, Ma."

"Who's happy?"

"Aren't you?"

"Your father and I are comfortable. Look. Take some advice and don't put so much emphasis on happiness. It'll only make you miserable. It's like Joseph Campbell says, 'It's important to follow your bliss, but sometimes you just have to make the best of what you've got.'"

"I don't think that's what he said."

"I got the video right here," her mother says. Renee can hear her mother shifting in a lawn chair, the squeaky sound of flesh on vinyl.

"Your father and I are worried about you," her mother says, when she settles. "Why don't you come for a visit? A vacation would do you good."

"I don't know."

"What's to know? It's warm. You can bring a bathing suit. You'll swim. Relax. Put some color back in you face. You'll have a good time."

Renee pictures her mother beside the aquamarine pool ringed with potted begonias. "Every time you tell me I'll have a good time, I don't. Not at Aunt Sonia's wedding. Not at my bat mitzvah."

"Such a good memory and this is what you use it for."

"Anyway, I'm busy this weekend." Static crackles on the line as her mother goes quiet with interest.

"You seeing someone?"

"I'm going to visit Gil, at the ashram."

"And why can't he come to see you?"

"He can't get away."

"What is this place? A monastery or a concentration camp?"

"Why do you twist everything into a shadow of the Holocaust?" There is a silence on the line and Renee knows her mother is considering whether to fight her on this one. Their relationship used to be composed of these little explosions, like gunpowder smoke signals they'd send out to one another from their distant peaks. But lately Mrs. Kirschbaum has mellowed. Ever since Renee's mother decided not to leave Renee's father, a thing she had been threatening to do as-soon-as-the-children-were-grown for as long as the children were growing, Mrs. Kirschbaum has softened. She has lost her edge.

Throughout Renee's childhood, her mother had kept a bag packed by the front door like Russians in the days of Stalin or the biblical Jews on the eve of the Exodus prepared to leave in the night, and once when Renee was eight, her mother had gotten as far as calling a cab. Renee still remembers how the headlights turned into the driveway in the middle of that clear March evening, how they shone through the bedroom window before arcing into the drive, like twin flashlights scrutinizing the home for valuables. Renee heard the sound of voices outside, the slam of the cab door, and the whining whir of the car engine backing down the drive. The headlight beams reeled like drunks back across the walls then slipped out, leaving Renee in darkness again. But the next morning when Renee got up for school her mother was there in the white-curtained kitchen, frying eggs and cursing the toaster and rushing Renee's brother and sister out the door before they missed the bus—her eyes only slightly more bloodshot than usual, her face only a hint puffier—as if nothing had happened. Renee never asked her mother about that night, but after it she fought with her mother regularly, over school lunches, dishes, curfew, boyfriends.

Now as she listens to the clinking of ice in a glass her mother is stirring half a country away, Renee realizes she is hoping for a fight, for someone to struggle against to know where she stands: the way it was in the old days, where you knew who you were by the side you were on. But her mother shrugs off the provocation.

"At least they got visiting hours," her mother says.

On Friday afternoon, Renee catches the van up to the ranch in front of the yoga center. The van is ordinary, blue, except for the stripe of white stenciled letters around its girth: OM NAMO NARAYANAYA CHANT FOR WORLD PEACE. She arrives early and takes a seat at the back, by the window. While she waits, she slips on a pair of sunglasses and ties a scarf around her hair in case she should pass anyone she knows. Women pile in over her, grabbing seats, arranging baggage, staking territory. The women are in their forties and fifties mostly, she thinks, ex-housewives and bohemian Upper East Side ladies looking for peace, meaning, skin tone. The driver is a handsome man, deeply tanned, with a shaved head, round wire-rimmed sunglasses, brown leather bomber jacket, jeans, and a silk scarf draped around his neck. He slips behind the wheel and chants three rounds of Tryambakam Yajamahe before starting the engine.

"I don't know how I feel about riding with a guy who has to pray before he drives," Renee jokes to the woman next to her. The woman glances at Renee without interest, then looks straight ahead.

As they enter the Lincoln Tunnel headed for Jersey, Renee thinks how ironic it is that Gil, of all people, should dump her for God. When they met five years ago, Gil was an atheist and an associate professor of wildlife biology at the University of Texas. Renee was college educated and underemployed. During the day, she cleaned houses. In the evenings she drove a van for a local sanctuary group, visiting warehouses on the edge of the city to pick up immigrants fighting deportation orders, who told harrowing stories of border crossings in the Arizona desert trying to evade vigilantes who menaced the U.S. border the way drug gangs did its other side.

After a few months, the local pastor and a few pious matrons were questioned by the Immigration and Naturalization Service, and the network disappeared like smoke. Renee kicked around town for a few months, waiting for the network to resume, but when no one contacted her, she gave up and applied to law school. That was where she'd met Gil, in a corridor of Townes Hall where he was trying to throw a coat over a sparrow that had mistakenly flown in and gotten trapped. He was thirty-three at the time, but his hair was already white. He made her think of a medieval gravestone rubbing from an English church, his face gaunt and elegant and sad like some long-extinct knight. He began picking her up on weekends to tour her through the hill country outside Austin and along the Gulf Coast, introducing her to the local flora as if this were his family. He drew her attention to varieties of plants and fungi, using their Latin names for the formal introduction and then, more intimately, leaning toward her to reveal their common names: rocky mountain jay, cottonwood, maidenhair, bolete.

"Being happy is a revolutionary act," Gil had said once, not long after they had moved in together. In those days, he often came home from class to find Renee seated by the radio listening to news broadcast from D.C., chewing her cuticles, a copy of *The Nation* spread open on the table.

"Tell it to the Burmese," Renee had said. But, in truth, she harbored a secret faith in their affection. Gil was her only consolation for all that was bitter and wrong in the world, as if happiness were a form of justice. In a world of melting glaciers, dying frogs, and extreme rendition, they developed a simple creed, a faith more modest than ideology or temple, in each other, as if the smallness of the act, their bond, would keep it safe.

That evening as they sat on the front porch, drinking sherry and watching the sky above the cotton trees smolder with the dying light, she'd asked him where their responsibilities lay.

"What will we tell future generations when they ask us how we let all this come to pass?" she'd asked Gil. "What will we tell them when they ask us what we knew and when?"

Her voice, she knew, had its familiar edge. It was the voice she used to quote nuclear winter statistics or factual inaccuracies from the paper over breakfast.

"I think there are people who can change the world," Gil had said carefully, "but I don't know who they are. All we can do is add to the right side of the world."

"How do we do that?" Renee had asked.

"Recycle?" he suggested.

"We are waffling in the face of history," Renee said.

On the interstate in New Jersey, they stop at a rest stop for gas. The driver tells them they have ten minutes, and Renee makes a beeline for the McDonald's across the parking lot in search of coffee. There is no coffee at the ashram, or processed sugar, garlic, mushrooms, onions; they are considered unduly stimulating. Before she can order, another woman from the van—a plump berry-brown woman with Rasta hair—joins her, and soon after the driver enters; they both tell him they're glad to see him.

"I was beginning to think we were the lone subversives," Renee says.

The driver laughs. He points to a Fred Astaire and Ginger Rogers poster on the wall by the entrance. "That's nice," he says.

For a moment, the three of them admire the irony of framed art prints—Turner, Monet, Hudson River School—in a McDonald's. Even the Muzak is Mozart.

"It's New Jersey," the Rasta woman says. "What can you expect?"

Renee doesn't speak to the driver again, but in the van, as they wait to pull out of the parking lot onto the highway, she watches the back of his neck where his scarf gives way to skin.

As they drive up into the foothills the air is redolent of warm apples, wind, and leaves. It is November but unseasonably warm. Autumn lingers. The low green hills in the distance are striated with blue and purple shadows. Watching the beautiful world become a blur outside the van window, Renee feels suddenly bereft. Her throat thickens and she finds it hard to swallow. When the Rasta woman points out some deer by the side of the road, Renee can only nod and look away.

It was in late December, a year ago, just a month after Gil's first visit to the yoga center, that Renee first began to notice the rift developing between them. They had recently moved from Manhattan to a brownstone on a tree-lined block in Brooklyn when Gil began coming home late—three, four nights a week—arriving at eleven p.m., at midnight, reeking of incense, aloof as God.

He began to dedicate fewer evenings to Renee and their ritual acrostic and more to chanting, folding his body into unusual positions without her. They used to talk about botany and Mahler; now their conversations pivoted on the Upanishads and obscure Hindu texts. He began rising at 5:30 a.m. to floss his nose, oil his gums, light incense, practice asanas, meditate.

At first Renee tried to take an interest in his "practice," as he called it. After a month of watching Gil spend evenings on his head in the living room of their apartment, Renee dragged out the teal sweat pants she had consigned to the back of her closet years before and went to sign up for a class. It was the day after Christmas and the city was tender with evening and snow.

Renee had expected the Center to be kooky and rundown, like the lavender-and-mustard-colored Victorian house that had doubled as a TM center and love commune off the campus of Texas A & M. But when she arrived after work that chilly December evening, she had found to her disappointment that the Center was drably genteel: a narrow gaunt brownstone wedged between identical brownstones, each with its own five-foot plot of cement fenced in by grillwork. The Center was distinguished only by an ornately painted "OM" that hung from a sign post and by the glass-enclosed announcement board nailed next to the front door listing class times and aphorisms: Serve, Love, Give, Purify, Meditate, Realize.

Renee had unlatched the gate and pressed the buzzer for admittance. A young dark-haired guy, dressed in a peach T-shirt and cotton drawstring pants, buzzed her in.

"It's $48 to become a member and you get a discount on the classes," said the skinny guy, who was busy entering names on a clipboard.

"If I make it a round $50 will you toss in enlightenment for free?"

"Sign here," he said, blandly, not looking up from his list.

Gil was taking a yoga class that night, so Renee hung around the boutique fingering the small brass deities and thumbing through the pamphlets on enlightenment, hoping to ride home with him, maybe convince him to stop for something to eat.

When Gil came down the stairs half an hour later, Renee's heart clenched. In those first few weeks after Gil started practicing yoga, every time Renee looked at him something caught in her throat. It was the way she used to feel when they drove together along the Gulf Coast of Texas and parked on a ridge above the dunes. She would hold Gil's hand and look out at that broad expanse of water stretching to other continents and her heart would ride out to all those places she would never go, knowing they were out there waiting to be visited, but not by her.

"I didn't expect to see you here," Gil said, and kissed her.

"That makes two of us," Renee said.

"Hang on a minute while I change and we can go grab some dinner."

Outside on the street the air was cold as a slap. Renee hunched over, her head retracted into her collar, bent against the wind, while Gil walked erect, humming one of the chants she recognized from the Center, impervious to the cold. Renee stole glances at the windows they passed, stuffed with elves in red felt suits, plastic reindeer, miniature towns winking with miniature Christmas lights, mangers, enormous aluminum snowflakes. It seemed to her there was something particularly disheartening about shop windows trimmed with holiday decorations the day after a holiday. They gave away the lie. The epiphany promised by ribbons and tinsel was a ruse. The trimmings were still there and we remained unchanged. They had not transformed us.

As they sat together over a dinner of moro rice and dim sum at their favorite Cuban-Chinese restaurant, Gil told her about his plans to move to the ashram. He had not wanted to move to New York

City, but when Renee decided to leave Texas, he'd left with her. Now, he said, he understood why. Why New York. Why Renee.

"Don't you see," he confided over the scattered plates. "I was meant to meet you. Otherwise, I never would have moved here . . . found the Center . . . yoga." He took her hand across the table.

"I feel like a karmic rest stop," Renee said.

All the way up in the yoga van, Renee thinks about how she will change her life, how she will propose she and Gil move back to Texas to the country he had never wanted to leave and had left only for her. All the way up on the van, she strategizes. She thinks of how she will propose they have a child, how she will tell him it is something that will last. But as soon as she sees him waiting on the lawn beside a white clapboard house, dressed in celibate yellow and smiling at her with abstracted fondness, she knows it is hopeless. That she has lost him.

"How was your trip?" he asks, kissing her on the cheek.

"I thought of you," she says and notes a flicker of panic cross his face. "We passed a semi that said G.O.D. on the side in four-foot-high silver letters. What do you suppose its cargo was?"

Gil smiles and for a moment Renee catches sight of the cynical former man she loved inside the beatific new.

"Let me take your bag," he says, hoisting the backpack on his shoulder.

"Gil," she says, touching his arm.

"What?" He turns only his head.

"Are you happy? I mean, here?"

Gil stares at Renee for a moment then looks away, up the grassy hill to the main buildings, surveying the place as if it would provide an answer he didn't have himself.

"As happy as anyone can be, I suppose," he says.

"Just how happy is that, anyway?" Renee asks.

"That's not really the point is it? Happiness."

"What is the point?"

"'It is neither our feelings nor our experiences that matter but the mute tenacity with which we confront them.'"

"Who said that? Augustine?"

"Godard," says Gil. "C'mon. I'll show you to your room."

The room Gil brings her to is on the second floor of the ashram's main house, a two-story white clapboard house at the base of a large sloping hill. Farther up the hill are two large red nineteenth-century guest hotels, reminders of the place's former life as the Hay Wire Dude Ranch. Renee's room is small and freshly painted; there is a wooden bed with heavy mismatched blankets folded across the foot. There is a rectangular mirror above a chest of drawers and on the wall beside the bed hangs a color illustration of the Indian saint revered by this sect, whose bald round head looks like that of an enormous cheerful infant. From her bedroom window, Renee can look out behind the house where the hillside continues to slope down for another mile past a tidy circular pond, a bramble of apple trees, a field gone yellow in the unseasonable late autumn heat, to a forest of aspen and birch. "Populus tremuloides," Gil had told her when they were hiking that first summer together in the mountains of New Mexico. "Quaking aspen." He loved to be able to give things names, to be able to say what was what. The first gift Gil ever gave Renee was a *Field Guide to North American Birds*. He'd said, "There are certain things you have to learn by heart."

"Listen," he'd said once, stopping on the sidewalk, one evening not long after they'd moved to New York. They were walking home up Broadway past Union Square. Renee squinted at the shadowed doorways and blank alleys pointed at them like rifle barrels from the surrounding buildings. Gil looked up at the empty sky. Somewhere Renee heard a scream, thin, shrill, faint.

"Did you hear it?" he asked.

"Someone screaming?"

"Night hawk," he said.

"In the city?"

"They nest on rooftops and cliffs."

She still wonders if he wasn't mistaken, if the sound wasn't a seagull or someone being mugged, which in his longing Gil mistook for something rare and loved and absent.

Dinner is served at five o'clock and held en plein air, under a striped tent on the front lawn of the ashram. A series of long tables of food stretches along one wall of the tent; the other side is crowded with wooden picnic tables. At least a hundred people have gathered to dine and the dinner line snakes across the hill. It looks like a country fair, ordinary, wholesome, except that a disturbing number of people are dressed in peach or crocus yellow, a color coordination that Renee cannot help but think of as vaguely creepy, cultish. If one is going to make a mess of things, she thinks, better to do it on one's own, avoid the crowd.

As they wait together in line, people come up and press Renee's arm and say she must be very proud of Gil. They wink at Gil and tell her, He's a wonderful man. He's great with a crowd. She knows that what they say is true, that Gil has a gift for putting people at their ease, blending wit with self-effacement. Jack-of-all-trades, he can change oil on a tractor, make cheese from raw milk, sew buttons, cut hair. Gil has raised his lack of ambition to the level of a calling. Despite his education, he remains heroically unprofessional. She loves this in him, and hates it.

As they pass under the tent, Renee notes that the driver is one of the food servers. He is in charge of doling out blueberries for dessert, one scoop per person the rule. When she reaches the driver, he holds Renee's eyes for a moment, before he heaps her plate. She cannot tell if he means anything by it, the look, that extra scoop.

After getting their food, she and Gil walk over to a small square table to pick up silverware before leaving the tent. As Renee pulls a fork from a molded plastic tray of cutlery, a woman from the van eyes Renee's plate, where blueberries roll around into the curried tofu and rice pilaf.

"It pays to have friends in low places," the woman says with a wink.

"What was that about?" Gil asks.

"Who knows," says Renee. They join a group on the hill.

Most of the ashram-goers have been bartenders, ex-junkies, most have experienced tragedy: There is the woman whose son died at prep school; the red-headed rock and roller who was a heroin addict. Renee wonders about Gil. What sorrows he has guarded that she never knew. She remembers a night last winter when he told her that he didn't want to come back, that his highest aspiration in life was to die for good and stay dead. "I didn't know you were so unhappy," she had said. "I'm not," he'd smiled.

When the driver comes to join them with his dinner tray, it is not a surprise.

He sits down, cross legged, in the grass next to Renee. There is a light stubble on his cheek, against his dark skin. She guesses he is Greek, maybe Spanish. When Gil asks him where he's from, he tells them Brussels.

"Belgium," the driver says, chewing, "has a two-to-one ratio of pigs to people."

"Who knew?" Gil says.

As Gil eats, he asks the driver how he came here, how he got involved with yoga, and the driver shrugs. Says he doesn't know. And

Renee knows in that moment that he is in it for the women. He isn't wearing peach or yellow like the others, meaning he hasn't taken vows of celibacy. He is one of the hangers on, the irreligious who haunt religious places.

"Is this your first time?" the driver asks Renee. "At the ashram, I mean." She says it is. He smiles and sets his fingertips gently on her thigh and offers to show her around.

"What a nice guy," Gil says, after the driver leaves.

Renee wonders if Gil is being ironic, but she knows that he has given up on irony. He believes it is "spiritually suspect," a phrase that sounds to Renee like a bad Buddhist spy movie.

After dinner, Gil goes to wash dishes and Renee goes to join the others who have gathered in the Krishna temple for *satsang,* an evening lecture and meditation. The small rodent-faced woman seated beside the harmonium in orange monks robes used to be an ad executive in Los Angeles and was called Louise Hickenbocker. Now she is Swami Gokulananda, named for a province in India where cattle are plentiful. She is in her early thirties but has skin as taut and radiant as a child's. All the swamis look like children, Renee thinks; they smile and show their teeth eagerly, crinkling up their eyes in identical crescents like well-adjusted second graders. These are not the kids that pushed when lines for the playground formed at the door. They did not fight for the rights of girls and scrawny boys to use the swings as Renee had. Even in the second grade, she had felt obliged to fight, to stand up to the vague, encroaching threat she could only dimly apprehend.

Gokulananda leads the group in a song about St. Francis of Assisi, then in meditation, then they read from *Mantras and Meditation* of Swami Vishnu Ramananda. Ramananda is the head swami in these parts. Last month he tried unsuccessfully to leave his body on a mountaintop in India and ended up living in London. One of the meditations is about *brahmacharya*, celibacy. Swami Gokulananda reads it aloud to the room. Afterward, she leads them in an elliptical talk about sex. Gokulananda says they shouldn't have it. "Sexual desire steals energy. Just like having a baby drains energy from the mother's body." Renee thinks about what the world would be like if everyone were so miserly about their bodily forces, so stingy with passion.

Renee has learned not to think about the baby she and Gil almost had. What she remembers instead is the hospital, the blue and white stripes of the curtains, the sharp-edged sunlight outside the window the morning Gil came to see her. They sat holding hands not speaking, looking out the window as if they expected to see something there other than the silver lamp posts sticking up in the parking lot like weeds.

Hers had been a sudden pregnancy, unexpected and unplanned. In the wake of the test results, Renee began to notice the women in shopping malls and the supermarket who pushed strollers and trailed toddlers from their hands. It seemed a remarkable act of courage to bring children into the world, to defy predictions of a nuclear holocaust, environmental apocalypse. Bringing a baby into the world, each of them dared the world not to let her child live. Sometimes, in the night, Gil would pass his hand over her rounding belly and she would wake to find him gazing at her like some new species of plant, amazed at the life before him. There was talk of marriage and baby names.

Renee began to neglect the obituaries in the local paper, to take long solitary walks at night and marvel at the deep purple of the sky and to feel once more—in what she thought might be merely an excess of hormones—a great thrilling hope, a joy solid as statistics, in the simple beauty of the world. She began to marvel at people in the street, that each one had come from some other one who had risked her life to give it life.

She felt the immensity of the spinning world beneath her, all its poignant possibility, and felt again the tremendous sense of promise she had known in her youth. Irrational, misplaced, the hope grew in her like the child she was carrying, and by the time Renee realized what was happening it was too late. Only later would she understand that her hope had been like her father's erstwhile faith in the Party, like her mother's belief in the man she'd married: fragile and fallible and misplaced.

After the lecture, they meditate. Renee breathes in and out and in and out until she is dark inside and still. She can feel the people around her, their breath, the torpor of their bodies. She can sense them in the dark behind her eyes. The cool blue emptiness of Gokulananda, like an ice field, remote and slowly shifting. Renee tries chanting OM in her mind, imagining the sound reverberating in the universe like a bass note. Gil has told her that if you find the proper pitch, you will be instantly enlightened.

She feels the vibration in her groin first. Then in her belly, then in her chest. A shivering heat moves up her torso, making her palms sweat. Then it ceases. The wave comes again, stronger. She feels the heat move up her body, as if it were traveling a corridor through the center of her, knotting then releasing, then knotting again, like an orgasm the length of her torso, as the heat rises from groin to belly to chest to throat out the top of her head in shudders. It ceases, only to begin again.

Later Gil will tell her that what she has experienced is *kundalini* energy rising, that it is a stage in enlightenment, one he has not yet achieved. "I thought it was a hot flash, early onset of menopause," Renee says. "No such luck," Gil says. "It's God." And Renee thinks that maybe it is and maybe it's not, but either way it doesn't matter. She has long ago learned that there are certain things you can put faith in and certain things you can't. As a child, she had believed in magic, in witchcraft and incantations, she'd even believed she had supernatural powers and would fly if she let herself freefall from her parents' roof. But like certain words that she had cultivated in her childhood because they could amaze her—plagioclase, comestible—faith was a thing forgotten in adulthood that left her with a faint disturbing sense of loss when she came across it now.

It seems to her now that the only thing that will always be there with her, for her, the only thing she can depend on, is the struggle, the fight, *la luta*.

Renee finds Gil sitting on the front stoop, studying his hands the way he does when he is worried. He wears a T-shirt, sandals, sweats. His hunched body looks vulnerable and young, and she feels a terrible urge to ask him to come home with her. To come home. *Marry me,* she wants to say, but instead she takes a seat. Together they stare into the darkness, into the grainy indigo air.

"How can I follow someone who won't be there to lead me?" he asks. Tomorrow Gil is to be initiated into his mantra, and he is angry because Swami Vishnu Ramananda is back on a mountaintop right now trying desperately to die; he may be dead by the time Gil takes him as guru.

"There will be others with you," Renee says, knowing they will not be her.

"The blind leading the blind," Gil says. He tells her that he feels abandoned to have come this far only to find that he may have to go on alone, that his guru is waiting for death in a cave in the mountains of India, listening to holy men read the epic *Bhagavatam*, twenty-four hours a day. "I just wish it could have been different," he says.

Renee looks out at the shadowy trees below them. A goat bleats in the dark.

"Take a number," Renee says.

"What do you mean by that?"

"I wish I were beautiful, that there wasn't a hole in the sky over Antarctica. Everyone wishes something were different."

That night, when she is sitting alone in her second-floor room reading by lamplight, she thinks of how she and Gil had talked of marriage once, just before they left Texas, when it seemed there were only two choices before them, splitting up or settling down. When she knew Gil loved her, it had seemed a simple thing to live without him, to leave him behind and move to this city by herself. "Being in love is just collaborating on a mutual fantasy," she had told him then. "Sometimes one plus one can equal less than two." Now she understands that it is always at the end, when things are coming unraveled between two people, that marriage is proposed. It's always in the face of loss that people look for signs.

When she hears a knock on the door, her heart, despite her, leaps, and she knows it is Gil come to talk things over, come to give her the chance she didn't think they'd ever have again but now thinks perhaps they will, the chance most people never get, to rewrite history and give it a different, happier ending. When she pulls back the door it is not Gil, but the driver.

"May I come in?" he asks, leaning on the door frame.

"Why don't we go out," she says.

She has no real desire to be unfaithful. She has never been before. She simply craves relief. Gil's slow withdrawal from love has been so painful for so long. An affair has the appeal that she imagines Reagan's reign had for Republicans—it offers an optimism untainted by concern for consequences, for who might get hurt.

She likes the fact that he is a driver, that it is his job to transport people. She wants him to take her somewhere, anywhere, fast. All her life she has taken comfort in the thought that she can leave, as had her mother before her. Renee has held onto the hope that if she works hard she will get somewhere. That has been the trouble with Gil all along. Her sense that they were getting nowhere, that they might drown in domestic contentment. His saintly disregard for ambition, his divine attention to inconsequential things, has made her suspect that there is nowhere to get to, that whatever Renee thinks she is searching for, is all, already, here. She is simply missing it.

The driver leads her down the creaky wooden steps out into the night, past the goat pens, past the trailer where Gil is asleep, to a field behind the Siva temple on the high hill where a phallic stone lingam rises out of the ground and the stars spin crazy overhead. They lie on the wet grass. He speaks to her in a language she does not understand as he removes her clothing and his own. His back is hard under her hands, his scalp like sandpaper, and she thinks of Alice, who told her that nothing beats sex with a bald man. "It's like fucking an atomic bomb," Alice said. But sitting on the belly of this stranger, her knees pressed into the grass as she sways under an empty sky, Renee thinks this act recalls nothing so modern, this reaching out in the dark for a hand to hold.

In the night, winter comes suddenly, belatedly, and the ashram wakes to ice. The leaves outside Renee's window hang like glass ornaments from the trees, which are bowed with frost.

Although attendance at the morning six o'clock meditation and eight o'clock asana class is mandatory, Renee slips on her boots and coat and steps out into the livid morning. She walks south along the main drive until she comes to a path that leads into a field and beyond that into woods. She follows it. She walks past the dry remnants of Queen Anne's lace and timothy grass, walking over bright red and yellow leaves shellacked to the path by ice.

As she walks, Renee thinks about the driver, whose name she does not even know, and about Gil, the man she has loved for so long it is as if he is a part of her. A limb she cannot stand to lose. It's not that she wants Gil back, she realizes; it is too late for that, she knows. She loves him but love is not enough. She simply cannot bring herself to give up the fight. She thinks of Swami Ramananda on that mountain-top in India at this very moment, surrounded by a dozen monks who chant without cessation from the *Bhagavatam* while he fights to die, to launch his spirit free of his body as she once hoped to push a child out of hers.

And then she sees it—something dark to her left—and stops. It is a bird. Perched in a bush a few feet from the path, on a branch bent low with ice. A tiny, black-capped Chickadee. Stock still. Renee has hardly ever had the chance to see a feral thing at such close range, and even though it is just a common bird, her heart pounds. She is so close she can look into its small, black eye; at the wrinkled lid, half closed; its black cap like a tiny yarmulke. Inky feathers fan across its throat, each one like a brushstroke. When she steps toward it, ice cracks off a branch into the snow, but the bird doesn't start. Renee clicks her tongue. Pitches a piece of twig. Until this moment, she hadn't thought it possible to freeze while in motion. She'd figured, if only you could keep moving, the encroaching cold couldn't stop you. A gong sounds from the main house, announcing breakfast, but Renee ignores it and starts toward the tiny bird—pushing her body into the tangle of branches, wading toward the overburdened bush—hoping against hope that it will be all right, knowing it prob-ably won't be.

At breakfast, she can't tell if she's imagining it or if people are really giving her dirty looks. Gil is cool, and there is a nervous twitch in his eyelid and he looks pale.

"You missed meditation," he says.

"I went for a walk," she says. "I needed air."

Everybody seems clumsy. Dishes clatter against silverware; peo-ple bump the table as they stand and leave. No one seems to be talking. The bus driver is nowhere in sight, but Renee doesn't want to ask. "How was your night?" she asks instead. "Did you sleep well?"

Gil keeps his face to his plate. Renee thinks maybe he hasn't heard her, and she is about to repeat herself when he says, "*My* night was uneventful." It's his tone, hard as river ice, that lets her know he knows. His left hand lies on the tablecloth and more than anything she wants to hold it, to be able to unmake whatever is being made here. To be, as they once were, *contra mundum*, to feel what she realizes she may never feel again—safe. But she knows it is too late for that. From the beginning it was too late. They will never be safe. They can only hope to be courageous.

The flecks of mustard seed in her scrambled tofu look like hard, black eyes. She pushes it around her plate, tries to swallow. The room is oppressively still. The light seems tacky and dead.

"Gil."

She wonders if the word came out of her mouth. It sounds so far away. Then she sees it is the swami, in the dining room doorway. "Can I see you for a moment?"

"Be right there," Gil says. He gets up from the table. Renee can hear his knees click.

"Gil," she says.

"What," he says. His eyes look red and tired.

"Nothing."

Renee is in the pantry, washing her dishes, when Gil comes in. He stands behind her, beside the table, and plays with the four green apples in the wicker basket there.

"The swami asked me," he says, "if I'd ask you to leave."

The water runs over Renee's hands, bubbling and cold. The hot water seems to have run out hours ago. She watches it swirl into the drain. She has always wondered what Gil would do if push came to shove, whether he would protect her. Or as her mother might have put it, whether he'd have hidden her if the Nazis came or said, "The Jew's in the attic."

"It's not personal, Ren."

"Of course it's personal."

"There are rules here. It's disruptive when people break them."

"What if the rules are wrong? What if the rules are stupid?"

"They're not stupid."

She hates Gil's tone of voice, his martyred calm, his reasonableness. "Fear of garlic is not stupid? Come on. You've undergone a conversion, not a lobotomy."

"Henry already left this morning," Gil says. Henry, she had not even known his name.

"You left a long time ago."

"I don't want to fight," Gil says.

"That's the problem. You won't fight. For anything."

Gil sits down in a chair and Renee leans against the sink. From here, she can see that the part in his hair is uneven and she wants to reach out and touch it, but she doesn't.

"I'm going to go pack," Renee says. Gil nods. He touches her back as she walks past.

When Renee comes downstairs, Gil offers to drive her to the pharmacy that serves as a bus stop in Wilmington, the town adjacent to the ashram. She tells him there is no need. The bus doesn't come till one. She has two hours and could use the walk.

"The road's pretty icy," he says. "It'd be safer if I gave you a ride."

"It'll never be safe," Renee says.

He walks her outside and they stand on the stoop, looking at the ice-glazed trees, the mountains wrapped in fog. When she turns to Gil, he opens his arms to her and she lets herself be folded into them. For a moment, she is safe. She knows that in another minute she will start to cry, so she stands on tip toe, kisses his cheek, then turns to go. She strides a hundred yards or more down the gravel drive before she lets herself look back. She is loath to look back, superstitious and afraid of losing love as easily as Orpheus did. But Gil is right there, standing on the chipped concrete of the stairs. She waves and turns away, knowing that he is behind her as she leaves him, that he is keeping watch as she reaches the road, turns the corner, moves out of sight.

When she gets back to her apartment, the day is already too far gone to salvage so Renee sits on her bed opening the mail that came while she was away. Among the requests for charitable contributions, a warning from her credit card company, she finds a brochure her mother has sent from a cactus zoo outside Phoenix, where all the plants have name tags. It is a thing Gil would have loved. *A Guide to the Garden.* She flips through the manila pages, glancing at the black-and-white photographs of leafy and spiny succulents: agave, *Opuntia phaeacantha* (prickly pear); *Mammillaria microcarpa* (fishhook pincushion); *Echinocereus engelmannii* (hedgehog); *Yucca brevifolia* (Joshua tree). In the background of each shot she can make out a desiccated landscape, austere as the surface of the moon, where against all odds the stubborn prickly things still grow.

Out the window, the sun is burning down on the other side of the Hudson and Renee considers the exquisite impermanence of it all, of her mother pulling the heads off begonias so they will flower and flower and flower, trying desperately to pass on their seed, and of Gil in the misty Catskills where the valleys are filled with pale vapor at this hour and the round-backed hills break the surface like breaching whales, and she knows that Gil is praying at this very moment, desperately, earnestly, as he once made love to Renee, when he still believed—as she now does—that feeling is a kind of knowledge and love an unregarded path to enlightenment.

MY LIFE IN THEORY

PHILOSOPHERS, IT WOULD SEEM, HAVE LITTLE TO TELL US about love; I know, because I am one. Despite the name philosopher—lover of wisdom—we are not known for our success in the realm of Eros. Truth is, our greatest minds have been losers when it came to love. Søren Kierkegaard, for instance, had just one sexual experience in his life and that a failed one, with a prostitute. Perhaps that's because philosophy seeks a system, and love—as any lover knows—is unsystematic in the extreme. Love's a messer-upper, and philosophers, on the whole, are a tidy bunch—at least I am, or was, until we met.

Kate, my girlfriend, introduced us.

I had been away at a regional APA conference, and for most of the flight home, I had been thinking about making love with Kate, the freckled expanse of her skin. So I was disappointed, when I returned home, to find her going on about a new reporter at the paper, recently transferred from one of those N-states in the West—Nebraska or New Mexico. I could tell from the way she spoke of him that she was a little infatuated, but it didn't worry me.

We liked to tell each other about our little crushes; it kept us on our toes, kept us honest. We had been together several years by then and shared a belief that we wouldn't stray so long as we kept our theoretical dalliances between us. Our revelations were like a ménage à trois without the social awkwardness, and we always made love afterward with the urgency of adulterers.

Kate and I had met in a Wittgenstein seminar five years before, where she'd impressed us all with her dry wit, long neck, and beautiful breasts. She is not what most people would call a beautiful woman—her expressions are too difficult, too interesting for that—but she is compelling. Though her mother is American, she grew up in South Africa, before her parents' divorce, and the African sun has left its mark—giving her eyes their squint, her mouth its premature lines. She had short copper hair and green eyes and could talk any of us under the table. She dated several of us that term, but I was the only one to last past qualifying exams, and I felt lucky, though luck is not a thing philosophers on the whole take an interest in. Superstition is largely outside our realm of concern. Although we traffic in abstractions, we think ourselves empiricists, skeptics; my peers and I snubbed the mystics among us (the Buberians—as we called them—seemed unrigorous, too sentimental for our taste). We favored Wittgenstein and Nietzsche. We grew up in the eighties after all.

The night I returned from the APA, as Kate described her new friend, I tried to imagine him, the way one tests a new flavor on the tongue. I tried to see what she saw in him, my interest in him an extension of my interest in her. It was not hard to imagine; she described his face, his voice, his body. "You know the type," she said, with the air of amused and proprietary dismissal that signals a crush, "beauty and the Beats—goatee, khakis, the collected work of Bukowski."

I wondered if she wanted to sleep with him. I wondered idly what he'd be like in bed. I'd slept with a few men before—in prep school and as an undergrad—there was something noncommittal in the whole exchange. We were friends, those guys and I; we didn't mistake sex for love. We were after pleasure, biding our time, until we met the right woman and settled down.

In *Philosophy Made Simple*—or PMS, as my students call it—the philosophy textbook from which I'm required to teach at the local university, love gets no mention in the index. *Remorse* does, as does *tyranny* and the *unmover unmoved*. *Rewards* are mentioned, *revenge*, *respect for others, paradoxes, pain, lying, heat,* and *happiness. Suicide, socialism, abortion,* and *sexual morality*. But *love* is nowhere to be found. To learn about love, evidently, you have to do your own research.

The majority of people seem content to love by rote, to acquiesce to cant—love is true (or untrue), men are dogs, women are nuts, love is hell or makes the world go round. Most do not need to ask what love is, any more than they question what is the good or the real. They live and love and ask questions later. But I couldn't help but wonder, even as I was happy with Kate, *Is this love? In settling down, have we merely settled?*

It occurred to me from time to time that the heart might not be the source of my troubles, but the mind. Ever since I'd defended my dissertation in the spring, I'd felt a dull dissatisfaction. The examined life no longer seemed worth living. Kate called it postpartum depression. But I wondered if it might be something more.

My colleagues at the university were little comfort. In the grim warren of grad offices my fellow adjuncts assembled like an accusation. This—they seemed to say—is what education leads to. This is the image of the examined life: frail women in cardigans, men with unruly facial hair and glasses. I had heard that one of my colleagues was once a homeless man. Now he had a long red beard and no plans to complete his dissertation. He joked about being unmanned by the microwave, offered me herbal teas.

Times were tough and the administration had shunted together the philosophy adjuncts with the English lecturers and comp instructors, and there was a subtle war on among the posters: Virginia Woolf facing off against Nietzsche, Joyce against Adorno. We held in common only our disdain for our subjugated status and student papers: "Marijuana should be legalized," one comp instructor said, "so that I won't have to read another paper about it."

Kate jokingly referred to this state of affairs as the Pedagogy of the Depressed. It's the reason she left academia. Maybe it's the reason I've stayed. Despair can arrest action: I didn't act; I only thought about it. That is, until I met Kate's new friend, Jake.

Kate introduced us about a week after I returned from the APA. We were leaving her office, when he came over to say goodnight. He was wearing a peach-colored sweater, something suggested—Kate would later tell me—by a men's magazine to which he subscribed; his hair was blond, cut in a sloppy shag that seemed meant to say, *I am handsome without trying, I am a free spirit trapped in a day job.* He was taller than me—six foot, I'd guess—with a lanky, cowboy's build. He had, of all things, a goatee.

It was dislike at first sight.

He told me his name and offered me his hand. "Kate has told me a lot about you," he said.

"She speaks well of you," I said, taking my hand back.

He smiled with only half his mouth, as if he were too hip to bother with symmetry. While they talked, I observed his languorous slouch, his half-closed eyes, lids drooping as if he were hypnotized by Kate's presence. I wondered if this routine often worked on women. I wondered what Kate saw in him.

"We should have dinner sometime," he said, his voice mellifluous as a late-night jazz announcer's. "The three of us."

I was relieved when Kate said we had to get going, she was starved, relieved to follow her after a brief flurry of goodbyes out the door.

On the drive home, Kate fumed about her day. When we'd first gotten involved five years before, sex had sustained us—we had more sex then than any three couples we knew combined—but over time our bond had become one of mutual indulgence. Sounding board more than sex partner. To be fair, she had a lot to complain about. The new features editor at the paper disliked "girl reporters," so Kate's beat had changed after his arrival. She used to cover environmental stories (illegal sewage dumping, unlawful development, Environmental Impact Statements); lately he'd assigned her coverage of stolen fava beans and cock fights. That week it was the national gay rodeo that was coming to town. For background, Kate wanted to check out a gay, country western bar in St. Paul.

"I've invited Jake to come along," she said. "You don't mind, do you?"

"Why should I mind?" I said, knowing that a question is not an answer.

The Townhouse Country bar was packed when we arrived a little past nine. At first glance it was hard to tell it from any other country western joint, with rough-hewn beams and cross rails enclosing the dance floor, a wooden bar and gambling in back. Men and women in cowboy boots, bolos, chaps, and spurs. But look closer and you noticed the rainbow flag beside the dance floor and that the predictable paintings of cowboys and Indians were actually beefcake pics of shirtless braves and cattlemen with well-oiled pecs beside a poster of k. d. lang, and those meaty cowboys gracefully two-stepping across the dance floor held other meaty cowboys in their arms.

As we leaned on the bar, waiting to order, a spark plug of a man with a handlebar mustache and ten-gallon hat approached and asked Jake to dance.

"I'm afraid I don't know that step," Jake said with an easy smile.

"He's *straight*," Kate shouted over the music.

"Can't blame a boy for trying," the cowboy winked, tipped his hat, disappeared in the crowd.

Around us a few people laughed in a nice way. And I began to like Jake just a little. His ease in what some might find an uneasy circumstance.

We found a table near the dance floor, a high small round table, the sort of impractical table that dance bars favor in order to discourage patrons from staying seated too long. We commandeered three stools and leaned our heads together to be heard over the music.

Jake told us ranching jokes and rodeo tales from the West. He told us that in Salt Lake City they serve a beer called Polygamy Porter, whose label features a naked man embracing seven naked women and the slogan Why Have Just One?

"The thing is," he said, smiling, "they'll only serve you one beer at a time. It's illegal to have more than one drink per customer on a table."

"Oh, it has a moral," Kate said. "I love an anecdote with a moral."

We laughed, and despite myself, I warmed to him. He had the appeal of the American West, a boastful self-contentment, an optimism and physical vigor that seemed at once decadent and innocent. It seemed to me that he had something like the delight that animals must take in themselves, a simple pleasure in the body, in life, which I had once taken in life too.

It turned out that Jake, like Kate, had been getting a PhD when he gave it up for journalism. "I don't believe in knowledge for knowledge's sake," he said. "It has to be applied."

"That's what I tell my students," I said.

"A man after your own heart," Kate said.

"So Kate tells me you're a philosopher," he shouted, when Kate went to get some more drinks.

"I teach philosophy. Just the basics: Platonic Forms, the Poetics, Ethics 101."

"So tell me," he leaned close enough that I could smell his faint cologne. "What exactly was the Greeks' position on sex?" He smiled his half smile.

I felt a charge pass between us, a thrill of desire.

"They had a lot of positions," I said, dismissing the question.

He laughed. "Is that a pun?"

"Not at all."

I looked away, watching the dancers on the floor, men in one another's arms.

When Kate returned, we drank another round, shouting over the music, but all I would remember later of that conversation was the heat between me and him, the pressure like a hand on my chest, real as the railroad ties that enclosed the dance floor.

If Kate noticed, she gave no sign.

"I'm going to go snoop around," she said. "You two okay here?"

"We're fine," he said.

"Hurry back," I said. But she was gone already into the crowd and we were left alone together, with the shock of desire arcing between us like a downed live wire and the awareness that whatever we said, we were saying something else.

The semester that Jake came into our lives, I was teaching two extension classes at the local branch of the state university: Introduction to Platonic Thought, from 3:30 to 4:45 Mondays and Wednesdays, and a course on Ethics 101 Thursday nights. I had eight students in each, which was just enough to ensure that the administration could not cancel. Enrollment is often spotty and sometimes my classes do not make and I have to pick up a class in composition or the dreaded Study Skills, in which underprepared students work through a soft-back manual comprising drills on procrastination and time management. I try to be philosophical about it. I take what I can get.

The extension classes with catchy titles do best: Love among the Runes—which purports to teach students "to divine one's destiny by casting ancient runes" (which are, in fact, brand-new, American-made, plastic bits with faux Norse symbols pressed into their surface)—always has a waiting list. So does Introduction to Astrology. There is a brisk trade in divination these days—astrological columns, palm readings—people seem less interested in preparatory contemplation than in foreknowledge, which seems to me to have it backward.

After all, what good is knowing what's to come if you're ill prepared to cope with it?

We began to see a lot of Jake. We became a threesome. He dragged us out to obscure Mexican joints in what passes for a barrio in the Midwest, insisted we canoe from Minneapolis to St. Paul by way of a chain of city lakes. We went to foreign movies: Ken Loach films that required subtitles; a film by von Trier that required Dramamine; Almodóvar. And each time we met I felt more acutely the tension between us, like a private joke we were keeping from Kate; I noticed that he took care not to brush my hand when handling the canoe in a portage, he no longer shook my hand in greeting as he had done before. I began to think about him more and more, to find myself distracted by thoughts of him. Things he'd said. To feel an embarrassingly adolescent thrill whenever Kate came home with stories about Jake from work, whenever he called.

I had thought he was gay when we first met, but the thought had passed. Now I asked Kate as we sat reading on the couch one night; she seemed not to have considered it.

"I don't think so," she said, continuing to flip pages in *The Nation*, "but I can see what you mean, I guess. The peach sweater."

"And the goatee," I said.

"Goatees are gay?" she asked.

"They're defensive," I said. "All beards are an assertion of masculinity. Goatees are lowercase masculinity. Ambivalent."

"Where do you get this stuff?" she asked.

"I make it up," I said. "To amuse you."

I considered, abstractly, the possibility of having an affair with Jake— but I dismissed it. I didn't reject the idea on moral grounds. Morality, in my opinion, is overrated, especially in the American empire. "Morality," as Adorno says, "may well appear self-evident to those who feel themselves to be exponents of a class in the ascendent," but for those of us who see little correlation between being powerful and being good, the issue is not so simple.

I didn't believe in monogamy. I remembered a drive that Kate and I had taken once along the shore of Lake Superior; we had driven past pine forests and root beer–colored waterfalls, waves breaking on the rocky shoreline, the sky overhead huge and swirled with cirrus clouds, and I had felt an almost painful joy. I'd reached out and pressed her hand with mine and said "I love you," and in that moment knew for the first time that what I meant when I said that was "I love *all* of this." And that to try to compress that joy and that desire into a single love is a kind of mutilation of spirit.

Honesty restrained me instead: Kate and I were scrupulously frank with one another. I wanted to discuss my crush with her, but something prevented me. Maybe it was a recognition that Jake was her friend, or that he was a man, or that mine was more than the usual attraction. In any case, I didn't mention it.

We'd been seeing Jake regularly for several months when we went to the U Film Society to see *Vanya on Forty-second Street*, a film about a cast of actors rehearsing a Chekhov play and the sexual intrigues among them. I was trying to keep my mind on the movie, off of him, when I put my arm around Kate and my hand landed on his shoulder by mistake, and we both started.

"Shhh," Kate said, setting her hand high on my thigh, nuzzling her head against me.

I looked over at him, his profile flashing in the light from the screen, his eyes forward, refusing to meet mine.

At home that night, I told Kate that it would be better if they went out without me from now on. I told her that I had too much work these days to join them, that I found him a little tiresome.

"You never like my friends," she said.

"Don't be ridiculous," I said. "You don't have any friends." I regretted it as soon as I'd said it, but it was too late to take it back.

To my surprise, Kate laughed.

"You're right," she said. "I don't like many people. That's why I wish you liked Jake."

I told her that I did, that I was just preoccupied.

She leaned up and kissed me. "A misanthrope and a hermit, we make a great pair."

When he came by after that, I contrived to go out. When they went out, I stayed in. I heard through Kate that he often asked after me; he asked her if I played racquetball, said he'd like to play a game with me sometime, if she didn't mind. She said she'd pass on the message; I told her I'd rather not. I avoided her office, picked her up at the curb.

I still thought about him, but I thought about him less.

In class, I often tell my students stories. Stories, I'm convinced, are what we remember, how we learn. Stories, like education, are a species of seduction: seducing students to care about something other than themselves. Drawing them out of their assumptions into a world of surprise.

That term, I began the class with the story of Zeno of Elea and his famous paradoxes. The fifth-century philosopher is not properly a subject for a course in Ethics, but his paradox of the arrow is a favorite story of mine so I told it anyway (such are the prerogatives of the pedant). Zeno pointed out that, if one reasons it through, one will see that an arrow shot at a target will never arrive: It will always be half the remaining distance to its goal (given that an object moving from one place to another must first move half the distance toward its goal, then half that distance, et cetera, he demonstrated that an arrow can never reach its mark). If you think about it, you can't get there from here. And yet we do. The arrow pierces the target, defying logic.

Zeno told the story to demonstrate the illusory nature of change by demonstrating the contradiction inherent in any description of motion. I told it to get my students to test philosophical assertions against the world in which they live.

The whole point of an education, as I see it, is to help you take the world personally, to put you on a first-name basis with history. But most of my students seem to think that a college education is an extension of adolescence, the intellectual equivalent of training wheels; they live in a state of semi-adulthood, while parents foot the bill.

When I asked one young woman recently what she was majoring in, she looked at me with frank disdain, as if choices were for losers, and said, with a shrug, "Y'know, Pre-life." Life in the academy, my students seem to think, is not the real thing. This is practice. This is only life in theory.

In early March, Jake heard from his landlord that his building had been sold and that he had thirty days to move, so Kate and I agreed to help him. The morning was wet and soggy with melting. As we walked up the steps to his building, I smelled the heavy scent of wild mushrooms. We were making good time, shuttling boxes down stairs, until Jake and I found ourselves alone in his apartment. The pale, March light poured in the French doors from the balcony and the room was very still.

"You've been avoiding me," he said.

I picked up a box. "I'm not avoiding you."

"What have I done?"

"Nothing," I laughed and pushed past him.

He caught my arm. "I must have done something."

"No," I said. "You haven't done anything. It's what I don't want to do."

He didn't ask me to explain. He raised his hand as if he meant to touch my face, when Kate walked in and we both stepped back. I joked that we were the prime movers unmoving. Kate said she didn't know how prime we were but we'd better move, because she wasn't doing this by herself. Afterward, we went to Jake's new place for pizza and beer. The two of them talked and joked, while I maintained an uncompanionable silence.

On our way home, Kate was cross. She asked why I couldn't be nice to Jake, why I had to be so difficult. I watched the sparkling of the streetlights, like orange emergency flares going up one after another. I felt the terrible weight of regret that sometimes heralds a loss. I told her, as gently as I could, that I was attracted to him, that I loved her but was attracted to Jake. She must have sensed that this was not our usual talk about infatuation. My mouth felt dry.

"Have you fucked him?" her voice was steady, emotionless, the tone she used to use in a heated seminar debate.

I shook my head. "Don't be ridiculous."

"But you want to?"

"Look," I said. "I don't understand it myself. I love you. This has nothing to do with us."

I wanted her to understand that it was like a philosophy problem. A question I needed answered: I wanted to understand what was between me and him. Early on Kate and I had agreed that we didn't want ours to become a small love, the sort of love we saw all around us, resentful, limiting, couples whose lives were less for all the sacrifices they'd made for the other. Guys who'd given up mountain climbing, women who'd given up jobs or ambitions. We promised each other we'd never be like that. But lately I'd had my doubts about us, and my attraction to him worked on those.

She asked if he felt the same way.

I told her that I thought he did.

We were quiet for a while.

"The heart has its reasons," I said, quoting Pascal, "which reason knows nothing of."

"You're so full of shit," Kate said.

When I woke in the night I heard her crying beside me. In the morning I told her that I wouldn't see him again. And for awhile, that seemed to be enough.

The philosopher Iris Murdoch once called marriage a "long conversation," but before I met Kate I treated my love affairs more like a drawn-out argument in which my task was to disprove the premise that ours was a viable relationship. I treated love like a suspect premise to be tested. My concept of courtship (a lawyer lover once told me) bore a strong resemblance to moot court.

With Kate, though, I was trying. I had my doubts, of course. But ours were not big problems, though we often fought about small things. Kate wanted us to go on drives in October to watch the leaves turn, to play miniature golf, buy a barbecue, get cable, and while there was nothing inherently sinister about any of these, I was thirty-three at the time and the thought of these diversions made me feel old.

For a while, though, things were better between us than they had been in a long while. We began going to concerts, to plays, and between us there was a new tenderness; we were both making an effort, even if the effort weighed on us a little. Kate suggested we meet in the afternoons for drinks; we made love on the couch, the sunlight pouring in.

When Kate told me that Jake was seeing the Sex Goddess, a lonely hearts columnist from a local alternative paper who emphasized toys and leather, I was happy for him and happy to find I didn't care.

When I ran into Jake a month or two later at Kate's office, we were polite.

"You're looking well," he said.

"Actually," I said, smiling, "I look like you."

He laughed.

It was true. We both wore jeans and men's v-neck undershirts and suit coats. He mentioned that his birthday was that weekend, that he'd be spending it alone (things having gone awry with the Goddess). It seemed only reasonable to invite him out for a drink.

"You should never age alone," I said.

I'd forgotten that Kate was going out of town to cover the Polar

Plunge in Ely, a fact I recalled only later that night at home. I considered canceling but decided it was better just not to tell her. I didn't want to upset her, and it hardly seemed worth mentioning. It was just a drink after all. So we met at the Lexington, a bar in St. Paul the three of us had liked, at the irreproachable hour of seven p.m.

We ordered martinis and sat at the bar. We discussed gin preferences. The virtues of a twist versus an olive. Slowly we relaxed. He told me about the Sex Goddess, who turned out to be a former gymnast from Cloquet, a Norwegian Lutheran with blue eyes and an uncannily flexible body. I told him about my latest idea for a *New Yorker* cartoon: If Philosophers Had Majored in Business, featuring Cartesian Waters (I Drink Therefore I Am); Platonic Girdles, For that Ideal Form; and Ecce Home Furnishings. He laughed, raised his glass: "I drink, therefore I am." I had forgotten how much I liked his company. I forgot the time. By one a.m., it seemed wise to accept his offer of a ride home. It seemed only polite to invite him in.

I made us coffee while he looked at the bookshelves, the volumes of Adorno, Nietzsche, Wittgenstein, Kant, German Idealists, English Empiricists. When I returned with the coffee, he took the cup then set it aside and asked if I would kiss him. It was a curious locution. He did not ask if he might kiss me, but whether I would kiss him—my volition the issue at hand. And I liked him for this, even though the kiss was bland. Even though I was aware of the hard length of his tongue, the musty gin taste in my mouth, and then I was aware of none of these things, only of the sickening lurch of desire in my stomach, his mouth, his smooth chest.

Desire confounds categories.

Systems fail us when it comes to matters of the heart. They leave out too much, lead us to false conclusions. We assume instead of knowing. Our only hope is to learn through experience. Kate was the one who reminded me that the phrase "the exception proves the rule," means not *validates* but *tests*. Desire proves love. Tests it. At least exceptional desire does, but isn't desire always exceptional to those engaged in it?

Lesbians are often accused of narcissism—our love of women blamed on a hatred of men or a hatred of our mothers or on a thwarted maturation that has locked one in pursuit of an adolescent mirror image of oneself—as if a woman simply loving another woman were inexplicable without reference to aversion or impediment. But this, in my experience, could not be more wrong. I have loved women because they are beautiful, because they are tender or brilliant, because I am moved by them.

When I fall for a man, as I fell for Jake, it is because he reminds me of myself.

The next morning, while Jake was in the bathroom, I called Kate on her cell phone, just to hear her voice. I told her that I missed her. She told me that I sounded funny. Was I okay? "I'm fine," I said. I remembered how she used to say, whenever I was away at a conference, "You can come home now, all is forgiven." I said it to her now. She laughed. "I didn't know there was anything to forgive." I wanted to tell her everything, but I couldn't. And the thought of that made me terribly lonely. I told her that I had to go, that I had a lot of papers to grade. But I didn't work that day. After Jake left, I sat at my desk watching the wind push the leaves around outside.

When Kate returned, I didn't tell her about the drink. But she must have sensed something. She seemed sad, and I felt a great desire to reassure her, because despite what I had done and was about to do, I loved her. My feelings for him, I wanted to tell her, had nothing at all to do with her. I was trying to find out about love, about what it is to be human, I was after evidence, the facts of the heart. Desiring him did not detract from my love for her, anymore than reading one book detracts from enjoying another. But I could tell her none of this.

She said she was having trouble at work. Her assignments were less and less relevant. In the last year she had covered a vampire convention of *True Blood* fans at the Hyatt. The theft of the butter bust of the Dairy Queen from the State Fairgrounds. The House Rabbit Society's Easter pageant. What she called "the cultural trivia of a trivial culture."

"We are the Romans," I said.

"Yeah," she said. "Look what happened to them."

Perhaps I only imagined it, with a lover's narcissism, but it seemed to me that the culture egged me on toward an affair with Jake. Everywhere I turned were exhortations to excess, refutations of restraint. Adultery began to seem like the social equivalent of second-hand smoke, a byproduct of a culture loathe to accept limits. Ford Motors, that quintessentially American company, whose slogan had once been We're Number One, now boasted, No Boundaries. Bus billboards pledged No Limit credit cards. Hewlett-Packard insisted Everything Is Possible. As if we needn't choose. As if choices had no consequences.

For a few weeks Jake and I met at his apartment in the afternoon and made love. I told Kate that I had student conferences, classes to prepare. Our meetings were largely wordless, a matter of gestures—mouths and hands, taste and touch. For hours after leaving him, I was conscious of my skin, dazed with arousal. Familiar streets took on a new brilliancy, the sky a new radiance; as I walked home along Garfield, each house, each sign seemed to possess significance.

But the more I desired Jake, the less we had to say to each other.

Grasping at desire, it seemed to disappear. After sex, I dressed quickly, eager to get home to Kate. I began to feel closer to her, more tender, protective. I began to notice little things she'd like—a Freud action figure, a biscotti recipe, books on South African history. I recalled how Kate's stories had amazed me when we first met—stories of her work with the anti-apartheid group the Black Sash, of her visits to remote villages and appearances before pink-faced judges to protest pass laws, of her uncle's strangulation by wire, the taste of blood oranges and olives eaten on a mountain hike. How she had wanted to be an Anglican priest because she liked the phrase "Peace be with you," passed around like a collection plate at the end of every service. I admired how she'd taken part in what Adorno termed "resistance," a refusal "to be part of the prevailing evil, a refusal that always implies resisting something stronger and hence always contains an element of despair." She seemed to carry in her the parched landscape of southern Africa, its desolation and its harsh beauty. I realized that the passion I felt for Jake was passing: Our sex was a little like getting drunk, liberating at first but tedious if done too often. I was embarrassed by the boredom I felt.

A month passed and another, before I admitted to Jake that I didn't know if I could do this anymore; he appeared neither disappointed nor surprised. He simply asked if I wanted him to change my mind. I said it would be easy, but that I'd rather he didn't.

And sitting there beside him, I missed him. More than missing him, I missed desiring him.

Kierkegaard—the failed lover—spoke of "the enthusiasm of a love that ever seeks solitude," and I wonder now if this wasn't the source of my disappointment in that affair; what I was seeking with Jake, I suspect, wasn't him—lovely as he was—but a more perfect solitude, a more complete sense of the world. I wanted the feeling that comes when you release yourself toward things—reading can do this and looking at a painting and listening to music or walking through half empty streets almost anywhere alone at night will do this. I wanted to stand in the radiant presence of desire, when all things, the black branches of trees, light falling on brick, the strains of a violin concerto, one's own hand, seem illuminated by a loveliness musical in its intensity.

When Jake called my office a few days after we ended our affair, I was surprised. He asked to meet at a pub in St. Paul. He sounded nervous; I noted that he didn't suggest we meet at his apartment.

When I arrived he was waiting in a booth. We ordered beers, chatted awkwardly.

"Have you run across my sweater," he asked. "The peach one?"

"I thought you'd thrown it over for a tweed," I said. I had not seen the sweater in weeks.

He didn't laugh.

"I've checked my car," he said. "I can't find it. I thought maybe."

"I'll check."

We drank pints of ale, and he flirted with the waitress, and it was clear that whatever had been between us was over now.

Kate was the one who found the peach sweater, the hideous thing had fallen behind the radiator in our bedroom, cast off, evidently, without attention. When she told me, I blushed, stammered. Confused by the implication, which—until she saw my reaction—she had not seen. When she asked me directly what was going on, if I'd slept with him, I couldn't bring myself to lie.

Kate sat on the couch and covered her face and cried as if someone she'd loved had died. And I started to cry, too. And it occurred to me that in all my careful reasoning I had left out one key thing: empathy. My formulation of the problem had been wrong, the premise flawed. I had been so concerned with the true and the untrue, the ethical versus the moral, action and inaction, that I had failed to consider the obvious, the simple fact that I might hurt the woman I loved.

I told her that it had nothing to do with us. That it was over.

"You're right," she said, standing. "It is." And she walked out.

For awhile Kate and I tried to patch things up. We got back together. Made love. Fought. Cried. Called it off and on again for a couple of months. Until finally we no longer remembered what it was we were trying to save, a time before things were over. I heard that Jake left the paper a few months later to return to school. I did not see him again.

Even now I prefer to think of ours as a temporary separation, not an ending. I take comfort in the thought that things haven't really changed, that Kate's absence is a momentary break, which time will heal—that change, as Zeno would have it, is illusory.

But every so often I remember the story in PMS of the follower of Zeno, who was lecturing before a crowd in Athens, gesticulating wildly as he made his points. The Zenoist was arguing that an object cannot move, because it cannot be in more than one place at a time. "If it moves where it is, it is standing still. If it is where it is not, it cannot be there," he said, when suddenly he dislocated his shoulder. A doctor was called from the crowd. Asked to fix the shoulder, the physician explained that it could not be dislocated: either the shoulder was where it had been and was not dislocated, or it had moved to where it was not, which was impossible. At which point the patient saw what should have been obvious all along: logic can mislead us. If we rely on reason alone, the answers we seek may elude us.

I remembered the story this morning as I watched my students write their midterm exams. It was one of those extraordinarily windy days in autumn and all manner of things were blowing past the classroom window, the flotsam of other lives—pages of newsprint, plastic bags like round white kites, twigs and cups and colored flyers—and in the midst of the maelstrom, I saw something go by, out of the corner of my eye, which must have been a twig, but which looked like a child's arrow, and I thought briefly that it could be one of Cupid's, or Zeno's—aiming for something it will never, ever, reach.

RAT CHOICE

LATELY LISA'S MOTHER HAS BEEN TELLING HER THINGS she does not want to know. Lisa's mother, who has told her little, now will not shut up. She follows Lisa out to the car, under starlight, to tell her that Lisa's father has been impotent for years. She tells her, at the kitchen table, about the pornographic film he has rented on his doctor's orders, about the penile pump.

This afternoon, she is telling Lisa about the drawings she has made. They are walking in Eloise Butler Wildflower Garden less than a mile from the house where Lisa grew up; it is October and the trees are a conflagration. Ocher. Russet. Orange.

The drawings her mother has made are crude, scrawled on typing paper in red and black magic marker. The first one is of Clara—the woman Lisa's father had an affair with ten years back, an affair he revealed for the first time two weeks ago. Lisa's mother slashed the drawing with lines and words. Slut. Cunt. Whore. Bitch. Then she hung it up in their bedroom.

"I told your father about it before I hung it up, so it wouldn't be a surprise," she says, as if consideration were the point here.

The second drawing, of Lisa's father, is stick figure with a huge erection and slavering mouth. Her mother titled it *The Unrepentant Rat* (Lisa laughs at this); she put that one up in the bedroom, too. "I realized," Lisa's mother tells her as they walk a familiar path through the woods, "that Clara wasn't the one who betrayed me. She didn't know me. She was a slut and a whore for sleeping with a married man, but she didn't know me."

What makes her mother angry, she tells Lisa, is not the fact of the affair but that Lisa's father will not apologize. He has told Lisa's mother that he is sorry that the news has caused her pain, but he will not apologize for fucking another woman. He claims not to re-member the details. When it happened or for how long. So Lisa's mother, her brilliant mother, her 190-IQ-mother-who-gave-up-a-career-in-medicine-to-marry-The-Unrepentant-Rat spends her af-ternoons scouring checkbook registers from 1996, 1997, 1998, 1999 in order to piece together the story Lisa's father will not tell. Her mother has deduced from these that the affair took place while Lisa's parents were in marriage counseling and her father was a consultant for a local electric company where Clara worked. He will neither confirm nor deny the allegations, her father, the lawyer, the dick.

Lisa wants to comfort her, her beautiful brilliant mother. But she does not know what to say. She wants to tell her not to take this per-sonally. That extramarital affairs are like an extracurricular sport in this country. Everyone is doing it. She wants to tell her that sex on the side is fashionable these days—that it is to the twenty-first cen-tury what Buddhism was to the fifth. It's a sign of the times, not a personal failure. These days, everyone is cheating on something or someone: income taxes, stock holders, husbands, lovers, wives. We are cheating ourselves. But what can she say on the subject of adultery that her mother has not already heard? The headlines are full of it. There is no comfort for the suspicion that it raises, Lisa knows this well herself: the suspicion that it is her fault that he wandered, that somehow she was not enough, that maybe nothing ever will be.

"The last erection your father had was with her," Lisa's mother tells her bitterly.

They are walking under pine boughs. A forest out of fairytales. The ground littered with brown needles. The sweet smell of pine and earth. Wood smoke rises from the chimney of the stone house that serves as a visitor center inside the wildflower garden. Lisa has walked these woods with her mother since adolescence. They are not out of them yet.

It is a month now since Lisa's partner, Richard, left her for another woman, taking with him the boom box on which they'd played Gluck's *Orfeo* and R.E.M., Smashing Pumpkins and Piaf; two boxes of books; his files; and their golden retriever, Jeff.

"This is why people get married," Gretchen, Lisa's best friend, says.

"Why? So they can cheat?"

"No, so they stay together when they cheat."

"Would that be better?"

"It would be different. It would be another choice."

Gretchen is getting her PhD in political science at the university where Lisa teaches composition and sometimes, like this term, creative writing. Gretchen studies Rational Choice Theory, why people do what they do and how to predict it. Gretchen calls it "Rat Choice" for short; the model, she says, is flawed, but it is popular. The *New Republic* ran a cover story on it just the other week. In Gretchen's field they talk a lot about "rational states"—a concept that pleases Lisa secretly. Whenever her friend talks about theorizing rational states, Lisa pictures a continent of tiny owlish people, scholarly and dour, a whole country governed by reasonableness. Like Swedes.

The crunch of leaves, the smell of wood smoke. Richard once called autumn an operatic season, and Lisa understands now that he meant the almost painful fullness of it, the bombast and the overblown beauty of the trees, the smell of fruit and rot, the leaves, the watery weight of the chill air. Thinking of him, she feels a lurch of desire in her belly, acute as a menstrual cramp. She tries to think of other things, of getting home, of getting food, of the class she has to teach tomorrow night for which she has yet to prepare. The cold walk has made her hungry. Her mother has fallen silent now. Lisa takes her mother's arm, hooks it in her own, and leans her head against the older woman's shoulder. Her mother smells of Anaïs Anaïs, a faintly floral French perfume.

"We'll be fine, Mom. You and I," Lisa says. "We are."

What Lisa is, in fact, is thirty-two and crying too often in the afternoons. When she is feeling Byronic and self-pitying, she tells herself that she is crying because she is childless, loveless, and middle-aged. When she is feeling more robust, she makes excuses: says she has lost the love of her life after a devastating six-year love affair; says graduate school is demoralizing; says it is performance anxiety. But she suspects it is both more and less than these, both more complicated and simpler. She wants to get beyond these woods and is afraid to.

The following evening Lisa stands before her class in a fluorescent third-floor room on the campus of a midwestern university, instructing thirty students in the basics of fiction. Tonight she is giving them an exercise. Lisa has asked her students to write down on index cards three things—a fear, a regret, a secret. Later, she will randomly redistribute these cards, each with one item, to the students as they write a character sketch of a person they consider virtuous or good. "They may or may not be good by conventional standards," she says. "But it must be someone you consider to be virtuous or good."

As they write their sketches, she sorts the index cards into piles—secrets, regrets, fears. After sorting them, she sits on her desk and reads through a few.

I am afraid of a world in which art does not matter.

I am afraid of suffocation. Of being suffocated.

Squirrels.

She laughs out loud, then apologizes to the few students who look up, their brows fretted with worry. The truth is, she is moved by these anonymous fears. Detached from specific people, they do not seem neurotic but become philosophical. Existential. Voices out of the void. Everyfear. They are such poignant and courageous proclamations. Despite a world in which art is disregarded, suffocation possible, in which there are squirrels, we go on.

She sorts through the fears, then the secrets. She does not have time for the regrets.

After they have written for five minutes, Lisa hands each of them a random secret to incorporate into the sketch. As she walks around the room handing out the cards, a few students begin to moan. "Can I have another one?" a guy in a baseball cap asks from across the room. "Okay," Lisa says, "anyone willing to trade with Nick? Anyone want to swap their fears, their regrets?" Hands go up around the room. "Can we trade with each other?" two women beside Lisa ask. "Okay," Lisa says. She allows the students one trade, either with each other or with her. "Oh, man," Nick says as Lisa hands him a new card, "I don't like this one either. This is worse." "Trade you," someone says from behind Lisa. "Would it were so easy in life," Lisa says. A few of the older students laugh.

"Don't just plop it in," Lisa tells them. "Work toward incorporating the secret into your sketch." This, she tells them, is how fact gets turned into fiction. This is how autobiography gets turned into myth—through the introduction and incorporation of random external elements (those casual pranks of the gods, she thinks). She tells them that it is an important discipline to accept random elements, not to try to control your material. When a thought comes up, it is important not to dismiss information about a character because you think, "That's not how I want it to go."

At the end of class, a student asks her what he should do with his cards; should he throw them out? "No," Lisa says, "I'll take them." She does not understand why she should want to hold on to other people's sorrows, but she cannot bring herself to toss them. She throws the lot of them into her briefcase. Shuts out the lights as she goes.

When Richard told her a month ago that he was sleeping with one of his students, Lisa had found the confession hard to believe. Like a bad plot twist in one of her student's stories, his phrases had seemed hackneyed, overdone. He did not tell her he was leaving her; that part had been her idea. He said, simply, that he was having an affair. Then he wept. "Who is she?" Lisa asked, her voice cold, as it is in the face of conflict. Emotion becomes remote to her when she needs it most, like a polite guest slipping out when the family dinner conversation takes too personal a turn. He told her that the girl was a former student, emphasizing the first of these two words. *Former* student. He told her he did not mean for this to happen. They had gone for coffee a few times to discuss—Lisa interrupted him. "Don't give me details," she said. "I do not want to know." One detail she will remember though, from what he's told her, one detail she cannot forget: The student he is fucking smells like ripe avocados. "We've lost the sense of wonder," he told Lisa, explaining why he'd strayed. "There are no surprises between us anymore." She told him that he was wrong. That she was surprised as hell; she was surprised that after six years of quasi-marriage he was going to leave her for a smell. She was surprised at herself for picking up a plate from the dinner table and hurling it at his handsome chest. She was surprised to find that she is a very good shot.

At home, after her class, she makes herself a cup of tea and stretches out across the bed that once was theirs. On the bedside table, a cairn of mostly unread books. The topmost one is *The Inferno*, translation by Ciardi, Lisa's version of pulp fiction. She likes the opening best: the forest Dante wanders through alone.

She can trace the origins of all her love affairs to books. With Richard it was Dante, Martin Amis, and Roland Barthes. Their first conversation had been about *A Lover's Discourse*, which Richard recommended that she read. He told her about his late nights staying up till four to trace the figures through the pages back and forth, his hands on the sheets, making notes in the margins. It could have been a body they were discussing. She had promised him she'd get the book that day. They were working that summer as interns for an august and long-standing lefty mag that worked them hard and paid them little; that was how they met. Checking facts and running down photos. They took pride in living well and on the cheap, in scamming press passes to the MoMA, cutting work to attend free screenings. She remembers this one day in particular: as they rode the elevator down from the ninth-floor office, they talked about their lives before that summer. Richard told her about growing up in LA. She told him about her summer spent in Italy on a grant.

"What were you doing in Italy?" he asked.

"The usual," she said. "I went to fall in love with the world. To recover from my education. I wandered around Florence thinking I was Michelangelo, thinking I was Dante."

He'd smiled. "Who was your Virgil?"

"I'm still looking," Lisa said. But it wasn't true. In that moment she thought that she had found him. Two months later he moved in.

Now, lying here alone, awake, at night, she goes over the narrative of their life together looking for clues, what she might have noticed and failed to, the tropes, foreshadowing, repeated imagery, all the things she tries to get her students to consider but cannot. She thinks about character, point of view, motivation, tense, how one action led causally to the next.

In class last week she told her students about fiction diction, which she told them differs from actual conversation in that there is always another meaning in the text. In fiction, unlike life, she said, you do not mean what you say. "A character does not come right out and say 'I do not love you anymore. I am leaving you for an undergraduate who smells like avocados.'" Her students looked at her, concerned. "The story would be over," Lisa said. "Instead, a character might say, 'Let's get a beer.'" They were reading "Hills Like White Elephants" that week, and in context, Lisa tells herself, the comment had made sense. Now she's not so sure.

Her life is a jumble of uncertain anecdotes, images, and scraps she cannot make into a whole; what she gets instead is a headache. Everything she struggles to get her students to do, she now tries. She looks for the moments of decision, the fatal flaw; she has explained to them the concept of hubris, with which they were not acquainted. She has introduced them to irony, which amazingly some hadn't heard of. *Welcome back to the Midwest*, she thinks. This, she told friends at college in the East, was why she was a sickly child, growing up in Minnesota, sorrowful and grim: She suffered from an irony deficiency.

What Lisa can't get over, what keeps her up this night, is how sudden it was. Their ending. Like a bursting pipe. Like the clutch that gave on her car last week as she was idling at a light. Sudden as a stroke her car had died. One minute she was moving, then paused at a light; the next minute there was no gear to shift into, just a growling as she frantically tried to stick the shift into a slot. She flipped on her emergency blinkers, got out, rolled the tin can that had taken her across the country a dozen times to the curb. The mechanic said it wasn't worth the money she'd spend to fix it. "Are you sure?" Lisa had asked. It seemed to her that people were altogether too quick to give up. Americans were always ready to move on, at the first sign of damage or dissatisfaction. "It's been a good car," she said. She knew the body was imperfect, dented, but the heart of it, its engine, had been good. "It's been a good car," she repeated. "Probably," the mechanic said, as if he were not sure. "If it was a cream puff, lady, I'd say maybe, but this is no cream puff." His hands were stuffed into his pockets. "If it were a cream puff," Lisa said, "I wouldn't have been driving it eighty down a freeway."

Still awake at four a.m., Lisa gets herself out of bed and curls up on the couch to work. If she cannot sleep, she can at least grade student papers. She hauls her briefcase onto her lap and tips it up to empty out the stack of papers, but index cards spill out instead. She gathers up the clump of cards and shuffles through them, sorting, reshuffling other people's sorrows. She tries to imagine some useful purpose for them. She envisions, for an instant, a board game like this: where you choose a regret or a fear, where you are dealt these cards and then deal with them. But what would be high, what low? How could you possibly win? For a moment, she considers mailing them to the nubile girlfriend of her ex, whom she has identified on campus, or thinks she has. She considers mailing them to enemies or friends. She considers sending them one by one, like postcards from a tropical vacation, to Richard.

Each morning her mother calls her with more news—the latest on her father's infidelity. She calls Lisa and leaves messages on her answering machine, messages Lisa does not return. Her mother's voice, when Lisa replays the messages, is an anxious blur. Lisa does not hear the words, just tone. Her mother's bitter cheer. "Hi, sweetie," she says. "This is your mother calling. Just wanted to find out how you're doing." She calls to remind Lisa that her sister's birthday is tomorrow. She calls to ask if she is coming over for a visit. Her voice is edgy with enthusiasm. All week, after their walk, she calls. Unanswered, she persists.

Lisa first learned about her father's affair two weeks ago, precisely two weeks after Richard told her of his own. The symmetry appalled her, the neat parallels of fiction cropping up in life. She was in the lobby of her therapist's office, waiting for her session, when she decided to check her machine. Her therapist's office has a courtesy phone on a table in the reception area, and Lisa is her father's daughter. She cannot resist a free call. In all the years she was growing up, she remembers her father best through his calls. Brief and out of the blue. He traveled most of the time, conducting seminars in tax law in Omaha, Baton Rouge. He was not around much, but he called. Whenever it was "somebody else's nickel." Whenever there was a company phone. Whenever he didn't have to pay. He would ask if there was any hot mail, any important calls, then he would ask for her mother.

Sometimes, when there are no messages these days, Lisa feels bereft. Sometimes she calls back just to make sure. Too often these days, when she is alone, time stands still. There is no movement. She feels cut off from the vital flow. That day, though, there were many beeps. Thank God. The voices are like ropes cast out to her to haul her back to safety. They give her a reason to go on; they keep time moving forward with their requests, their invitations, their calls for help. An editor had called to tell her he had a book on his desk he'd like her to review; there was an invitation to a party; and there was her father.

Her father had called to tell her that they were back in town. They had been to a couples' workshop in northern Minnesota for the past week. Now they were back.

"Your mother and I have returned from the Northwoods," he boomed. "Actually, we haven't been in the Northwoods, we've been on a voyage into ourselves. We're back," he said, "and we'd like to share with you some of our discoveries. We'd like to introduce you to the new parts of ourselves. Give us a call," he said. "Stop by."

This, Lisa imagines, is the sort of thing that happens to affluent, educated people in their seventies—these enthusiasms. In another era they might have become pious. But her parents gave up religion long ago, read the existentialists, studied physics and the brain. Long ago, they secularized their longing. What religious fervor must have been to another century, faith in self-help books and PBS are to her parents and their kind. They read Joseph Campbell and listen ardently to Bill Moyers's specials; they take an interest in theories about the goddess within; they believe the opinions in the *New York Times*. It is not so much faith they seek as a decline in incredulity. They have believed in nothing but their own efforts for so long that their spiritual faculties have atrophied. They cast themselves about with ill-gotten fervor, like adolescents in a first brush with love. Nevertheless, Lisa had been disappointed to discover this sappiness in her father, the high-powered lawyer. In her mother of the 190 IQ.

On the way home from therapy, Lisa dropped by her parents' house. Her father was seated in the living room, reading the local paper when she walked in; he said from the couch that he was delighted she'd stopped by. They'd had an exciting adventure, he said, gained many insights into their relationship and into themselves that they'd like to share with their children. Lisa felt vaguely nauseated as she took a seat.

"I'm happy for you," she said. "But I don't want to know how you feel about your marriage. I'm your daughter," she said, thinking she should not have to explain this.

"Well, then you don't have to listen." He shifted his bulk on the cushion. Squinted at her. "I was disturbed," he said, in his skeptical, lawyerly tone, "to learn from your mother this weekend that you once suggested that she have an affair."

There was a glint in his eyes, as if this were a game, the way he used to look when he'd test Lisa and her sister with torte-law dilemmas over dinner. "I don't recall having said that," Lisa said, "but if I did, I suppose I meant it. She needed more than kids for company, Dad."

Her father's eyes softened, grew unfocused.

"So let me ask you a question," Lisa said. "Did you ever have an affair?" It was an idle question, but the subject—given Richard's recent revelations—was on her mind. Lisa's sister had once speculated that their father had had an ongoing affair with a lawyer he worked with in Louisiana. Lisa hadn't thought it possible then.

Her father smiled at her. "Yes," he said. "I did. Ten years ago. I told your mother about it this weekend." He looked delighted, as if he had won a debate. It was not the confession but his evident delight in the confession that appalled her. He seemed pleased to have cheated, and pleased to tell her so.

The garage door opened, went up, went down.

Her father said, hushed and quickly, "Your mother's coming." The door to the kitchen opened behind them, and they heard Lisa's mother come in.

"Hi, sweetie," she called from the kitchen. "How are you?"

"We were just talking about Dad's affair," Lisa said, looking past her father, defying him to shut her up.

"Oh," her mother said, coming into the living room. Her tall and lovely mother bent in half and sank onto a cushion on the couch;

she looked tired, worn out. "I was pretty upset when I first learned about it. But then I realized," she turned to Lisa's father, "we've done worse to each other." Her father raised his chin, frowned as if interested in this equanimity, in the novelty of this response. Lisa wanted to punch him.

"But," she said, turning back to Lisa, "the workshop was very exciting." She told Lisa about the rules of the couples' workshop. Everything, she said, was defined in terms of E/A: Encounter and Acceptance. Experience and Analysis. Enlightenment and Acknowledgment.

"I don't believe this," Lisa said.

"What don't you believe?" her father said.

Lisa ignored him. Faced her mother as if they were alone.

"Dad has just told you he had an affair," Lisa said. "What are you going to do?"

"We're trying to work it out," her mother said.

"Jesus Christ," Lisa said, inexplicably angry. "I have spent my entire adult life getting the divorce you didn't. I have spent my whole adult life leaving your marriage behind. I want another kind of love than this."

"Good for you," her father said. He beamed at her. "I love the daughter within me."

"What is he talking about?" Lisa had no idea. Her mother explained that this was Weir-speak—which Lisa will thereafter refer to as Weird-speak—more from the couples lab. It is called "percept language" and reflects the belief that no one ever really knows anyone else, only one's perception of them. Hence, her mother told her, it is impossible to say, "I love you." You can only say, "I love the image of you I carry within me. I love the daughter within me."

"That is ridiculous," Lisa said. "That is absurd." People, it seems to her, are always doing this to reasonable ideas, distorting them until they become parodies of themselves. They have done this to God, to karma, now to Wittgenstein. It is one thing to acknowledge that perception is a factor in relationships; it is another to deny the possibility of self-transcendence. "Love is about self-transcendence," Lisa said. "To say 'I love you' is to make a gesture beyond narcissism; the whole point is to move beyond oneself, to say it is you I love." But she gave up. She knew her parents did not know this other kind of love. Nor did she.

"E, A," her mother said.

"I love the daughter within me," her father said.

Lisa said, "I am going home. I am leaving now. I'll call you later, Mom."

When she tells Gretchen about this later, she will make it comic-operatic, their three voices an absurd chorus. But the truth is, she finds nothing funny in it now. She is ashamed that they are none of them better at love than this.

Lisa should be studying or preparing for her class, but she sits among the library carrels studying the girls instead. She wonders who it is that Richard beds now. She watches as they pass her—on the sidewalk, on the street, the ones in cars, in hallways, carrels, in the stacks; everywhere she wonders, *Is it her?*

Her mother calls to tell her there have been muggings in the park; the woods are no longer safe to walk. A man was held up at gunpoint. A housewife has been raped. Her mother thought she'd want to know. "It's not safe," her mother says, speaking to the machine. "Stay out of the woods." Her mother calls her as she's heading out the door to pick up her car that has been fixed. Lisa does not pick up the phone but she listens to the words broadcast out into the room. The voice asks Lisa to stop by. And since Lisa has lost the trick of time since Richard left, since time holds still now and she cannot see the point in doing anything or going anywhere, except to class, she goes to see her mom.

It is a week now since their last walk, and the leaves in the garden are mostly fallen. The woods look skeletal as she drives past. But she is happy to be going home. She will drink coffee, she will eat cottage cheese and toast. There is this compensation in her father's recent revelations: They know the worst of one another now and can go on.

Truth is, she doesn't judge her father for it. For wanting more. She understands it. Though she's sorry for her mom.

But Lisa's wrong. The coffee is not brewed when she arrives. Her mother doesn't offer lunch; she offers news instead. She reels off a litany of betrayals, as Lisa stands there peeling off her coat: It was not just one affair, it seems, but a career of infidelities—blow jobs, hand jobs, phone sex, graduate students. Her mother tells her everything as her husband has told her. They sit at the kitchen table, whispering.

When her father walks into the kitchen for his lunch, Lisa's mother hushes her. "Hey, Lee," her father says. "I didn't realize you were here, hon. How are you?" He opens up the fridge to forage. "Fine," she says. "We're just talking about what a dick you are." "Ah," he says, apparently unruffled. He pulls out a plate from the bowels of the fridge and faces his women. "Anyone going to eat this?" he says, holding up a plate to them.

At home, Lisa calls Gretchen and tells her all about it. Gretchen says it must feel terrible to know those things about her dad.

But in truth, Lisa thinks, it does not. She is relieved to know her father wanted more. More than the lawn, the car, the house, the wife, the kids. She is relieved that he wanted more than this and got it.

"It's funny," Lisa says. "In a weird way I'm relieved, y'know?" Lisa says. "And it makes a kind of sense."

"What does?"

"Richard. The Avocado." This is how she refers to Richard's new girlfriend these days, and sometimes, when especially aggrieved, she calls her just the Smell.

"How do you mean?" Gretchen asks.

Lisa can hear Gretchen chewing, tart little toothy sounds. "What are you eating?" Lisa asks.

"Sorry," Gretchen says through a mumble of food. "Rice cake. I didn't think it'd be so loud." There is a hollow swallowing sound. "So what makes sense?" Gretchen asks.

"My father was a philanderer," Lisa says. "I appreciate their charms."

Alone on the couch that afternoon and dazed with hunger, Lisa considers what Gretchen has told her of Rat Choice. According to the theory, developed in the 1950s from neoclassical economics, people are predictable. The theory assumes that humans are rational beings, and that given a set of exogenously given preferences (assumed to be universal, unchanging, and self-serving), a person's behavior can be predicted. Everyone, according to the rats, has a set of definable interests that can be ranked hierarchically, and everyone can be depended on to act so as to maximize these. Sometimes the theory worked. According to the article in the *New Republic*, rational choice could tell you why drivers join AAA—because the organization offers member perks. But it is at a loss to explain idealism— why, for instance, comfortable, middle-class, white kids from New England joined the Freedom Riders in the 1960s. The theory cannot account for this. The rats know nothing about it. Self-sacrifice. Hope. Altruism. Crazy love. This is precisely what the theory cannot account for. The model would call them irrelevant, inexplicable as hope, love, fidelity. In the theory, interests are simply given and are assumed to remain constant over time. Nothing, it seems to Lisa, could be farther from the truth.

⟫➤

Lisa has forgotten to eat, for a day at least, she thinks, or maybe two. Her fridge is empty save for mayonnaise, old eggs, expired milk, and capers. At times like this, the body is a total pain. Like a pet, it demands its feedings. So she's forced out into the world to get some groceries. It tires her to have to eat; the need seems unending. Each day, her body makes the same demands anew.

She grabs her coat, walks out the door. The sky is a quilted gray. It looks like snow. As she walks the two blocks to the grocery store, Lisa thinks about her visit with her mom. She cannot help but note how radiant her mother has become—toned, vibrant, luminous in her misery, alive with pain and desire. At seventy-two, Lisa's mother is having more sex than she is.

Lisa first learned about the body from her mother, as she learned from her the plays of Beckett and Brecht, learned etymology and ants. The body, when they considered it, was discussed as if it were a car one must keep well tuned. Her mother spoke of exercise, of calories, and fat; she spoke of folic acid, zinc; the latest from *JAMA*. When, as a child, Lisa had asked questions about sex, her mother answered her with a cold and clinical accuracy. She never spoke of passion, and Lisa had not imagined her parents in the clench of a strong desire. Even when Lisa grew up and came to love, kissed the girls and blew the boys, desire remained for her abstract, remote as a rumor.

Across the street from her childhood house, her best friend's parents fought. The father slapped the mother's ass as he passed her where she tended the barbecue grill. He kept a mildewed archive of *Playboy* in a room off the laundry room—a room empty but for the stacks of slick magazines, which Lisa and her best friend perused till desire became, in Lisa's mind, linked with the smell of mold, the cold damp of a small white room, a cement floor, exposed pipes. Something chilled and damp.

≫►

At the grocery store she hauls things off the shelf, indiscriminate. Apple juice, potato chips, Milano mint cookies, ground chuck, and wheat bread. She throws them all into her cart. Tangelos, marshmallow fluff. Stuff she has never considered eating, never even considered food, she takes.

The check-out line at the grocery store is long, and her thoughts are unruly. She keeps wondering how it started between Richard and the Smell. Where did literary criticism turn to love? She wonders if they might have taken up doing something as simple as shopping. She was, he'd said, a *former* student; outside the classroom, where was it that they met? Beside her are racks of *Seventeen*, the busty images of *Cosmo*. She wants the details now. Specifics, she thinks, will give her satisfaction, peace. Contain it for the moment, at least. Without them, it bleeds into everything. In every café grocery store classroom bus stop she imagines them meeting here. In every street. Was it here, was it here? A madwoman's mantra.

She pulls out the index cards to distract herself from thinking. And then they spill. Pouring into the *Cosmo* rack and across the gum-rubbed carpeting. "Fuck," she says, and squats to pick them up. The guy behind her squats to help, and she tells him it's okay, she's got it thanks, but still he tries. When she straightens up, recovered now, he holds out several cards to her, face up, their writing plain as day. *I am afraid . . . I regret . . . My secret is . . .* He glances at the cards he holds, returns them to her with an air of stifled interest. The smile he gives her looks like a smirk.

He is a short Semitic guy, with a buzz cut and wire-rims, a gray tweed coat, chapped lips that are trademark grad student, a dry flakiness around his eyes, excessively long lashes. She guesses from his pallor that he's in the sciences, or a student of some Slavic language or other—Russian lit, maybe the classics. He has the desiccated smug affect of the grandiosely studious.

He chats her up in line. Asks if she's at the university. About her field, the focus of her research. She wants to tell him her field is love, her focus infidelity. Instead she tells him she's not very focused these days. He offers her his hand to shake and gives his name as Matt. She doesn't offer hers.

In the parking lot, he rattles up behind her with his cart, and asks, not facing her but more as if he's asking the whole lot, if she'd like to get a cup of coffee? Despite herself, she's touched.

"Thanks," she says, "but I have errands."

"Forget it," he says, bitterly, as if she'd led him on. As if he'd known for years that she would fail him. His eyes are on the tar of the parking lot as he walks away. His shoulders bunched up like shrubbery around his throat. A tweedy hump of resentment, moving off.

Richard used to say she was reliable. That with her, he always knew what to expect. At first this was a compliment; later it was not. She thinks about Rat Choice, which makes her think now not of Swedes but of a maze. The rational choice model posits interests as given and unchanging. The things the theory can't account for are the things that count: altruism, love, grief, irrational hope.

"Wait," she yells at Matt's resentful back. "Wait up." She takes long running steps to catch him. "Sure," she says. "Coffee sounds just great." She feels so sorry for them both. And for a moment, seeing his expression, she is almost hopeful. A whole new theory starting here, she thinks:

Irrational Choice.

Matt is not an attractive man, not by a long shot, but she feels a certain kinship that might approximate attraction in a pinch. His hurt is so obvious. She feels a keen longing to alleviate it, the way she imagines nuns must feel, a selfless desire to relieve another's suffering. She decides that if he asks to sleep with her, she will say yes, though she feels no desire for him. When he opens the car door for

her, he asks, "What is your name, anyway?" She lies to him and tells
him: "Beatrice."

Sunday would have been their anniversary, and Richard calls her,
drunk. His voice is sad and felty through the phone. He asks if she
remembered; she tells him, yes, she did. He says he doesn't ever expect to feel that way again, the way he felt about Lisa. "I can't imagine
feeling that way about anyone ever again," he says. "I can't imagine
feeling that in love." Talking to him, she feels time lurch, resume its
unsteady trot. He sounds so familiar. "Not even with me?" she asks.
"Not even with you," he says. He tells her he has concrete around
his heart. It hurt so much to leave. "But you left me," she says. "It
still was hard." The girl and he have broken up. And Lisa, trying to
disguise her glee, asks, "How old was that chick anyway?" "Twenty-
nine," he says, "but she seemed much younger. Or maybe I'm just
feeling old," he says. "You'll never be a child prodigy," she says, quoting back to him what he had said to her when she turned thirty. He
laughs. And suddenly they are relaxed, familiar again. They tell each
other jokes. He says the local bus company has a new slogan, has
she heard? In an affected German accent, he says, "Vee have vays
of making you valk." She laughs. "That's good," she says. She tells
him her latest idea for a *New Yorker* cartoon: a man showing trophy
fish points to one and says, "I caught that one in the stream of con-
sciousness." He laughs. Then Lisa tells him the one about the parrot that started to curse a blue streak. His owner threw him in the
freezer as punishment. First he heard a frantic fluttering, then silence. The owner opened the freezer door, peeked inside. The parrot was sitting inside, contrite, legs crossed, wings folded. "Are you
ready to come out?" the owner asked. The bird nodded. "No more
cursing?" The bird nodded. "Okay," the owner said and replaced the
bird on its perch. "Just one thing," the parrot asked. "Tell me: what

did the chicken do?" They strangle on their laughter. For the first time in weeks, she sleeps.

On Monday morning Lisa's mother calls, and Lisa unthinkingly picks up the phone. She asks Lisa how she is, then she tells her that she has begun reading Virginia Woolf's diaries. Lisa's fave. She likes them enormously, her mother says, "all that she suffered, blow on blow." It seems a bizarre reason to like Woolf. For a moment Lisa is offended, the way she always is when she hears art explained away as the by-product of suffering, not work. Years ago Lisa gave her mother *To the Lighthouse* to read, and now she asks her mother if she liked it, if she ever read it. Her mother says she liked it, but that now she appreciates it more, knowing it was based on autobiography, knowing that she suffered so.

Lisa can hear her father shouting cheerfully in the background. "Tell her I say hello," he says.

"Did you hear that?" her mother asks. "Your father says hi."

"The bastard," Lisa says.

Her mother laughs.

"Is Dad being nice to you?" Lisa asks.

"Oh," she says, airily, "we're working things out."

Her hopeful mother.

She has read too many Russian novels to believe in happy endings, but still she does. She thinks they will get back together. She thinks they will meet on a bus, or in a bed. She is a stupid with hope. Umberto Eco is reading at a local church, and so she goes, thinking maybe she will run into Richard there. The room, when she arrives, is full of men who are not him. She scans the pews. Eco looks like an egg with a beard. Eco says he usually appears with his translator, Will Weaver, and that it is strange to appear alone. Eco reads two pages from *The Island of the Day Before* in Italian, "to prove I can read

Italian," he says. Afterward he reads in English about jealousy and about hell. Hell, one tormented character says, is not what we have been told. It is not unremitting despair but unending, useless hope.

After the reading, Lisa drives uptown to KinhDo to get some take-out Vietnamese. She gives her order to the guy at the cash register, pays, then stands there waiting for her food, scanning the room, when she sees them. She doesn't know if it is the Smell or someone new, the speed with which we move on dizzies her. All her imaginings, she sees now, have been wrong. She has never seen this girl before. She has never seen Richard so happy. The two of them are tender, unreserved—*bodied*—as they never were. Their lips are wet and smiling; they snap the heads off shrimp. Their fingers glisten with oil.

It is nothing rational that prompts Lisa to start toward them, but more like reflex, like the day she'd pitched the plate at Richard's chest; choosing what her mother hadn't chosen all those years—to make a scene, make a fuss, make a mess of things but *try*, to love this man who once loved her. When Richard raises his eyes to her, they seem filled with happiness, and for a moment she thinks he's glad to see her, as if they'd intended to rendezvous, that maybe this is not a date.

But when Richard says her name, it's not in welcome but in warning: "Lisa." He slides from the booth and stands like a bodyguard between her and the dark-haired girl, but nonetheless it reaches her, the faint scent of avocado. Her skin aches with what might be anger or grief.

"I didn't expect to run into you here," he says, hands on hips; it's a new gesture, unflattering; she wonders if he's picked it up from her.

"That makes two of us," Lisa says. "Or rather, three." Lisa stretches out a hand to the girl, stepping around Richard as she does. The girl is not what she'd imagined: black hair to her shoulders, freckles, black-rimmed glasses; thoughtful, bookish. Such confrontation is more suitable for daytime TV dramas than for life; the books Lisa loves avoid it, but she's tired of avoiding things. Of rational choices.

When Richard moves to intercept her, he is fast but clumsy and a little off balance: his left arm swings back toward the booth and collides with a water glass, a soup bowl, and liquid is everywhere—hot broth, iced water.

"Fuck," says the girl, jumping up and colliding with Richard.

"Are you okay?" he asks, his arm protectively encircling her. A waiter races over with a rag.

"No worry," the waiter says. "Clean up fast."

"You okay?" he asks the girl again—and suddenly there's nothing more to say. He's said it all. By reaching for someone other than her.

"God, I'm so sorry," the girl says, reaching for Lisa with napkins in her hand. When Lisa doesn't take them, the girl takes his hand instead and says, gently, smiling, "I'm Becky," clearly clueless that there was ever anyone but her.

Lisa walks out without waiting for her order.

Outside on the street, the sky is inky black beyond the orange sodium glare of the street lamps and Lisa is disoriented. Every direction she looks in seems like the wrong one, every street a dead end. Cars race past in front of her on Hennepin Avenue and her heart throbs in her chest. There is a buzz in her throat, a pressure behind her eyes that makes her think she might cry. She walks to the parking lot at the side of the building and goes to her car, which—like herself—looks worse for wear, but still it runs. She gets in and shoves the key in the ignition. She hesitates before starting it up. She hasn't the slightest idea where to go from here.

She leans her head on the steering wheel and tries to cry. She sits there, willing the tears to come, dry-eyed and ridiculous, forehead to the wheel. To help herself along, she tries to remember "telling details," as she coaches her students to do. She recalls how she and Richard had nearly driven off a cliff on their way to see Mount

Rushmore in a January snowstorm last year during their Kitsch Tour of the Midwest. She remembers how Richard phoned her, after her kitty disappeared, and meowed to the tune of the "Internationale" to cheer her up, insisting it was a collect call from France. She recalls how they used to eat fat California burgers and drink cold beers in a dark neighborhood bar around the corner from their place and did not need to talk; the sex they had on his office desk and once in the elevator on the way up to their department; how she once saw him pick up a rubber duck in a bath shop (where she'd come to buy a gift) and turn it over and over in his hands, scowling at it from every angle, as if even this merited serious consideration; she remembers things they have eaten, bottles of wine they tried, positions in sex, the taste of the biscotti they made together and his wine-poached pears—simple physical things.

But it's no use. She cannot cry. Her body and mind are not on speaking terms. So she starts the car, shoves it in gear, and drives. She'll go to Gretchen's or to her mom's. Or she could pull over at a pay phone and call up Matt, the guy from the grocery who gave her his number after coffee and asked her to call. Her heart is pounding; her throat is tight. Panic, she recalls, was named for the god of wilderness. She heads for home.

She takes the parkway fast, rounds a lake and then another and then she is in the woods. Passing Eloise Butler Wildflower Garden and Bird Sanctuary, it occurs to Lisa to stop, but she has spent too much time already in this dark wood; she is ready to be done with it. She'll find no Virgil there to guide her; she's going to have to make her way alone for now and maybe for years to come, alone, and the thought of this—of herself alone, without Richard, in the vast stretch of time that is her future—makes her, finally, cry. She sobs big, ridiculous, hiccupping tears. Her vision blurs, and she reaches for her bag, fumbles inside for a Kleenex, and finds the cards instead. She pulls them out and drops them in her lap, and slows.

The curves of the parkway are gentle, and when she rolls down her window, the cold autumn air feels good against her wet face as she drops her speed from 45 to 35 to 25 to 20 to 15 to 10 miles per hour. Then 5. At this speed, when she holds the stack of cards out the window, those accumulated sorrows in her hands now, they do not slice away from her and scatter like buckshot, but rise gently from her palm, lifting away, fluttering briefly, before they begin their inevitable descent. In the rearview mirror, they look like enormous moths, or like a flock of birdless wings, like some strange new creature making its way, awkwardly, hesitantly, for the very first time, into the terrible beautiful bodied world.

SMALL BRIGHT THING

ON CHICAGO'S SOUTH SIDE, JUNE KIM'S MOTHER IS COL-
lecting Oriental rugs. When June calls to discuss her upcoming visit
home, her mother tells her about her latest: a garnet-and-green flat-
woven kilim from a small mountain village in Turkey. Her mother
describes the care she will give it, how she will spend the morning
rearranging furniture to make room—a thing she never does on the
occasions when her children visit. June has to wedge herself into her
mother's new life like a splinter.

When the conversation turns to flight times and specific dates,
June detects a note of anxiety in her mother's voice. "That is if you
still want me to come," June says. "Of course. Of course, I do," her
mother says, and then—in one of her motherly reversals—she grows
eager, almost conspiratorial, as if she has a secret to impart, but if she
has, she doesn't reveal it by phone, and as the weeks pass and the date
of June's visit approaches, June begins to hope her mother won't.

In the past her mother's revelations have been painful—June's father's infidelity; her parents' impending divorce; her mother's dona-

tion (after June left for college) of all June's childhood belongings to charity. "You're only young once," her mother reasoned, meaning June wouldn't need the toys again, but June sometimes wonders if she has ever been young. "I was thinking of having children," June said, hoping to wound. "Oh you were not," her mother laughed. And, as always, she was right. June can't imagine having kids. Having a mother is enough.

June flies into Chicago on December 23, the busiest flight day of the year. LaGuardia, from which she departs, is crowded with cranky passengers burdened with gifts and tired children and the grim resign that major holidays inspire. CNN broadcasts airport delays and snow. Sometimes June thinks she sees Greg, the guy she has been dating, amid the swirling crowd, but it is never him, just some other lanky, six-foot guy with chestnut hair that falls into his eyes and a sexy, melancholy droop to his neck. Sometimes she thinks she sees her shrink.

Despite a three-hour flight delay, June's mother meets her at the O'Hare gate, cheerful as an elf and reassuringly unchanged: defiantly unfashionable in a navy parka and jeans, her gray hair still worn long past her shoulders. At fifty-three, her mother insists on dressing in grad-student gear circa 1973, the year June was born.

But something about her mom is different, like a picture hung at a tilt, and it unnerves June. Ever since she inherited a small fortune from a wealthy aunt six months back, June's mother has been behaving strangely. Often she is out when June phones her; when she's in, she's often giddy and vague. It has crossed June's mind to wonder if her mother's doing drugs again; her mother was a flower child in the sixties, before June was born, and now that her mom's been freed from a day job, June fears she's headed for a flower-power relapse. But June knows better than to ask.

Her mom greets her with a brisk hug and a "Long time no see. You look terrific. How've you been?" as if June were a long-absent friend, a person with a life and a past of her own, as if her mother weren't the central feature of her twenty-seven years.

"I'm fine, Mom," June says, conscious of eyes on them—the willowy Korean daughter and her short, squat, Anglo Mom. "Can we go home?"

Exiting the parking garage, as they wait in line to pay, June's mother reaches for her billfold and pulls out a photo, a snapshot folded in half.

"I have a surprise for you," her mom says.

"I hate surprises."

"Oh, June Bug," she says.

For a moment, June feels oddly sick, afraid of what the photo may reveal, afraid that this time—at long last—it will be a man.

Since her parents' divorce fourteen years ago, her mother has not so much as dated. "What do I need with a man, when I have you?" she'd said to June and her brother, Sam. But June fears a change is coming, slow as tectonics, and as world-altering.

June takes the photo in shaky hands and squints at it. She should've known: a rug.

"What do you think?" her mother asks, breathless as a girl. "It's a Norwegian kilim, eighteenth century. Dowry rugs like this are very rare."

And very weird, June thinks. To the Moorish template of geometric forms has been applied the palette of an Easter egg—pastel pink and green and yellow and orange. The combination looks somehow wrong: the cheery midwestern colors applied to a Near East design. On the back are scrawled its dimensions (4×6), a merchant's name (Menendian), and price ($10,000).

"Wow," June says of the price.

"Isn't it?" her mother says, taking the photo back. "That's just the word for it: it's a wow." She stares for a few seconds at the beloved image as if she can't bear to put it away, then does.

The apartment—where her mother has lived since the early seventies when she was a young mother and a student of East Asian history and June's father was a professor of economics—looks much as it always has, except the coffee table is piled high with back issues of *Oriental Rug Review* and June's old room looks like a seraglio.

Her mother has transformed June's room in her absence. Now the bookshelves are lined with volumes on textiles, her old bed heaped with cheap printed Persian rugs her mother purchased years ago—before receiving the inheritance—which she can't bear to throw out but has no use for.

"I felt precisely this way about Henry before the divorce," her mother says, referring to June's dad, as they sit drinking sherry in the living room. "I could see all the flaws in the manufacturing, but I couldn't bear to get rid of him."

Her mother addresses June in an exhausted, sentimental tone, the tone June as a child heard her use with friends on the phone, and it is clear she has decided—in the way her mother has of making up her mind about how things are going to be without telling others involved—that June is old enough now to be her friend.

June's mother hums as she refills their glasses, smiling to herself, and June wonders if her mother's drunk.

"How's your young man?" her mother asks, handing June back her glass.

"Greg," June says. Her mother never calls him Greg. June wonders how he is. "He's fine, I guess." June wonders if Greg is happy now; June wonders if she is. Despite her therapist's best efforts, June is not convinced of the merits of happiness. Despair, June believes, is a crucial part of her personality. Her shrink says this is depressive

logic, but June thinks happiness is overrated; she suspects a pharma-
ceutical plot: "If we're in a war on drugs," she's asked her shrink, "is
Prozac war by other means?" Her shrink has made meds a condition
of her therapy, but June is pleased to find they have had no effect: despair has not abandoned her. The only consequences of note are dry
mouth, appetite loss, and a jittery feeling in her legs when she turns
out the light. Sorrow is still with her, like a twin.

June's mother talks about politics and rugs and inquires politely
about June's job at an educational publishing house; she asks about
the raise June had been promised after her annual review. And June
politely answers.

Her family's formality used to shock June's friends, as had her
mother's blue eyes, her English features and oatmeal-colored skin.
They found it cold. But June knows it's a code for love, like any
other, a pattern they make. Beneath the formality born of her father's
Korean discretion and her mother's New England reserve is fierce
feeling, a small bright thing, like the candle her father used to light
before the image of his ancestors.

June's mother has tried to teach her about rugs, but June retains only
the nomenclature, which she adds to her store of family hieroglyphs,
the meaning of which she has yet to decipher. She takes the words
away with her from these visits, carrying them home along with the
gifts of clothing her mother gives her, things that June will never wear
(crocheted vests; calf-length formal dresses with large, abrupt bows;
skorts—part skirt, part shorts).

June's mother has taught her that yarn may be twisted clockwise,
in an S-spun, or counter-, Z-spun. That wool is the most common fi-
ber used in Oriental rugs but silk is better and, as in clothes, to avoid
rayon. She has learned the difference between rectilinear (composed
of angular geometric figures) and curvilinear designs (composed of
floral motifs and often more intricate).

She has learned that rugs—like all territory, like tiny nation states—have borders and fields (the large open spaces at the centers, where the principal pattern is).

She has learned to name the parts of a rug (warp, weft, fringe, kilim, field, medallion, main and guard borders) as once she learned to name the parts of her own body.

She even knows the seven categories into which each pattern fits: the medallion (at the field's center); the repeated motif; the all-over pattern; open field; panel rugs; portrait rugs (from the end of the eighteenth century, depicting landscapes, historical events, European paintings); and prayer.

As June goes to sleep on the pull-out couch in the living room that night (her old bed too heaped with textiles to be cleared), she feels toward the rugs, which hang on every wall and cover nearly all the floor, an almost sibling rivalry she has never felt toward her brother, Sam. The two of them were more like long-term lodgers who shared a boarding house. After their father returned to Korea and their mother went to work, they had each gone their own way, passing one another quietly in the hall, each seeking a singular kind of comfort. Her brother—now a senior at Reed—found it in Buddhism; June—an assistant editor at a small educational publishing house in Manhattan—found it in books. Their mother took solace in textiles.

At breakfast, they split the paper like an old married couple. June takes the science section and her mother the front pages of the *Times*. Occasionally her Mom looks up to share some bit of news about Sam (who's spending Christmas at a Buddhist monastery) or the polity.

When June looks up from her scrambled eggs and toast, she sees a man's photo on the fridge. Where June's report cards used to hang beside her brother's drawings is a small black-and-white of a man in a tie. June's eyesight isn't great and she doesn't want to stare. But she can see full well it is a man. And not her brother.

"Want some juice, Mom?" June asks.

"No thanks, bug."

June rises from the table and goes to the fridge. At the door, she looks at the photo and sees it's not. It is just a JPEG from the Web: a nineteenth-century etching of a gentleman in coat and tie, beneath which is the caption: "Ask Doctor Kabistan: Advice for the Ruglorn."

June laughs.

Her mother looks up from the *Times*.

"What's funny?"

"Ma," June says, "you're obsessed."

After breakfast, her mother takes her through her latest acquisitions, pointing out familiar details—noting the popular motifs of boteh, herati, Mina Khani, Memling Gul. Her mother speaks not of price but of personalities—which, like price, depend on many factors: material, origin, design, condition, rarity.

Her mother praises each rug's qualities like she's praising a child's. She offers "rug rules," as another mom might offer beauty tips: Silk—she says—is best, not only for its sheen and fineness, but for its adaptability to dyes, its natural resilience. Avoid antique washes, which like bleached hair, cheapen. (It is desirable to have dyes fade with time and use, but faking it is a fault.) Condition counts: Has it been damaged? Has it been skillfully repaired? Has it aged gracefully? Origins matter: not just the country, but the weaving district and availability of others from that region. ("A rug should not forget where it comes from," June's mother says.)

Post-tour, June goes to the bathroom and when she comes back, her mother is staring into space. She has the deflated, slightly disoriented look she developed soon after the divorce. Sometimes June would come on her mom in the laundry downstairs, stopped half-way through folding a sheet or a towel, the cotton bent over her arm as if she were a waiter attending table, stock still and staring. She has that same look now, having come to the end of her rugs. And June knows that her mother needs her. There's no one else. No man. No drugs. Just them, like always. For always. And she feels flushed with love and a desire to protect her tiny mom—her generous, vulnerable, compulsive-obsessive mom.

"Ma," June says, setting a hand on her shoulder.

"Oh," her mother says. "Yes? What?"

"Want a cup of tea? I'll make us tea."

"Oh, no," her mother says, "No, thank you, June Bug." Her mother looks around the room, filled to overflowing with patterns and books and rugs. "What now?" she asks. It is a big question, expanding like a hollow bubble in the room.

"Simple," June says, taking her mother's hand. "We get your rug."

"Oh, I couldn't possibly," she says.

"But you can."

"It's the day before Christmas, the streets'll be mobbed. They're probably closed." Her mother looks a little gray, saying this, "Maybe somebody's already bought it?"

"Let's try."

In their excitement, they leave without their coats. The frigid air beneath the gray sky is bracing, but it feels good as they race together for the train.

The rug merchant, Mr. Menendian, greets June's mother with the mandarin courtesy of the Muslim; he offers tea and opens his hand to indicate seats for them, two plump kilim-upholstered chairs. Before retrieving tea, he unfurls the precious rug like a banner at their feet.

He explains to June, as if introducing a guest, that the rug is a Norwegian dowry. He points out the date woven in the border (1793).

He explains that the girl likely wove it for herself, for her trousseau, in hope—or perhaps in preparation (he smiles at June)—for marriage. Then, after a decorous inclination of his head, he withdraws.

June's mother points out details—the girl's initials, the rarity of such a rug. But she needn't bother. June can see for herself the beauty of the thing, which seems to possess—in its very weave and weft, in the delicate but urgent colors—the ardor of a heartsick girl.

"It's very expensive," her mother says, crouching beside the rug.

"You should get it," June says.

"Do you think so?"

"I do."

To own it, June thinks, would be like owning love itself.

The Norwegian dowry kilim—which is not large, even rolled and wrapped in paper and plastic, it's no larger than a bulky coat—has a chair to itself at the Kyoto Gardens, where they go to celebrate their purchase and Christmas Eve.

When her mother goes to the restroom to wash up, June orders hot saki. The place is filled with variously Asian faces and Jews, the only ones out tonight. The smell of ginger and wasabi and soy and hot tea fill the room, and June feels a rare moment of pure contentment.

Years ago, June's shrink asked her what she loved ("love is a good place to start," she'd said), and June was hard pressed to answer: she's never known what she might want as much as her mom wants these rugs. The only thing she's sure she loves is them—her crazy mom and long-absent dad, and for a while there, she thought, just maybe, Greg.

She's scrutinizing the menu, trying out tastes on her tongue, when her mother returns.

"June, I have someone I want you to meet."

When June looks up, her mother is standing beside a tall, smiling, bald man.

"Isn't this a wonderful surprise?" June's mother says.

June wonders if it is a surprise or if this is her mother's way of breaking bad news.

"June, this is my good friend Mark Goldberg. Mark, my daughter, June."

"Nice to meet you, June," Mark says. "You're as pretty as your pictures."

"Isn't he a charmer?"

June wonders if he's a gold digger after her mother's cash, but she guesses not, given that he has no hair and is not a looker and wears a shirt of dainty pinstripes, a navy cashmere coat slung over one arm. Fiftyish, she guesses. He's probably a shrink, she thinks, no, worse, a csw. He has the latter's sheen of professional kindness, solicitude billable by the hour.

"Won't you join us?" June's mother asks.

Mark looks at June. "I hate to interrupt," he says.

"Don't be silly," June's mom says. "You're not interrupting. We'd be thrilled."

June looks away.

"So this is the rug," Mark says, patting the roll, as he takes a seat.

"Do you have rugs?" June asks, meaning, does he collect, but it comes out wrong.

He touches his balding pate.

"Think I need one?" he asks, cutting his eyes at June's Mom, then he laughs good naturedly, as a man in a toupee would not. June watches the two of them laugh.

"So," June's mother says, "what looks good?"

"I'm not hungry," June says.

"You were starving half an hour ago, bug."

"Must be the drugs," June says. "Imipramine kills your appetite."

June's mother raises her menu a little higher, like a shield. June knows her mother hates this subject, hates even to hear meds mentioned. June's despair is like a stain, a sign of damage, of poor repair, which her mother shies from, perhaps feels incriminated by.

But Mark takes it in stride.

"I know the feeling—all the drugs I used to take in college made me scrawny as hell." He pats a solid belly. "Hard to imagine now."

June loathes these fifty-somethings with their chummy recollections of the sixties, as if they were forever young, which he is not.

"I'm going to go wash up," June's mother says. "Order me a whiskey sour, will you?" she places her fingertips on Mark's hand as she rises.

For a few moments they sit in awkward silence. And sitting there, the old feeling returns—the furious swollen ache that feels like a terrible itch, as if her soul were allergic to her body, or she to the world, a terrible straining against the skin, which her therapist has told her is anger. It's this anger that drove her once to try to cut her way out when she was fifteen, to slice her arms, like a nineteenth-century physician letting blood. All she wanted was a little more room. But there's no more room.

"Tell my mom I didn't feel well, will you?" June says, rising from her chair.

"June," Mark says, beginning to stand.

"What?"

Perhaps it is the tone of her voice that stops him. He sits back down.

"Good to meet you," he says. "See you around."

June takes the El home, comforted by the clatter of the tracks, the sway of the illuminated cabin, which slides like a fat bullet over the streets, with her body safe inside; like the others in the car, she sways into the turns like delicate seaweed, like the plants in the aquarium she kept as a child. Gone now. She thinks perhaps the aquarium was meant as an object lesson, to teach them young about loss. Soften the blow. But it hadn't. She'd been shocked when her father left when she was thirteen. Shocked, too, when Greg broke up with her last month without warning or excuse. Despite practice, nothing softens the blow. The clatter of the wheels on the tracks reminds her: loss is loss is loss is loss is loss.

Sometimes it occurs to June to wonder what her ancestors would think of her. Not the Korean forebears her father lit candles to, but the ones off the other boat, the Mayflower Puritans, the Soules, from whom she's also come (on her mother's side). The DAR never imagined her. Her tobacco-brown face, her soft tea-stained skin, the delicate epicanthic folds of her eyes.

At home, she stands in the bathroom, whose structures seem to her surprisingly low and cramped, not at all as she remembers them from childhood; it's as if the rooms were under pressure, squashed, or as if she has expanded, grown ungainly, gargantuan. She studies her face in the mirror, looking for the link to others, to her mother, finding none.

Others have called her beautiful. She can see that she is pretty, her oval face, her almond-shaped eyes. She recalls the Korean grocer on Seventh Avenue, who addressed her in Korean, speaking to her in a tongue not native to her, who asked her name, and when she said June, he'd said, no, no, her real name, her Korean name. When she said she didn't have one, he'd snapped at a clerk and turned away, annoyed.

She washes her face, pats it dry, brushes her teeth, and spits.

June is getting into bed on the fold-out couch in the living room, when it occurs to her that she doesn't want to be here when her mom comes in. She doesn't feel up for a heart to heart, so she goes into her old room and drags several rugs onto the floor and makes a bed. She strips the linens from the couch and fits them to the pile of rugs. She pulls a small prayer rug onto herself, comforted by the familiar sense of weight. It's a pity, she thinks, to keep all these and not have any use for them.

Unlike her mother, June cultivates detachment—recycling each day's paper, keeping only half a dozen books at any given time (bringing those she's read to the Strand to sell). When Greg phoned her a few weeks back, she hadn't cried (he'd said he was so glad she was okay with this. He'd hoped they could be friends, as they had been, and she'd said, "Sure, why not," and had been glad she was okay with it as well). Okay. She is okay.

And then she is asleep.

She wakes to snow falling, the hush that as a child seemed so promising. She opens the window and the cool pillowy winter air pushes back her hair from her face like a gentle hand, it moves the nightgown around her as a lover might. She hears her mother come in, hears the kitchen faucet turn on, turn off, a giggle and a shush, the toilet flush, then her mother's bedroom door open and close.

When the house is quiet again, June goes into the living room, as she did as a child on Christmas morning, trying to catch Santa in the act. But this year there is no tree, no stockings—her mother must imagine she's outgrown all that. There is only the rug—like an honored guest—regally sprawled across the couch. Did the bride make it for herself, June wonders, or was it a gift her mother made? Was she engaged or merely hopeful when she began to fill her trousseau?

And then she sees Mark's coat, navy blue cashmere, slung over the back of a chair, and her stomach drops, like she's in a fast-rising elevator.

June steps back into the bedroom. The rugs on the bed, where once June slept, look all wrong, with their borrowed patterns, cheap copies of ancient designs, trite facsimiles of what once had meaning and use to the families who made them. When she hears a noise from her mother's room, she pictures them—her mother and the man—

and she is immediately sorry. She tries not to think of them, but trying only makes it worse.

She thinks of what this apartment contains: rugs and books and patterns, a mother, a boyfriend, a daughter. In the bathroom are razors, pills, bleach under the sink. In the kitchen are well-sharpened Trident knives. Beneath June's skin, a familiar itch.

And it comes to her. What she must do. It's not destruction she's after, but an opening, to let something out or in.

It will be hours and hours before her mother and the new man rise; June has lots and lots of time. As she steps into the living room and passes the couch, she wonders if the dowry rug maker ever married, or if she wove to fill her waiting. Waiting that became a way of life.

June goes into the kitchen and selects the sharpest paring knife, then she settles herself on the living room couch, beside the costly glorious rug. She gathers the dowry rug into her lap as if it were a child, strokes its rough surface with the palm of her smooth hand. She pushes up the sleeve of her nightgown and draws the knife across her forearm, as a lover might draw a fingertip, testing the sharpness of the blade, giving in to the painful pressure, which is almost like pleasure, before she raises the tip and drives it in. At first it is difficult to fit the blade under the tightly woven yarn, the weave is close and holds on. Clinging to what it has always been. But bit by bit, it gives. She begins to unravel the tiny knots at the back, letting them pull free of the strain they have been under for so long, and as June cuts, it seems to her that she can hear each knot give way beneath the blade with a sound like a relieved sigh.

THEORY OF TRANSPORTATION

WHEN THE TWO OF THEM WERE YOUNG DANCE PARTNERS IN a De Mille revival on Broadway, Christopher looked like a sailor out of *Querelle*, packed and muscly and beautiful, with a plump round face like Sluggo, the cartoon character. "You do not realize how much a face can change," Tuni will tell me later, but what frightens her that day in the hospital is how little Christopher looks like himself. How generic illness makes one, how in the end the very old and the dying young look alike, as if it were not life but particularity that ebbed away, and its lack that finally kills us.

As they walk down the hall to his room, there are friendly catcalls and wet smacking kisses from the doorways they pass. "*Love* those hoofer legs," calls a six-two brunette in room 504 whom Christopher introduces as Leroy. "Charmed," Leroy says, getting up from a make-shift vanity on which he has arrayed face creams, waxy lipsticks, powders, to offer Tuni a soft, pawlike hand. "Just visiting?" he inquires.

"Just visiting," Tuni smiles.

"Lucky you," says Leroy wistfully.

Christopher has made a lot of friends here in part because he spends a portion of each day distributing to other guys the gifts people send to him. The rest of the time he keeps busy redecorating the nurses' stations and ordering in remarkable foods. When they reach his room, an order of pickled herring and cheese pierogi has just arrived from an East Village Ukrainian restaurant that never delivers. "Dan, up the hall, had a hankering. So," Chris says as he fishes for cash in the pocket of a coat hanging in the closet. "I know the owner at Veselka's. I called. Made a little deal." He gives a twenty to the delivery guy and waves away an offer of change. "I figure, since I'm here I might as well have a good time." He picks up the brown paper bag and starts out the door. "I'll be right back. Make yourself at home."

Tuni sits down on Christopher's bed and begins examining the various bottles on the night table when Leroy, now in full makeup with a bedpan on his head and a flower behind one ear, runs past the door, shouting, "Can we get some help in here?"

"This is really sick," Tuni says, when Christopher returns.

"That's why it's a hospital, dear," he says. He takes her hand to lead her to the cafeteria. "Don't worry about the grub," he says. "I've ordered in sushi."

In the cafeteria they set up their picnic at a window-side table with a view of the river. The trees below look skeletal in the winter light and the water is gray as a cadaver. Christopher seems not to notice, absorbed instead in the slow dissection of a California roll.

"My sister from Cincinnati calls me every day to console me," he tells her. "She says, 'Christopher you're *dying*. My little brother's dying.' Then she bursts into tears and hangs up." He looks up from his plate. "I suppose it makes her feel better to be able to pity me."

"Jesus," Tuni shakes her head.

"Anyway, it takes her mind off the bastard she's living with. She was always envious." Christopher spears a cylinder of rice encased in seaweed and inspects it for a moment on his fork. "Thomas has been fabulous since all this started." He looks up at Tuni. "Honestly, I don't know if I'd do the same in his shoes."

"You would."

"Don't try me."

"I won't."

For a moment they can't seem to find anything to say, and Tuni feels the silence spreading around them like a rising tide, threatening to strand them on separate shores. She wants to ask him about the medications he's taking—what the blue pills are, the pink. She wants to make a place for him to teach her about the world as he did when they were younger and stood together in the wings of the Majestic practicing lifts and falls.

"It's funny," Christopher says, finally. "People keep telling me I'm dying, and I really resent that. 'Cause I'm not. I'm living."

Tuni wouldn't like it if she knew I was telling you this. She says she has copyright on her life, that I'm moving in on her.

"You know what I'm talking about, Fran," she said over coffee at the Barbizon Hotel one afternoon late last summer after I'd picked her up at work. It had become my ritual to meet her at the clothing store where she was working then. Our rendezvous being the only sure thing in my otherwise unpunctuated week. I'd recently quit my job as a copy editor, my cat Waldo had died of a stomach ulcer, and my lover of five years had announced that she was leaving me for God. It always rained when I met Tuni at work, but I'd go anyway. Inevitably I'd catch the wrong train and have to walk ten blocks in a downpour along Madison from the East Sixties to reach her. That day was no exception. I ducked into doorways. Ran two blocks at a stretch against the lights. I arrived soaked to the skin and had to stand just inside the entrance, dripping on the welcome mat of the beige boutique full of beige women in beige clothing.

"This is my friend, Fran, who is embarrassing me," Tuni announced to the room of beautiful clerks at the wrap desk.

"We really need to buy you an umbrella, sweetie," she said, kissing me as she eased my sopping bag from my shoulder.

"Try an ark," I offered.

"Lena," Tuni said, grabbing one of the nubile youngsters at hand. "I want to introduce you to my friend Fran."

"*Ahhnn*, so *you're* the famous Lena," I said mimicking the emphatic nasal cant of Tuni's kin, known as rabbi-speak.

"God, you guys sound so much alike," Lena effused. "Are you two sisters?"

"Just friends."

"About to be enemies if this keeps up," Tuni said.

"I borrow Tuni's personality on occasion. When mine's at the dry cleaners. It shrinks in the rain."

Lena smiled at us in good-natured confusion. Tuni and I smiled at each other venomously.

"Friends often begin to sound like friends when they spend a lot of time together," I remind her later at the Barbizon.

"This is different and you know it. You've taken over my personality."

"Don't sell yourself short," I say. "You're not so readily duplicated."

She talks about me like I am a virus, replicating her cell by cell, replacing her with a bad copy. Telling her stories, stealing her lines.

Every Wednesday since I moved to the city, Tuni and I have met at this same cafe to tell each other stories. We have covered a lot of ground in two years: we have swapped rape stories, discussed Balanchine's upper lip, the surrealists, the Hasidim, Tuni's unwavering desire to have sex with rabbis, our wavering desire to have sex with each other, Coptic art, the Diaspora, god, history, favorite breakfast cereals, literature, always literature. Last Wednesday she told me about Christopher. Christopher who has lymphoma but is careful to say he doesn't have AIDS. Christopher, the former soap star, former Dance Machine producer, the perfect date who brought her roses and didn't ask her to suck his dick. The last of her dancing partners, the one-who-wasn't-dead. Christopher who has been shy around Tuni for years, avoiding her, because she is the sort of woman he would fall in love with, he told her once, if he did that sort of thing, but he doesn't.

The café is on the border of the West Village where wealth becomes this city. Not far from here beautiful men in pairs and trios stroll the streets and the windows are dressed to kill: teddy bears bound in leather chaps and studs, faux Fabergé eggs, shops given over entirely to roses and chocolates. The homeless are here like everywhere, but fewer. And slumped beside the illuminated crèche at the corner of Carmine and Bleecker or against the windows steamy with heat and dressed with tinsel and lights, even the mendicant can seem picturesque as they do in foreign countries where one doesn't have to take suffering personally.

I arrived at the café at the usual time, a few minutes before eight, and took a table by the window where I could look out at the traffic drifting north on Sixth Avenue and the gold peaked roof of a midtown building lit up in green and red floodlights like a Toulouse-Lautrec whore.

Tuni arrived a few minutes after me, looking foreign and regal in layers of black velvet and brocade with a tall velvet hat like a Parisian stovepipe.

"Why do the Kennedys always have tears in their eyes during sex?" she asked, setting her Batman lunch box on the table. I shrugged and smiled. "Mace," she said. Most people tend toward platitudes in despair, Tuni inclines toward vaudeville. So I know when she is funny, that something is awry. That night she leaned across the table to tell me condom jokes. Safe sex puns.

"What's up?" I asked. She turned from me to watch the red swarm of taillights beyond the window. I watched her watching the street.

"Isn't everyone I know who's going to die of AIDS dead already?" she asked after a while. When she finally looked at me, her eyes were watery and her mouth was straining as if she were about to smile. "Life's so uncertain," she said.

I know what she means. Last spring my lover, Margaret, announced that she was leaving me to become a monk. It wasn't that she didn't love me, she said. It's that love doesn't last. "I want to make something of my life," she told me. "I want something that will last, that will count."

"Don't I count?" I asked her, the room blurring with tears.

She put a hand to my cheek. "We always knew we were just crossing paths."

"I didn't," I said. "I didn't know that."

That night, after coffee, I took a cab home all the way to Brooklyn. I wanted to feel protected, to feel I could afford to be taken where I asked. Cab rides are a pleasure specific to New York: One feels exempt, taken care of. In the back of a yellow cab heading anywhere—crosstown along Houston, or up Sixth to Central Park—you can drop your guard. For an instant. Let go your bag. Unlock your jaw. You can read the name of the cabbie on his permit posted by the meter and forget it. For once you don't have to look with an eye out for mug shots, for police lineups. You don't have to look into faces in case you'll have to remember them later. Cab rides in New York are like a love affair: one surrenders oneself to the care of strangers, trusting that they will take you to the right place. To the place you cannot get to on your own.

❧ ❧ ❧

"*Love* your boots," Christopher says when he opens the hospital room door. "Inappropriate for every occasion." Tuni laughs and thrusts a bouquet of daisies toward him. "Tell me what I should do with these," she says, awkwardly holding the flowers before her like they might be contagious.

"I forgot you're the woman whose idea of nature is a potted plant," Christopher says, taking the paper-wrapped bouquet as Tuni steps in.

"Did I ever tell you about the time I tried to go on a vacation in the country?" she asks. "I took a train all the way to Vermont and spent an entirely miserable weekend. I kept trying to hail a cab. No one would sell me a knish." Christopher laughs and closes the door behind her. It is one of his good days, she can tell. By now she has grown accustomed to the cycles of illness. The paranoia and despair, the euphoria when he is convinced he'll be the first person to come back from this. At first she didn't believe Thomas when he said you get used to it after awhile. But she has. It's amazing what you can get used to.

❧ ❧ ❧

When I arrive at the café the following Wednesday, I find Tuni browsing the obits in the *Times, Actors Equity News*, SAG. She scrolls down the page, points out a dancer she worked with under De Mille, a famous Irish actress who was always trying to sleep with her ex-fiancé, someone from summer stock in Connecticut.

"It's weird," she says. "I read these things and get really depressed. Then I become elated. Then I buy an unnecessary hat."

"Nothing like an obit to make you feel alive," I say, and lean down to kiss her. Tuni is beautiful and sometimes when the city is tender with evening and falling snow I remember that once we might have been lovers. We met five years ago in summer at a Buddhist monastery in northern New Mexico, just the other side of the Colorado border. We spent an afternoon together on the front porch of the zendo, sitting in the shade, watching the red-tailed hawks ride the thermals in that ultramarine sky, while Tuni told me about growing up in the ballet. She explained to me the distinctions between the Kirov and Bolshoi; fouetté pirouettes; why all ballerinas hate Audrey Hepburn. "She was what you were supposed to be and never would," she confided. "She was Balanchine's ideal. He married four of her, you know. He had four wives all with long necks and small round heads. Like neolithic art objects. You could never measure up." I read her passages from Frank O'Hara's *Lunch Poems* and Virginia Woolf's *The Waves* and told her stories about fish fries in country taverns in Wisconsin. Two days later, when we were lying naked beside each other in a cold stream in the middle of an unmown field, she told me I was brilliant and had perfect breasts and asked me to marry her. She offered to fly me to New York, no strings attached.

"It's not an offer I make lightly," she said. At the time Tuni was performing off-Broadway and was, what she called, a "minor celebrity." She knew how to make an impression. But I was already falling in love with Margaret. I said I would think about it. And I have.

"Did you see Kay Boyle died?" I ask, taking a seat.

"Yeah," she says. "Who's gonna replace those guys?"

"Who knows."

"No one has politics anymore," Tuni says. "Not the old school politics where it's part of the way you live. I mean look at Ben. He's this hugely successful playwright and still he lives in the same crummy apartment on Twenty-first Street and eats tuna sandwiches. He has those deep socialist values where you can't decide anything unless five people have discussed it. The man lives by committee."

"People don't have politics anymore," I say. "They have parties."

"Of course then there are people like Lena who should never become involved in politics," Tuni offers. "She thinks a party is a social event. 'The Communist party? I'd love to come. I have a fabulous red dress. The Nazi party? *Love* to.'"

I smile and watch her talk, her white moon face suspended above the black marble table. I know what she means. Still, I think it's not politics, but something less tangible that we've misplaced. We do not know how to live our lives anymore, if we ever did. We paste them together from scraps, odd bits. We fake love affairs. Develop routines. Go into therapy. Visit the zendo, the ashram. Adopt Japanese religions and French literary theories. We borrow, we beg, we steal. We miss the point. We long for it.

I think of a night last year after one of these meetings with Tuni, just after our big young country had declared war on a small old country. I was on the subway platform at Christopher-Sheridan, one a.m., with two sailors in spanking white uniforms trimmed in navy blue stripes and round white caps like dog food dishes. They were drunk and yelled at the elderly black man behind the glass who was selling them tokens. They wanted directions.

They were oddly anachronistic, the two sailors, arrogant and naive and so very white. They looked like they'd been scrubbed with bristled brushes and soap, their faces were creamy, matte red at the cheeks, they looked like they would smell like babies, new and moist. Like sheets.

They seemed to be posing for pictures no one was taking, pictures they had seen: pictures from another war we won, their fathers, my father, the war that came *after* the war to end all wars (spoken of like an august and distant relative—Great Uncle, Great War). How odd to see them then—half a century later—stepping through the turnstile straight out of a Gene Kelly flick. Playing victorious as if the last fifty years hadn't happened: No House Committee on Un-American Activities, no civil rights movement, no Selma, no King, no Dylan or Leary or acid or Beatles or Stonewall, Marilyn, Joplin, Nicaraguan Revolution. Done with change, they would turn back the century as if it were a time bomb on which the clock was running down.

For three weeks after Christopher is discharged from the hospital Tuni calls his apartment and leaves messages on his machine, but he never calls back. Then, one Saturday evening, Thomas answers the phone. She can hear Christopher in the background, asking who it is and a muffled sound as Thomas covers the receiver. "Tell them I'm dead," Christopher says. "They can save their sympathy for the starving children in Crown Heights or Somalia or wher*ever* it's chic to be starving these days. Who is it anyway?" When Tuni offers to bring by some Chinese food, she can hear Christopher instruct Thomas to tell her thanks but no.

"He's really not up to seeing anyone. I'm sorry," Thomas offers.

"Don't worry about it," Tuni says. "Well, I'd invite you out Tom, but I'm sure you wouldn't want to leave Chris."

"Invite me out," Thomas whispers.

So they meet at a Greek diner at the south end of Central Park. Thomas, who is only twenty-eight, looks drawn and tired and aged. He slides into the red leather booth and kisses Tuni chastely on the cheek. They chat for awhile about mutual acquaintances, how funny the weather's been lately—hot then cold—the hole in the ozone layer, give their orders.

"I want you to know that it's not that Chris doesn't want to see you," Thomas begins when the food arrives. "It's just been a rough time for him." He circles the rim of his coffee cup with the tip of his index finger.

"For both of you," Tuni says, but Thomas continues to stare at his cup as if he hasn't heard her.

"His sister slit her wrists in Ohio," he says matter-of-factly. "The day Christopher was released from the hospital."

"Christ, Thomas."

"She wasn't handling Christopher's illness very well," he says, tapping the saucer with the back of his nail. "It's so ironic, isn't it?" he looks up at her. "I mean, here's Christopher fighting for his life and his sister kills herself."

"I don't know what to say."

"That's because there is nothing *to* say," he tells her. "Nothing."

The hospital discharged Christopher because they said there was nothing more they could do for him. "Can you imagine being so sick even a hospital won't take you?" she asks. "I guess for them he's just another guy they can't help, but for Chris it's his only life."

"What would you do if you were dying?" I ask. "Not that we aren't."

"You mean imminently?"

"Yeah."

"Depends."

"On what?"

"Of what?"

"How about diphtheria?" I propose. "Influenza? Anthrax."

"Burn the fields," she says, roused by the mention of her favorite disease.

"Dutch Elm," I press.

"I'd go to Holland and buy wooden shoes and dance in the Amsterdam ballet. How about you?" she asks. I think of what I might have said a year ago, how I might have imagined Margaret beside me reading. Now I think I will die on my feet, traveling.

Ever since Margaret left, I find I spend a lot of time on subways. Just riding them. Last Saturday, I crossed three boroughs on the F and 7 trains, riding from Nathan's Hot Dog stand at Coney Island to the Chinese pastry shops on Main Street, Flushing, and back again. I ride at all hours—three a.m. with the musicians, the transvestites, the nurses in their scuffed orthopedic shoes going home from the late shift; just before dawn, among the sleepy brown workers who catch a few extra winks on their way to low-paying jobs with lousy hours.

At first it was by mistake. I was coming home after work a few months ago, reading a book and thinking about Margaret and why she had left and what I could've done differently, when I found myself at Far Rockaway, just having forgotten to get off. Then there were other times I'd jump confidently onto a train only to find it was going in the wrong direction, Uptown instead of Downtown, or to Queens instead of up the West Side. After a while I just stayed on. The train would pull into my station, the doors would open, and I would sit there, with all the other people going to other places, going with them.

Christopher comes in and out these days. Sometimes he is incredibly lucid, like a drowning man who understands he's going to drown. They say there is this remarkable clarity when you're facing death. Time slows down and you see everything happening. As if your life had nothing to do with you. As if it were someone else's story you were telling that bore no relation to your own. Sometimes Christopher is like that, Tuni says. With this uncanny clarity. And then there are other days when he's demented. He'll march the three of them out for ice cream at Häagen-Dazs and when they get there he'll start raving about the absence of his favorite flavor, or he'll force Thomas to take him to Chase Manhattan bank only to refuse to make a deposit and it will take an hour to find out that he's forgotten his account number and had been too embarrassed to say so.

"I need to talk to Tuni Lewis," Christopher announced two days ago, after a week in a coma. Thomas, amazed, brought Christopher the phone.

"Hi, munchkin, how're tricks?" Christopher asked Tuni.

"*Fine*, Chris. And how are you?"

"Oh, fine, you know. So when am I going to see you?"

"Name a time."

"How about tomorrow morning?"

"I'll be there."

When she arrives at eight the next morning, Thomas leads her to the living room where Christopher is arranged on the couch among oily pillows and yellowing linen. He has not eaten in two weeks and Tuni tells me that she is amazed that a person can look like that and still be alive. Thomas leans over to wake Christopher and tell him Tuni's arrived.

"I'll leave you two alone, I guess," Thomas says. "I have a couple of errands to run."

"Sure," Tuni says. "We'll be fine, won't we Chris?"

"Of course," Christopher says, eying Thomas. "Who's *he*?"

"I'll be back in a few hours," Thomas says, and he turns and walks away down the hall.

It is terrifying to watch someone die slowly, Tuni will tell me later. You think they cannot go on, but they do. If something doesn't come along and kill you, you can last a long time almost dead.

Pumped up on the morphine that he injects during his frequent visits to the bathroom, Christopher is cheerful and vague throughout the morning and early afternoon. When he slips into sleep, Tuni goes to the kitchen and makes them tea. When she returns to the couch with a tray of cups and saucers and a steaming pot, he gently takes her hand and places it on his chest, clasping it to his bony sternum, so she can feel his heart throbbing under her palm.

"It hurts here," he says simply.

She asks him if he remembers Jessica Ro, a former lover of hers and a former dancer. "The Korean chick with no hair," he says.

"Yeah," Tuni says, relieved by his recollection. "She's working with me now, selling our clothing line on the West Coast."

"My friend Tuni owns a clothing company, too," he says.

"I *am* Tuni," she says.

"Well, I *told* him I was happy to go see a drag show, but not *that* one," Christopher exclaims. Then, abruptly lucid with pain, "Can you help me to the bathroom," he asks. "I've got to go."

"Sure," Tuni says.

After his shot, Christopher lies back on the couch. "See you two later," he says, although Tuni is the only one there. "Bye-bye, munchkins. Bye-bye. Bye-bye, munchkins."

Among the things Margaret left behind when she left me was a sweatshirt I had given her depicting a pair of bespectacled rabbits on ice skates skating round and round and round. It still has her smell in it, a smell of incense and wood smoke and flannel. Lately I've taken to wearing it around the house, sleeping on Margaret's side of the bed, I spend a lot of time reading the books she left behind. Wondering what she saw in them. Christopher Isherwood on his guru, Yeats's translation of the Patanjali's Sutras, Buddhist poets, feminist theologians.

I am reading in the living room early one evening when I catch a glimpse of myself in the mirror above the hearth. For a moment I think it is Margaret seated there, in her rabbit sweatshirt, reading

Isherwood. But then I realize it is only me in disguise. Only me pretending to be someone else.

Tuni is standing in the foyer, wearing a black cape and an enormous black sun hat with a broad floppy brim, when I arrive at the International Center of Photography.

She tells me Christopher's back in the hospital. The chemo they've given him has ruined his bone marrow. He's not producing enough red blood cells. They have to give him new blood. There's the chance of a marrow transplant, but it's an experimental procedure and his insurance company isn't sure they'll cover it.

We walk up a curved staircase to the gallery where the photos of Soviet Jews are on display. People in suits and leather bomber jackets are shuffling through the rooms carrying plastic glasses of red and white wine close to their chests. The people in the photos are crowded too: pressed against door jambs, cowering under chandeliers, dwarfed by their bookshelves and Kurdistan rugs.

When we reach the last of the rooms, I launch into a monologue on the evident influences. Cartier-Bresson. Vuillard. The French fascination with moral claustrophobia.

"*It* was *bri*lliant," I pronounce in full-blown rabbi-speak.

"I thought they were pretty nice," Tuni says, in what I imagine she imagines is my family's Midwestern dialect.

"Are you imitating me?" I ask her as we move toward the exit.

"Well, I thought *some*one here ought to be representing your personality. It had to at least put in an appearance, don't you think?"

We push silently through the bodies. Through other people's perfume and cigar smoke and nervous human smells.

"I miss you," she says quietly when we reach the top of the stairs.

"I'm here."

"No. You're not."

I feel around in my pocket for bits of things and try to identify them: a dime, the stem of an apple, a bank machine receipt.

"I don't know who I am when I'm with you anymore," Tuni says.

"I'm not trying to move in on you."

"You've taken over my personality."

"I've adopted your verbal mannerisms, that's all. I do that with perfect strangers. Don't take it personally," I say.

"Fran," she says angrily. Then more softly, "I depend on the people I love to be who they are." I think of how little she knows about me, how in all the time we have been friends we have never had an ordinary conversation, a simple, plain, brown-paper-bag conversation, the sort of conversation I routinely had with Margaret by the stove, eating chips from a bag, walking to the subway. Tuni and I have performed for each other, like tightrope walkers; afraid to fall.

"I wouldn't know how," I say. But she has already turned to go. I admire the rippling of her cape as she descends the broad red-carpeted staircase.

On the subway home I sit beside the door in a narrow single-person seat wedged between an armrest and the conductor's box. Across from me a young black woman wearing a velvet hat sleeps, her head falling onto her chest, her lips parting. Beside her is the Hasid in his black coat and felt bowler. His yellowed beard unravels over his chest as he sleeps. He has wire-rimmed glasses; a few brown age spots show on his cheeks. But it is his hands I notice. How his right hand is spread open on his knee, palm up as if in supplication. The fingers of his left gathered together like the hooked beak of a tulip tree blossom, and twisted out from his leg in the wrong direction. It is a small gesture, this wayward hand. But significant. Defying convention. I study him across the aisle before I begin to draw the fingers of my left hand together and lay them against my knee, turning them outward. My right hand open upward on my other knee. I look over at the Hasid again to check that I've got it right and find him staring at me. His eyes moist and bloodshot. He yells something in what I take for Yiddish and swats his hand in a gesture I could not possibly misunderstand.

In the final week before Christopher died, whenever he walked—which was not often—he floated. His feet hardly reached the floor. His was not so much a death, Tuni will tell me later, as an unbecoming. "He unbecame himself." His body did not so much give out, as erase into the air.

I imagine, sometimes, how it must have been the night Christopher died. How Thomas spent the wee hours of the morning walking around Manhattan by himself. If he thought about it, it might have occurred to him that he was putting himself in danger, in harm's way, tempting hurt to hurt him more that he might feel something. It is the feeling nothing that frightens him, I think. The great weightlessness since Christopher's heart stopped. I imagine it is because of that, because he cannot feel anything anywhere on his body, that Thomas walks that night through the streets of Manhattan from the hospital at Seventy-sixth to a theater in the forties, where he can sit in the dark and watch people move and let someone he will never know touch his body, which he no longer recognizes as anybody.

THE THREE CHRISTS
OF MOOSE LAKE,
MINNESOTA

IT'S NOT LIKE WE BELIEVED THAT THEY WERE THE SONS
of God or anything, but for awhile (before Dr. Davidson and all
the publicity, before it became a story, when we were still just folks
caught up in the mystery of the thing), we felt kind of special—chosen, you might say—to be host to the three Christs of Moose Lake,
Minnesota. I felt—I don't know how else to put this—blessed. It
brought Karen to the hospital after all, and what can I call that if not
a blessing?

You've probably heard about them by now. The three guys at the
Moose Lake Hospital for the Mentally Ill, who all claimed to be the
son of God, aka Jesus Christ. It was Dr. Davidson's idea to bring
the three of them together to see if "confrontation with a similar
delusion" would shock them back into reality. That was what Karen
told me anyway. I wasn't in on the details of their therapy, of course,
being an orderly. My job was to keep things in line. To help patients
into the toilet and hold them up under the shower and tie them
down when that kind of thing was necessary. It isn't glamorous work,

I admit, a glorified bouncer really—the sort of work you might expect a guy like me to do, if you saw me in the Piggly Wiggly—but it's honest and it's a step up from the life my father led.

Of course some of what you hear about the Christs is just plain wrong. Nothing more than publicity seeking by some of the staff, looking for their fifteen minutes. It's not true that the hospital's bricks wept blood or that the Virgin Mary appeared in the parking lot. (Mr. Martinez's son has the Virgin of Guadalupe spray painted on his rear windshield, like those Jesus Saves vanity plates you see sometimes. Amazing, maybe, but hardly miraculous.) It's not true what they said in the *Weekly World News* either, that when they gave the three Christs the Myers-Briggs personality test, one of the Christs scored clear off the charts: neither ENTJ ("The Executive") nor ISFP ("The Artist"), but INRI.

INRI? Give me a break.

But certain things did happen. That pretty, young nurse Pederson was caught in a compromising position in the linen closet with one of them (I think it was the Viking Christ, which we call him because of his big red beard). I didn't see it myself, so I can't be sure, but they say that when they pulled her off him she was wearing only orthopedic shoes, reenacting what she called her favorite temptation. It's not true that her name was Magdalena, though. It was Helga. Helga Pederson of Verdon. For the record. In case somebody out there's keeping track.

To tell you the truth, I wasn't much interested in our little trinity until Karen came around. She arrived in Moose Lake a few weeks before Dr. Davidson to set things up. She had been his assistant in the Twin Cities, a "psych resident," she called it, having just finished up a degree at the university. She was there to observe, she told us, to take notes, to get a lay of the land. We figured she was sent ahead to make sure Dr. Davidson wasn't embarrassed, to make sure our guys were the real thing and not some publicity stunt, as they'd started to become. Somebody had been leaking stories to the local paper and TV news and we'd been fighting off reporters for most of a week. There was starting to be a lot of talk about miracles. A local kid claimed he'd seen one of our guys under a full moon strolling across the surface of Moose Lake. But of course there was never any proof, and those of us at the hospital knew better. Let's face it: Miracles don't happen here.

It's not that ours is a bad town; it's just unexceptional. If you overlook the fact that our principal industry is locking people up or tying them down (of the 2,126 people in town, 592 are in the prison or our patients), we're like a lot of little towns up here north of the Twin Cities—farm towns and fishing towns along Highway 35, which runs like a shaky line north to Canada—places city people stop for gas or fishing tackle and drive on past on their way somewhere else. Sometimes when I'm driving home after work, looking at the buildings in town—one-story aluminum sheds, fake log cabins, tractors on the main street alongside the cars—a place long and low as a distant train whistle, I feel a longing like heartburn. An ache right there.

But like I said, I didn't pay a whole lot of attention to any of it till Karen showed up. We were still keeping the three Christs apart in those days to avoid any trouble; each one was in a separate group-therapy session, each one sleeping on a separate corridor. When Karen arrived to observe afternoon group, I was assigned to help restrain some of the bigger patients if things got out of hand, as they sometimes do.

She wasn't what I expected. I was thinking she'd be older, sort of stern as the medicals often are. But she was kind of pretty and really young. I felt sorry for her actually, sure the patients would roll right over her. She had straight brown hair that fell like a curtain; that first day, she wore a skirt the burnt-red color of the autumn leaves you could see beyond the bars on the windows. She looked like a teacher or a mother. Or a school girl. Not like a doctor at all. "Stoical," that's how she looked; it was a favorite word of hers. I looked it up after she'd said it a few times, like I did a lot of things when she was here.

Which is why—after group that first day, when I showed her to the cafeteria and she asked me if I wanted to get lunch—I said, "Sure." Staff don't usually fraternize with medical, but she wasn't a doctor yet and she seemed nice, like she meant it, and of course she didn't know anyone here. I could feel some of the other guys looking at us, when we walked up to the line to get our trays, especially the new guy, Jackson, but I didn't care. I felt a little good about it even. Sort of proud, special. She asked a lot of questions about the hospital, the Christs, the other patients and staff; she asked a lot of questions period. Personal things, like how I got here and why this line of work. But I didn't mind the way I usually do when a woman starts asking me a lot of questions. She was a good listener, and I found myself telling her all kinds of things. Things I don't usually think about, let alone *talk* about.

She asked if I'd grown up in Moose Lake and I told her how I was from Chicago and how for years I couldn't figure out what my Dad did for a living. My mother said he was in merchandising; I thought he played golf. All I knew was that I used to wake up in the night to the sound of the garage door opening and from my window I'd watch trucks unload TVs and boxes and stuff into our garage, things that disappeared a few days later. I was fourteen before I figured it out, understood what should have been obvious, that he was kiting merchandise, a fence; I was twenty before it occurred to me to ask a friend on the force to run my dad's Social as a favor; he came back with a rap sheet long as my arm. She said that must've been hard, to find out something like that about your father. I shrugged; it's better to know the truth, I said. Still, I don't judge him; a man does what he has to. Let's face it, times are tough. These days even being the son of God is a competitive business: survival of the unfittest you might say.

🦋 🦋 🦋

We'd been warned to keep the whole thing quiet to avoid the kind of controversy that could get our funding cut. The head honchos in Admin said local religious folks might get the wrong idea, think we were trying to cure people of their faith in God. You got to wonder what goes on in the minds of some people. I mean, these are the same folks who want to stop little kids from trick or treating in Ohio, where my sister lives, because they think Halloween's a kind of devil worship. "Pagan" is the word my sister used. Now I ask you, what kind of person thinks like that?

If anything, having the three Christs around got us more interested in religion.

They got us talking. The usual divisions dissolved. Suddenly it didn't matter if you were kitchen staff or janitorial, ward nurse or nurse—briefly, we were all of us in it together, guardians of the sons of God. Heated conversations went on even after we'd punched out on our time cards. Almost any night of the week in those days you could walk into the staff lounge off the kitchen and find two or three of us chain smoking and speculating on the three Christs.

You could tell a lot about a man by his opinion of our trinity. Jackson, the new guy, made jokes. He has those movie star looks women fall for, a real Brad Pitt type (Brad Pitt with a mullet)—all blond hair, blue eyes, and Old Spice. He said (to make the nurses laugh) that when you got them together in group therapy they'd "be beside themselves." He said, "When you get those three together, they'll crucify each other."

But others of us were of a more serious turn of mind. We wanted to know if God returned, what would he be like? (One of the younger nurses insisted God could be a she.) What would God want? What would God do?

Karen had her own concerns. She told me about them sometimes as we did our rounds together, as we walked the halls or grounds, we'd talk. She wondered if it was kind to cure them. "We all have our illusions," she said. I asked if she believed our boys were the real McCoy. But she said I misunderstood, that she meant something else entirely. She'd studied literature at college, like I mentioned, and was often quoting beautiful things other people had said. There was a guy named Ibsen who had this idea that he called "the vital lie," the thing we need to tell ourselves to get out of bed in the morning. She wondered if we were really curing these guys or simply robbing them of "the illusions that sustain a life," if we were restoring sanity or just a more acceptable craziness.

And she got me thinking, I mean, what's so wrong with believing you're the son of God? What harm does it do? If it weren't for the linens they kept pulling off their beds for robes, they'd have been pretty nice to have around. They weren't violent or anything, except for the occasional stigmata scratched into a palm and a tendency to bellow the Psalms in group. Mostly they were a quiet bunch.

A lot of the staff preferred the red-haired one—the Viking Christ—a little spark plug of a guy, muscly, maybe thirty, with bright green eyes and a bushy beard. He's the least self-righteous of the three, which is how I like to think God's messenger would be if I met him. Mostly he smiled and raised his hands over us and said, "Bless you, Bless you"; he hummed little songs to himself. He never gave me any trouble.

Mrs. Weimar, our resident theologian, preferred the skinny Ethereal Christ, a young Swede, twenties, blond and tall and scrawny. He was serious and sad and quoted scripture to the others. She said he was a dead ringer for the real thing.

The Angry Christ, as we called him, was our least favorite. He was a big guy, a bruiser like me, but older, maybe fifty, always raging about how we are squandering his father's gifts to us. One week he broke out of art therapy and ran into the hall shouting, "We must love one another or die" (which Karen said is not even scripture, but poetry, some guy named Auden). He had a point maybe, but he seemed a long way from holy. Another time, not long after he arrived, the Angry Christ escaped from rec therapy and Stevens caught him in the parking lot kicking the bumper of an SUV (shouting "Selfish, Ugly, Vain" over and over). When the president gave his speech about the need to bomb other guys before they bombed us—preemption, he called it, or presumption, something like that—the Angry Christ got so pissed he had to be removed from the common room. The TV shorted out as they took him past, and I felt pretty sure the Angry Christ was behind it, that he'd given the set a good punch on his way by, just before the screen went black. He's tall enough to do it. And he is mad as hell.

It's weird to be guarding the Christs. It's rare these days that we got to keep *any*one around, what with deinstitutionalization and all. Most of the adult admits are in and out in less than two weeks, "assessed and stabilized" they call it. So we were kind of pleased to get to keep our Christs. Only about one in ten stay on here, and that's only because they're what they call "nonresponsive" or a "difficult placement." So maybe that's what happened with our boys.

I'm not what you'd call religious. I don't spend much time in church, though I've been with friends, y'know, at Christmastime here in Moose Lake. Everyone goes to the services at Good News Lutheran; everyone who's at liberty that is. But my father was a Jew; Cohen was his father's name, which he changed to Corn when he settled in the Midwest, convinced it was as Middle American as you could get. Not wanting to stand out.

But who knows, maybe if the son of God did come back, he would go crazy from the mess we've made of everything. The air pollution and the poverty, the suffering and the wars and the waste. We've learned so much and what have we done with our knowledge? After two thousand years in the Christian era, what do have we to show for ourselves? Lady Gaga.

Now I have never been a religious man and I don't want to claim that I became one. It seems to me the ordinary physical world we live in is hard enough to tackle without going looking for the supernatural to contend with. I'm not an educated guy. But Karen, who knows more about these things than I do, seems to think that the two things aren't so different; she says that the material things of this world are just energy looked at from another angle, moving at a different speed ("think of $E = mc^2$," she says), and that we make too much of the distinction between what she calls "the solid and numinous worlds." She says, "Divinity is found in the most unexpected places." I didn't claim to understand all she said, but when she talked I felt my heart lurch. I began to look up words, to read in bed at night instead of falling asleep to the TV; I began to want to be better. With Karen, it seemed, I might be and that life might after all be miraculous.

This was not as crazy a hope as it sounds. I'm not saying that I'm so great to look at, but I have inherited some of my father's gangster charm. I got a nice enough mug, a decent build, I work out with weights. I was a skinny kid, but since I hit my thirties women have liked me. Pretty women. Helpful. Looking for a fixer-upper. I've been flattered, and sometimes I have mistaken that for love. But when I met Karen, I knew it hadn't been. Not the kind of love you see at the movies, that kind of big love you come to resent after a while when you begin to believe that the truth of the matter is nobody in real life loves like that—big as the sky over cornfields. I knew that I had never been in love before, because I loved Karen like that. With her I had the feeling that anything was possible; that I might surprise myself. That we all might.

In time of course we began to get critical. To debate the fine points.

There was talk about scriptural accuracy, complaints that the Angry Christ was not playing his part well, that he was "untrue to type." Mrs. Weimar called him "anachronistic," "too Old Testament." She said he had it all wrong, that any self-respecting Christ would "leave God's fury and the suffering of Job to the Jews." I didn't understand everything she said. But I got the gist: Christ was a nice guy and our Angry Christ was anything but. He was more like that billboard you see in the cornfields outside Northfield, the black one with white lettering that reads: "God is coming and boy is he pissed." Our Angry Christ must've had a look at that before he lost it.

The whole thing must've been getting to me, because one night around that time when I was doing night rounds—checking that lights were off, doors locked—I passed the room of one of the Christs and out of the corner of my eye I saw this, well—radiance. This glow. I pushed open the door and looked in, but the room was dark, lights out. I figured it was probably a streetlight, reflection off the hood of a car outside. A trick of the light. I was disappointed. I'd hoped to have something to tell Karen. We'd been spending a lot of time together, and I found myself saving up things to tell her. Interesting things I'd observed about the Christs or the staff. Little stories about my dog, Herman. I began to try to be, y'know, better—to read the newspaper, look up the words I didn't know instead of skipping over them, I began to drink eight glasses of water each day, lift weights at the gym, eat broccoli. Floss. I started to hope that maybe she liked me, or could.

⫸⟶

I wasn't the only one who started imagining things.

Maybe it was all the talking we were doing, all the hours of speculation, but after a while some of the staff began to see signs. The giant TV in the rec room, the one suspended out of reach of patients, which only the staff can control, started switching channels spontaneously. Others claimed their watches stopped. A car that had been stalled in the parking lot for days started up all of its own.

Some of it was easy to explain away. The Angry Christ is a big man, over six feet, and he might have slapped the TV set with a palm as he went past that one time, shorting out a wire. Watches run down; they break. As for the car stalled in the lot for three hours waiting for a tow, Karen said that "outside of Pascal good luck does not prove God's existence." She called it "Deus ex jumper cables." No miracle there.

Still, I understood the desire to believe. I was hoping for a miracle myself.

I have observed that if you give a man a mystery you will end up with one of two things—a cop or a philosopher. Because one kind of man will look for someone to blame, he'll try to find a culprit to punish until everything is under control again; the other kind of man will marvel at what he hasn't seen before. That's why the young are naturally philosophical, why kids wonder where they were before they were born and why a banana is called a banana; kids can spend hours watching clouds. Everything amazes them.

People argue about what distinguishes man from the lower animals now that we know that chimps can sign and elephants remember and dolphins think and chimpanzees kill for sport (I saw this on a *National Geographic* special the other night). Karen said that what makes us unique as a species is that we make art, but I think maybe we're the only ones who pray and who wager, which, depending on how you look at it, maybe boils down to the same thing—faith in a power beyond our own, whether God or luck.

So it's not surprising that it wasn't long before people started to calculate the odds. At the height of it, the irreligious were placing bets (which Christ would crack first and how); the religious were praying for a sign. The miracle I prayed for was for Karen to fall for me. I had a vision of our life together, how I'd maybe go back to school—community college in Minneapolis or Fargo, y'know, two-year, then maybe move up to something bigger. Study anthropology. Maybe teach in a high school. I could see our house, a living room with a fireplace and a set of *Encyclopedia Britannica* and dinner parties with educated people, where we'd discuss philosophy and politics and all the big questions, like what distinguishes man from apes.

Then a week before Dr. Davidson's arrival the trouble started.

The Christs were getting to be a handful: Keeping them apart was taking up more and more time; we had teams assigned to supervise the activities of each and a careful schedule that ensured they would not meet even in passing on the way to lunch or art therapy or rec hour. Karen and I were spending more and more time together. Then one day I came in and saw on scheduling that Jackson had been switched with me, assigned to Karen, so that I could assist in electroshock; I ached with disappointment.

And the next afternoon, as I was returning from C Ward, I came around a corner and saw Jackson all cozy with Karen in the hall. His hand braced against the wall above her head, his face dropped down near hers in a way that made me want to strap him into a straitjacket, and I was thinking about doing just that when we heard the scream up the hall and saw Mrs. Weimar race out into the corridor with a Dixie cup full of a liquid dark as blood. Mrs. Weimar claimed it was the miracle at Cana all over again, that she'd given the gentle Christ a glass of water and he'd transformed it into wine.

Jackson stuck a finger in the cup and popped it in his mouth and shook his head like a dog shaking off water, then said, "Yup, it's wine all right. Pretty shitty wine, but wine."

The desire to believe is strong. And for a while, we all believed in the wine that Weimar found in that Dixie cup. We wanted to believe those things are possible, that things like that could happen to people like us.

It wasn't until the night shift came on that one of the nurses glimpsed a bottle of Manischewitz in Mrs. Weimar's locker and phoned the director at home. Turned out Weimar had a big bet on the gaunt Christ being the real McCoy. They searched her locker, quietly let her go.

I wasn't around for the confrontation, when Dr. Davidson brought the three Christs face to face to face. But I understand that it was quite a sight to see. They got the whole thing on video, but I can't bring myself to watch; still, I've heard all about it from Jackson, who likes to tell the story. From what I hear there were intensive sessions for five days straight that week; our boys didn't come out for hours at a stretch; at first they ignored each other, wandered around the room like the others weren't there; when Dr. Davidson finally made them sit down and introduce themselves, things got ugly; evidently there was a lot of shouting—the Viking Christ insisted that the other two were frauds, that he was the one and only real son of God; he tried to punch out the others to prove his point; the gaunt Christ quoted scripture about how people in glass houses shouldn't throw stones and something about a bean in the eye. The Angry Christ was un-usually quiet—maybe someone overdid his meds—but he didn't take much interest in the proceedings, from what I hear; he played solitaire, made little low under-the-breath comments about pearls and swine; evidently he tried to bum a cigarette from Dr. Davidson, which just goes to show the guy's completely delusional since this is Minnesota and you haven't been able to smoke inside a public building here in thirty years.

Karen says it was like watching people move through the stages of grief when facing death—denial, anger, bargaining, grief, acceptance. I imagine how hard it must have been for them; how each of those guys must have clung to the hope that he really was the one; waiting to be recognized for who he is, waiting to be seen in his true colors, waiting for the moment of truth when the other guys are shown to be fakes; but eventually you just face facts; realize that you are not the man you thought, the man you'd hoped you'd be.

I don't know exactly what went on in those sessions, but I think I understand how those guys must have felt, giving up their delusions. I imagine they felt real bad losing the hope that they might be special after all, like I did when Karen introduced me to her fiancé—a skinny guy with wire-rimmed glasses, tall and lanky with a bowl haircut like the Beatles had and an Irish accent I swear to God was faked (love is a mystery)—and I realized how crazy I'd been to think someone like her would ever choose someone like me.

When it all was over, a reporter asked me what I'd learned, and I told him the truth, though he didn't print it. I told him that what I'd learned from the three Christs of Moose Lake was that no one is really that special. Not any one of us is. And the sooner you get over thinking you are, the better off you'll be. I told him the trick to life, the key to staying sane, to not going clean out of your stinking mind, is not to expect too much of yourself or others. You'll only be disappointed. "Ours is a technological, not a miraculous age," I said. I didn't say I was quoting Karen. Miracles just don't happen.

So I suppose you could say that reason triumphed in the end. Though Karen said maybe it was narcissism that won out. It is evidently better to be an ordinary schnook than to have to share an identity as one of three sons of God.

Now things are a lot quieter. Karen went back to the Cities with Dr. Davidson. I hear that the gentle Christ was contacted by MTV producers looking for the newest face to play lead for a "crossover" group trying to appeal to both "the Goths and Christian rockers," that's what Karen wrote in a letter she sent from St. Paul; they have a Mary Magdalene on guitar whose a dead ringer for JLo, she says. Rock of Sages is their name.

The Viking Christ is in a half-way house in Minneapolis; I hear he's a clerk at a food coop, part-time. I hope he's doing well. I really hope he makes it.

The Angry Christ is ours. Of the three of them, he's the only one who failed therapy, though the medicals don't like to call it a failure. He was "unresponsive," Karen would say. They had to intervene. Which is to say they shocked him. I was off that day, so I don't know what exactly went wrong. Some sort of feedback, reverb they could not explain. Evidently, they sort of short-circuited his brain. That's the story I got anyway. He had no family so they didn't need to worry about a lawsuit, and the publicity had pretty much died down by then, so no one was paying much attention and no one has called to complain or protest. Still they cured two out of three, which isn't bad, so you might say our story has a happy ending.

But lately I've been feeling kind of gloomy. I don't know if it's the return to the everyday routines of strapping down and restraints, the mops and spills and Dixie cups and rounds. Or if it's the fact that Karen's gone. It's been almost a year now so you'd think I'd be used to it. But some things are hard to get used to. Time doesn't heal all.

Since the shock treatment, the Angry Christ has been pretty quiet. Mostly he watches TV. He sits in the rec room on the yellow couch. The TV stays to one channel now, unless one of the staff changes it. The clocks keep time. Sometimes I find him in the rec room, just sitting there, with tears streaming down his face for no apparent reason. And I admit that when I'm feeling sort of bad myself, because the dog is sick or the streets are lousy with snow or like that day a few months ago when I got the wedding invitation from Karen, it's almost comforting to find him weeping silently like a stoical fountain. Sometimes, I think I almost understand where he's coming from.

And maybe that's the reason that I don't want to tell the others what happened last night, maybe it's because I feel kind of sorry for him and don't want them to shock him again. Or maybe I'm afraid of the publicity the news might bring, because that might bring Karen back and I couldn't take seeing her right now, not yet. Or maybe it's that I want to keep this for myself for a little while, to hold on to the possibility that I've been wrong about him, and us, and everything. Whatever the reason, I didn't note it in his chart.

But the day Karen was married—yesterday, that is—when I was doing my evening rounds, coming round with extra water for the patients after the nurses had distributed the meds, I brought the angry Christ his little Dixie cup of water. He looked almost regal, radiant on those pillows, and for the first time in weeks he looked right into my eyes with an expression of sane sorrow, as if he understood my pain, as if he almost felt bad for me. And when I held the cup to his lips, he took it in his own hands, unassisted, and drank it down. I watched him swallow, watched him stick out his tongue and raise it to show me he hadn't hidden anything. He did all this with an expression of such dignified sadness that for a minute it crossed my mind to wonder which of us was nuts—the man who believed he was the child of God or the one who was bent on convincing him he wasn't, that no one of us is special after all—and maybe it was all the stress with Karen getting married, but I'll be damned if when he handed back that cup, I didn't see in its bottom, plain as day and unmistakable—palpable as longing, hallucinatory as love, or like a sign that we are, after all, maybe more than we might seem—the faintest trace of wine.

GRAVITY

THROUGH THE DOORWAY OF THE SYNAGOGUE LIBRARY that opens onto the main hall, Richard can see his sister Rachel clacking up the temple corridor from the dressing room. She is frantic, looking for things that have not arrived: her bouquet, her mother's pearls, the groom. She moves in a rustle of taffeta and silk, beneath a pearl-beaded cap and a tent of cream lace, like a perambulating cake on a mission from God. That, at least, is how Richard will put it to Brian when he speaks to him later tonight, long distance. It is not a good simile, Richard is aware of that. It is rather overdone and straining for effect, but that, he thinks, is apposite to the occasion.

This marriage—Rachel's second—has come after a long and arduous courtship and there is more than a little triumph and enmity in the proceedings, which Richard imagines must resemble the emotions in a calf-roping ring. Richard likes to think of things being like other things. He does not like to think of things being what they are, in themselves. That, at least, is what Brian told him recently. He had not put it quite that way, of course, being Brian, but that is what he meant, Richard thinks, when he said, "You're always loving what you left."

What Richard Has Left is a category, Richard reflects, which now could be said to include Brian, the man he loves and lives with and left two days and some two thousand miles ago to come to this wedding alone. Richard had not expected to attend. As a rule he avoids weddings, but when his father announced a few weeks ago that his mistress would be coming, Richard agreed to take part.

He told Brian that he was going for his mother's sake, to hold her hand. He told himself he needed a vacation from life with Brian. But now that he is back in Minneapolis, back in this town he vowed never to return to, Richard struggles to remember why he has returned, he who has spent a lifetime leaving this place and these people he loves behind.

When he left the Midwest fifteen years ago, first for college then medical school, Richard vowed never to return. With the naive conviction one can nurse only in one's youth, he believed that he was making a clean break. He imagined his family would fade for him as a lighthouse beam fades when a ship pulls out to sea, diminishing to a weak trail across the air, then vanishing. Their lives seemed small to him then, their choices inspired by fear, not the sharp desire he had discovered and traced over the skin of men, desire like a cord deep in his gut that had strengthened, grown taut, pulled him with a jolt into his body, his life. Now that he's back in this the city of his earliest sorrows, he finds it difficult to account for his time since he left; it seems to him that no time at all has elapsed since he was home for his sister's last wedding, since he last saw his family, that he has always been—may always be—in waiting.

From the library where he stands looking out onto the foyer, watching the preparations his sister and mother make, Richard can see that Rachel is more nervous this time than the last. She is anxious to get the details right: She double checks the corsages in their box, she counts them twice; she scrutinizes the commas on the programs, harangues the caterers by cell phone. She makes a show of her guttural "h" when she pronounces chuppah, as if it would prove her an observant Jew, which she is not. He cannot help but notice how careful they are of ritual this time around, superstitious maybe or simply aware now of how fragile such vows are.

When Rachel turns toward Richard with a pleading look, he gives a little flutter of his fingers and smiles at the Divine Pastry and, with a relief he would rather not consider too closely, starts toward her.

Halfway across the foyer, Richard's mother intercepts him like a bad pass.

"I need to speak with you," she says, voice low.

Across the foyer, Richard's father has entered with Uncle Leonard and a relative he does not recognize, a large woman in beige. "Rachel . . ." Richard begins to say.

"Can wait." His mother bends her mouth into a smile and turns a radiant look on Rachel and the all-but-empty foyer, as if they were her audience. Then she grips Richard's arm above the elbow and starts toward the chapel. But she is too late.

"Hey, kids," Richard's father shouts, as he crosses the room to them.

His mother stiffens. For as long as Richard can remember, his father has called them kids—his mother, his sister, him—and despite his mother's protestations, the term has stuck. "Kid," he can hear her say, as she said throughout his childhood, "is an inappropriate address for a woman, even a beautifully preserved woman, of—." It's an old argument, Richard thinks, an old wound. But then they all are. Scar tissue, he often tells Brian, is the materia prima of family.

Richard knows this must be hard for her: Though his parents pretend that nothing has changed; though they have not yet mentioned divorce and Richard's mother disdains even to speak of the mistress scheduled to appear later today, Richard knows the subject cannot be far from her mind.

When Richard's father reaches them, he embraces Richard with that excess of enthusiasm he has taken to employing since his son left home, an enthusiasm Richard conceives is meant to compensate for his absence in Richard's youth and to suggest an intimacy they have notably failed to achieve, a public demonstration of a mannish understanding they plainly lack.

"How are you, son?" he asks. Then, turning to Richard's mother, "Lydia," he says, almost shyly. "You look terrific." He kisses her on the cheek.

Richard's mother runs her tongue over her coral pink lipstick. Impatiently.

"Excuse us for a moment, won't you?" She holds Richard's arm in a vice grip, as if clutching a banister on a precipitous descent.

"Of course," his father says. "I'm sorry. I'll catch up with you later, Rich."

Inside, the chapel is hushed and mahogany. Richard notices the narrow band of indigo blue carpeting with absentminded approbation. His mother sags into the first pew.

"Wouldn't you know," she says, "the one time your father is early it's with her."

"That's *her*?" Richard should have known, of course, but he cannot link the word *mistress* to the bland, beige woman in the hall.

For a moment they share the sepulchral quiet, then Richard takes a seat beside her.

"My god," Richard says.

He is appalled less by the fact of a mistress than by the woman herself. Though he'd never tell his mother this, Richard was relieved when he learned of his father's affair. When his mother phoned to break the news, speaking with the remarkable equanimity she maintains in the face of crises—*Your father has a mistress. He's asked her to*

the wedding. Please come home—Richard had been torn between out-
rage at his father, grief for his mother, and relief. Here, at last, was desire he recognized and shared. Growing up he had despaired that his
parents asked no more of life than the bland false emotion of respect-
ability and dull suburban comfort, which looked to him like loneliness, a joyless match. Their marriage had made him wonder if the
passionate life he hoped for was mistaken, *more than we could ask*.
All they appeared to require was the semblance of happiness, which
seemed to him no life at all. But here was proof—painful proof—
they'd wanted more. The news confirmed for him a long-held suspicion that things are never what they seem. That none of us is.

But he knows that for his mother the revelation has been a shock,
and his heart breaks for her. His mother has believed in the image
of things—the right fork, the right wine, Julia Child; she's believed
that abiding rules will redeem us, that being right is—if not the same
as being happy—at least compensation for unhappiness, imagining perhaps (as Richard so often had as a child before he fell in love
with men) that happiness is beyond them. But seeing his father in
the lobby with the woman who absurdly must have been his lover all
these years, Richard thinks perhaps it's not. Perhaps happiness is out
there still, waiting for them, in the foyer or the world, like the plump
woman in beige.

"How's Rachel taking it?" Richard asks, trying to shift the subject
from mistress to bride.

"She doesn't know," his mother says. She picks a bit of fluff off her
dress.

"She doesn't *know*?"

"I didn't want to upset her," she says. "She's been so tense, so sure
that something will go wrong."

"She'll be furious, you know," Richard says, "when she finds out."

"She won't find out. Why should she? Your father's very good at
keeping secrets."

"She'll have to find out sometime, Mom."

"Sometime," she says, "not now."

The way she says it makes Richard think that his mother is the one who'd rather not have known this, known sometime, but not now. He takes her hand in his and holds it. It is cool and dry and seems impossibly fragile, and he wonders when her skin grew thin, her veins blue and protruding, vulnerable beneath the surface, a few brown spots here and there.

"I'm not sure I'm going to be able to make it through this," she says softly.

Richard strokes her knuckles gently. "Of course you will," he says.

"Nothing is a matter of course anymore," she says.

Someone opens the chapel door behind them and there is a sudden burst of sound from the foyer—the sound of guests arriving—and then a quiet "Sorry, I didn't know anyone was in here" and the soft sound of the door closing.

"How long have you known?" Richard asks.

She shrugs. "I've known for awhile that your father had 'friends.' I didn't know about *her* until Rachel announced the engagement. He said he wanted *her* at the wedding. It's been six months. I would've told you, but your father made me promise not to. He said he wanted to tell you kids himself." She smiles up at him, as if she might cry. "Now you know."

She draws a sharp breath as if she might sob, and Richard pats his pockets for a Kleenex, but she doesn't cry. Instead she tells him what she knows about the mistress, the woman named Betsy with whom his father has been involved for years. She is divorced, a former executive secretary at General Mills, a woman his mother remembers meeting once years ago at a fiftieth birthday party for Richard's father, which Betsy helped coordinate; Richard's mother remembers thinking her sweet, if rather bland.

"I just wish I had a little more time," she says wistfully, and Richard understands that she means more time with her husband, time to make it work between them. He feels suddenly how difficult this must be for her and his throat aches.

"Just an hour," she says, "that's all."

"With Dad?" Richard asks, his voice soft with sympathy.

His mother looks at him with irritation, as if this were an unkind joke. "Without him," she says. "I want your father out of here. That woman can do what she wants. But I want him out. The liquor store at Byerly's called to say the champagne order is ready. Do me a favor, will you? Get him to drive you over and load up the coolers? For me? Please."

"Of course," Richard says. He stands and walks to the door, then he turns to look back at her, at her tiny fragile figure on the hard wooden pew, as it seems he has always done—turning back to look at her as he is leaving her behind.

"I'm so sorry, Mom," he says, door handle in his hand.

"Don't pity me," she says. "Your father's a prick."

Richard knows that he should be angry with his father, but what he feels is awkwardness, a slight unsociable embarrassment at all that is unsaid between them. Richard and his father don't speak as they cross the temple parking lot under the humid blur of a Minnesota midday sun, and Richard hopes that his father won't try to disburden himself of details, to pass on his secrets to Richard, like family jewels. Richard is curious, it's true, about his father's other life, but it is the faint unsatisfying curiosity that one reserves for the tragedies of strangers. He does not really want to know. It's enough to know that they hold this thing in common: infidelity.

"Some heat we're having," his father says, irrelevantly. He clenches his fingers and a faint beep issues from a car in front of them. Richard's father is a handsome man, the sort of picturesque old gentleman that foreign tourists snap photos of. His father's favorite story from his travels abroad is the one about the cluster of Japanese tourists who surrounded him once in a street in Paris and took his picture as if he were a national monument, thinking him the quintessential Frenchman in his red beret, his handsome face, his pouty frown. He delights, as Richard does, in being mistaken for someone else. As if a false, even a mistaken identity, might be more promising than the ones they have.

Richard's father is a great believer in family, in the notion of family, a thing Richard thinks may characterize those who are unfaithful—this faith in family they cannot seem to keep. As they drive up Hennepin, heading for Excelsior Boulevard, Richard remembers a night many years ago when his father drove them through a wooded area near their home. The swatch of park was part of a campaign by the city to preserve the last remaining wild lands in their bedroom community, and as they took a curve by the small swampy lake where Richard had first kissed another man (a boy really, lanky and tough, with white blond hair, who tasted of Marlboros and peppermint schnapps), a shape had bolted into their headlights and they'd felt the thick dull weight of a body clip the grill of the car before it bounced off the bumper and into the grassy ditch.

It was a scrawny deer, legs skinny as fishing poles, a thing that seemed meant by its delicacy to be broken; its side heaved frantically, smudged with mud and blood. Richard had stroked its coarse brown fur, crying stupidly, pointlessly, over what was already lost. His father had clicked his tongue. "Damn it," he said. "Goddamn it." Across the road Richard saw a second deer waiting near the trees, watching for this one to clear the road and come, innocent still of loss. For a reason they never discussed, they decided not to tell Richard's mother. As if it had been some sexual indiscretion, a shameful indulgence, this accidental death. "We don't have to mention this," his father had begun. "No," Richard agreed. And they never had.

But Richard thinks of it now, driving with his father once again.

He remembers how his father had looked stern and moved and solemn as they drove home and how he had said, the only mention of it he had ever made, was to say, quietly, distractedly, "I never saw it coming." Which is how Richard imagines he feels now, about all of this, all of them, even his own life, though he does not say it. It makes Richard feel tender toward his father and he lays a hand on his Dad's thick shoulder and gives it a light squeeze and his father frowns at him, eyebrows raised, wonderingly, and then smiles and says, "I'm glad you could make it, son."

By two-thirty, the foyer of Temple Beth Elohim is clotted with guests who arrive in large shiny rented cars, feathered hats, polished shoes, accessorized with leather. Rachel has retired to the dressing room and Richard stands alone by the chapel door, armed with programs, squinting at the blaze of the ozone-depleted summer sun reflected off the asphalt parking lot.

His mother, Mrs. Lydia Klein (née Morris), stands greeting guests as they arrive. She is a formidable woman, even from here, even in the face of adversity. Her authority is apparent and impressive, her casually correct posture, elegant and unrigid; the taut skin of her cheeks glows like polished leather. Tan and toned, she has—he thinks—the resolute bearing of the unhopeful, like a Civil War general leading troops into a losing battle. Her small figure has always seemed towering to him, even after he grew well beyond her five-foot-five height. When she looks up at him, he still feels she is looking down. Even now, especially now, seeing her in a shift of Prussian blue linen, a string of pearls at her neck, the diamond of her wedding ring catching the light so it glints.

It has fallen to Richard to hand out programs. He stands by the chapel door, trying to soothe the gentiles. He slips the folded program with its inset sheet of Hebrew prayers into the hands of his mother's Methodist kin, knowing there is nothing a Methodist fears more than not being able to comply with the rules. He notices several on his mother's side freeze when they glimpse the unfamiliar Hebrew letters. The idea of having to sit through a communal prayer without being able to hold up their end clearly unnerves them. His aunt Elizabeth, his mother's elder sister, looks positively stricken, as if she might turn back, until Richard points out the transliteration on the back. Still, once the ceremony is underway, it will be rough going for the gentiles, the Orthodox contingent spitefully upping the tempo until it is difficult for even the Reconstructionists to keep up.

The last time Rachel married, the groom was an Anglo-Catholic and the wedding was held before the family hearth with a justice of the peace presiding; a string quartet played Bach in the kitchen, and the Methodists—on his mother's side—were right at home. The Jews—his father's New York kin—were grim; they came late, left early, wore yarmulkes through the service, though there wasn't a rabbi for miles. Richard's mother had orchestrated the whole affair. The reception was held at a good French restaurant and involved large quantities of poached salmon, pâté, endive, baby vegetables. There were ice sculptures in the shapes of fish and swans, loaded down with caviar, hard-boiled eggs, and shrimp. The wedding cake was a monument of scalded sugar, built of profiteroles stuffed with cream. It was all very comme il faut, Richard thinks now. They had joined the New York family for breakfast and dined with the Minneapolitans at night for cocktails, and the divisions, like the scotch his aunt Elizabeth drank by the quart that long weekend, were neat. But this time something has shifted and Richard is uneasy; he feels lost, relieved for little things like the card that will be on the linen tablecloth tonight, to tell him where, if anywhere, in all of this, he belongs.

The Jews arrive like conquering heroes, loud and exuberant, wearing large hats. His Uncle Leonard, his father's elder brother, sports an Italian silk suit, a handkerchief in his breast pocket, a skimmer; he slaps Richard on the back as he accepts a program and asks after the bride.

Standing in this crowd of unfamiliar relations, Richard feels disoriented without his props: his desk, his white lab coat and surgical blues, his nurses and reception, his apartment overstuffed with books and tasteful costly art; he feels lost without Brian. Though they fight on trips—unflappable Brian annoying in his equanimity while Richard loses his mind—Richard misses him. Brian is a handsome, charming guy and is great at working a crowd. Richard imagines his lover in the foyer and feels a twinge of domestic pride he can rarely feel when they're together.

Brian and Richard were friends for years before they became involved. They met while doing their residencies at the same hospital in New Haven before ending up at the same hospital on the other coast. In the years before they got involved, they'd lunched together occasionally, been fond if distant friends. Then, two years ago, they'd drifted into their love affair like flotsam washed up on a beach after a particularly nasty storm. Each having survived a bad breakup had turned to the other first for comfort, then for love.

Their first few months as lovers, they had been careful with each other, solicitous and gentle, the way one is with the ill. They bought each other flowers, tied with ribbon and raffia. They tucked little notes under the windshield wipers of one another's cars, into lab coat pockets, desk drawers, on clipboards among patients' histories. At home and out with friends, they called each other absurd pet names: sugar bean and pumpkin, honey and cupcake. They made a show of their domestic bliss, as if to prove their exes wrong. Their sex was passionate and urgent. It left Richard weak-kneed, given to fits of the giggles. But at some point he cannot yet discern, it changed between them. Settled.

These days their sex is more like flossing, a prophylactic regime, regular and suburban as lawn care; Brian never wants to fuck in the kitchen or on the edge of the tub or among the file cabinets of Medical Records as they once did. He does not like to use words like *fuck* when talking about sex. Richard's handsome lanky lover wants Doris Day sex. That, in fact, is what they call it, the Doris Day. *Is Doris coming today?* they quip. *Y'know she comes whenever she can.* Richard finds he misses his last lover, a small ugly pug of a man who fucked with a kind of Genet-like brutality. When he dreams of desire, as lately he often does, it is this man—not Brian—who holds him, this man whose force, like gravity, draws him magnificently down.

Across the foyer, in the far corner, by a potted palm, Richard's father is looking uneasy; every so often he turns to scan the crowd, as Richard was doing before catching sight of him. Beside his father is the woman in beige, who appears to be studiously avoiding scanning anything at all. She smiles vapidly up into the rafters, with what seems to Richard to be a vegetable placidity, staring not at the high second-story ceiling, not at the crowd, but at some indeterminate place in between.

What appalls Richard about his father's mistress is not what he'd expect. It is the fact that she is ordinary. The word *mistress* hangs about her like a tacky boa, an ill-fitting dress. She is short, plump, dressed in a tan suit and skirt with a pearly synthetic cable-knit sweater underneath. Shaped like a butternut squash. Beside her, Richard's mother is a monstrous beauty and Richard thinks that this may be the point. The mistress is no threat. She looks intelligent but not too. Attractive but not too.

His father sees him and gives a wave and they start over.

Richard's father looks misty-eyed, and Richard wonders if he's regretting having brought her.

"Son, I'd like you to meet Betsy."

Betsy takes Richard's hand in both of hers as if to demonstrate her sincerity. "It's awfully nice to meet you, Richard. Your father has talked about you for—well, all the time. You've made him very proud."

Her hands are soft and powdered. Her hair is salon sculpted, a dull false brown. He is sure she has white couches in her house—worse, a condo—with large floral patterned curtains and glass tabletops.

"And you have made him . . ." Richard begins, when he is interrupted by someone tugging on his arm. He has no idea what he might have said, how that sentence would have ended. He was in a freefall of verbiage, waiting to hit ground to see what sort of sound, or mess, he'd make. But he never lands.

It's Sasha, his childhood chum, at his arm. Tugging playfully, as in the old days, when they were kids, and later, in high school, sweethearts.

"We'll see you later, son," Richard's father says, obviously avoiding introductions where he can.

Richard hands a program to a Methodist wavering in the doorway, then turns to Sasha.

"You look wonderful, Richard," she says. "Running away from home agrees with you. I, on the other hand, am a mess. I gained sixty pounds with Lizzie. I never lost the weight and now." She shrugs.

Whenever Richard meets his high school friends, people he pretended to know because friends were necessary as clothes—they made it less embarrassing to go out in public—he feels a twinge of self-consciousness, an embarrassed moment when he finds himself wondering what they know about his life now. It's not that he's ashamed about the fact that he is gay, quite to the contrary, he imagines rather fatuously that this preference marks him out, makes him part of a lineage of Baldwin and Wilde, Shakespeare and Socrates, confirms some long-held but vaguely and never quite articulated sense that he is different from the others, born for some remarkable end, which he is only now beginning to suspect he is not.

In the psychology textbooks he had read during his medical training, he recognized this as a Napoleonic Complex, but nevertheless, the feeling has remained, haunting him, especially now when the first blush of youth has passed and his life is rutted with the emotional potholes that soon become one's path in life, and he can no longer imagine himself as anything other than what he is now—a respectable gay radiologist with a handsome husband, a thirty-year mortgage, and a stable, loving, monogamous relationship from which he sometimes strays.

It is not embarrassment then, but something more like shyness that he feels at the prospect that once again, as throughout his schooling, people might imagine that they know him, and are wrong. It's not as if he isn't out to his family, they have absorbed the news like leukocytes massing on a foreign body, surrounding it and making it their own. They have produced from the bourgeois surplus of their lives an excess of enthusiasm for Brian. Holiday cards come addressed to them both, as do invitations to Thanksgiving, a set of knives, his and his bath towels, flannel sheets printed with cartoon barnyard animals.

Richard smiles at Sasha and wonders what she's heard and from whom and in what form. He recalls that she was once very close to his mother. He had been envious of her then.

"How's Brian?" she asks, answering his unasked question.

"He couldn't come," Richard says, though that is not what she's asked.

She nods. Scans the crowd. Her profile is still flawless, Mediterranean.

"I didn't invite David," she says, referring to the husband he's never met. "Not that he would've come."

Richard feels something in him unknot beneath his rib cage and a warmth take residence there. He'd forgotten how likable Sasha was. Her frankness. Of course he realizes that she may simply be one-

upping him with honesty, sensing in her uncanny way his own dis-
sembling, and to counter that impression and deny her the opportu-
nity for superior candor, he adds, "Brian had a gastrointestinal conference to attend in San Diego."

"Ah," says Sasha.

He wants to ask her if she is disappointed in the way things have
turned out, but she would ask him in what way—how *what* has
turned out—and he would not be able to explain.

He thinks about their childhood as green—bands of grass and
dense forests of oak and elm and fronds of wild asparagus. He wants
to tell Sasha about the tour he made yesterday of their old haunts, the
woods where they smoked dope and the railroad tracks that held a
glamour for him then that trains still hold, their old neighborhood
with its greenways and bike paths and warnings to yield. As a kid, he
had tried to be careful, which is what the acres of tidy green, those
pristine forests stocked with bunnies and does were intended, he
thinks, to convey. The harmlessness of things. They promised what
life never could deliver: that if only you stayed in your yard, if only
you stayed on the path, you could avoid damage.

The ceremony is mercifully brief; the couple—to his surprise—
are untraditional and have dispensed with the chuppah and most
Hebrew prayers. The only remnants of religion are the *tallitot* and
yarmulkes worn by the rabbi and groom. Judaism reduced to sarto-
rial inflection. Watching the couple take their vows—his lace-fes-
tooned sister and her portly graying groom in a ponytail—Richard
feels a dull tug of recognition, as if he were trying to recall something,
when he realizes with a start that what he's recognizing is the disturbing similarity between the groom and his father's mistress. They are
the same shape. Both members, it would seem, of the squash family,
and now his.

⋙➤

After the ceremony, dinner is held in the basement of the synagogue—a large, dim, beige room in which have been arranged dozens of round tables with white tablecloths. Rachel's father-in-law leans back in his chair, twirling the stem of his wine glass on the table so it makes a neat, indented ring on the cloth.

"Be a sports writer," he tells Richard, evidently confusing him with someone's nephew, a reporter for the local *Tribune*. "All the truly great writers started out writing about sports."

"I'm a physician," Richard tells him. "I'm Rachel's brother? I don't like sports."

"Boxing," he says. "Now there's a sport."

The immediate family are seated with the bride and groom, except for Richard's father, who has defied his place card and sits now beside his mistress a table away. He chats to her, Richard notes, as if she were a distant but delightful cousin. A maiden aunt. He is cautious in the extreme. Rachel, who has begun making the rounds of tables, greeting her guests, appears not to notice this change in seating—or perhaps she is just too preoccupied, or too exhausted, to care.

Richard can hear his aunt Elizabeth at the next table ranting about indigestible bean sprouts. The first female aeronautical engineer in the country and a one-time consultant to NASA, she had been Richard's favorite relative. He loved her for her excesses in this moderate family: drinking too much, chain smoking, she could argue any of them under the table. But now she's gone half mad and in her familiar righteous tone is declaiming the vice of vegetarianism.

"People think that stuff is good for them," she raves. "There are more toxins in raw broccoli than in a pack of cigarettes. And peanut butter? You might as well eat plastic."

There are raucous toasts, then dinner is served.

Neil and Rachel tip their heads together and make a show of love throughout the meal, and Richard recalls the morning when he first met Neil fifteen years ago, just after Rachel left her first husband, just before Richard left for college. Rachel was twenty-three then, a few weeks divorced, and you could see still a band of pale skin where her wedding ring used to be. It was a weekday morning in late spring and Richard remembers a thin blue sky through cold glass windows, a chill in the air. Richard had been helping Rachel settle into her third-floor apartment. (A fact that seems significant now: Everyone he's ever known who's divorced and taken an apartment has chosen rooms on a high floor, as if more at home in midair.)

She sat on the blond parquet wood floor, her legs folded to one side, unpacking boxes and chain smoking Dunhills, while Richard put dishes away on the cabinet shelves. It was approaching noon when Neil emerged from Rachel's bedroom wrapped in a blue velour robe, wearing moosehead slippers with brown felt antlers. He scuffed sorrowfully across the parquet, his fists dug deep into the pockets of his robe, antlers flopping.

"I overslept," Neil said, looking at the moose. "I have to call work and tell them I'll be late again."

"Poor sweetie," Rachel said.

"You're not going to send me to the home for the motivationally impaired, are you?" Neil asked.

"Oh, sweetie," Rachel said, embracing the man she'd later marry, "This *is* the home for the motivationally impaired." They'd laughed then and for a moment clung to one another amid the litter of boxes and their image became indissolubly linked with Richard's worst suspicions about his family. Months later, when he packed up for college and left, it was this that he believed he was escaping, leaving behind him forever: doubt and its attendant compromises that pass for love.

That is what Brian has failed to understand these last two years; Brian has taken personally Richard's reluctance to domesticate. He doesn't understand that what Richard is trying to leave behind isn't Brian but the thing his mother and sister settled for. He's spent his whole life trying to get free of these same bonds, to resist the gravitational force of family that demands such compromises, that makes insouciant sex into infidelity, homosexuality into a family embarrassment, all the compromises and scars that come of belonging and wanting to belong. Brian takes it personally, but he's wrong to do so. Richard simply wants a bigger life than this, than what he sees around him here in the basement ballroom of Temple Beth Elohim.

Across the table, Rachel rises from her chair taking her new husband by the hand. Turning to the klezmer band set up behind her on a platform decorated with crêpe paper and balloons, Rachel blows a kiss to the band leader, a skinny saxophonist who winks at her and blows a deep note, and the band begins to play the Carpenters' "We've Only Just Begun" in a slightly dissonant, minor key, klezmerstyle, played as it might have been sung in a Polish synagogue a century ago—like a hopeless prayer; and turning to her new husband, Rachel begins to dance.

Richard is not sure how long he watches them, the couples twirling around the room like the carnival rides he watched as a kid, thinking the motion beautiful—synchronized and bright like small bouquets—and wanting to be part of it. But he holds back now as he did then, knowing rides are disappointing once you're on, the dipping and spinning as if the world has come unmoored, knowing that the dancing couples are beautiful only because he is on the outside looking on at the fine patterns they make.

Instead, Richard gets up from the table and crosses to the bar in the corner. The bartender, in his little red vest and black bowtie, behind his little portable bar, looks bored and for a moment Richard is annoyed that he should see this affair as just another gig, another schmaltzy wedding with a lot of boozy guests, instead of Richard's family.

The bartender asks what Richard will have and then, before he turns to get it, he holds Richard's gaze a beat too long, a fraction of a second, but it's enough. Richard smiles. The guy is not unattractive. Maybe a little young, twenty-six, twenty-eight. As a rule, Richard prefers his lovers to be older; he prefers to be the younger man. The ingenue. But it will do. Besides, it's just flirtation.

"Always the groomsman, never the groom," the bartender says, with half a smile.

"You don't know the half of it," Richard says. He stuffs a bill into the tip glass, thanks him for the drink.

The bartender sets the bottle of Jim Beam on the bar between them. "Take it," he says. "It's got your name on it."

"Which would be Richard," Richard says.

"Nice to meet you, Richard. I'm Ed."

Richard thanks Ed again and goes to sit down at an empty table. He eases off his shoes and pours himself a drink. Then another. And another, enjoying the soft feeling that comes after several drinks when the walls bend like wax, the room slowly collapsing onto itself.

Every so often, as he looks around the room, he glances over at the bartender, who is almost always looking back at him. Their eyes meet this way several times until Richard realizes he's been staring, and the bartender staring back, for something approaching half a minute, each waiting for the other to turn away. He tells himself it's not sex he's after here, but the familiarity of the gesture, the connection made between strangers that defines his other life, which is composed largely of this bravado and self-invention—like the routine he learned as a resident for taking case histories—"playing doctor," he still calls it.

He's had to learn this, over time. It is, he thinks, a trick picked up in medical school, where it was necessary *not* to think about the cadaver disemboweled before you as a person who once played golf, played bridge, ate tuna sandwiches, made love just like you. He'd understood then that sometimes it was necessary to turn things into other things in order to go on. And it worked in the world as well. It helped, he found, to imagine himself the hero of some great adventure, his couplings and courtships prelude to some great love affair, to imagine the future as a place in which fulfillment was imminent.

He's skilled at impersonation, and knows it. But it has its drawbacks: it makes him wonder what, if anything, is authentic between people. Looking around the room at all these people related to him by blood and genes, he cannot help but wonder what if anything they have in common. On the plane, he'd read in *JAMA* about the latest studies on twins, and had thought then, looking at the evidence, how fragile and unpredictable are the things that bind us to each other, how irrelevant often and absurd. Lawn furniture and neighborhoods, stamp collections and a preference for parting one's hair on the side. What struck him about the studies was what was rarely noted in popular press renderings of the research: how inconsequential are the bonds between people in the end, how tenuous and insignificant, even for those more genetically alike than most of us will ever be, how—for all the genetic dicta—we share so little of significance.

When Richard decides to go over and speak to the bartender, it's not with any conscious intention of picking him up. It's not premeditated, he tells himself. He's just playing a part. It's just one of many things he will pretend away, make into something else: an excess of joie de vivre, a drunken and fantastic absurdity, rather than infidelity. Truth is, he loves Brian, but infidelity has nothing to do with love, he thinks. It's more like stepping out for a smoke, an invigorating break.

As he passes the head table, Richard overhears his aunt Elizabeth telling his mother about dark matter in the universe—the powerful, unseen substance that gives galaxies their shape, that mysterious force that holds stars and planets in their orbits with its fierce gravitational pull.

Later, as Richard stands in the dewy grass outside the temple's classrooms where as a child he'd learned the Hebrew alphabet, unzipping the bartender's pants, he thinks of Brian with sudden and intense longing, the thought arriving as a weight on his heart, but to his surprise it is not unpleasant but a thrilling anticipation that merges in his mind with his arousal and the soft yellow blur of streetlights in the distance, the firm satisfying rump in his hands.

Back inside, in a corridor of the basement, Richard phones Brian, but there is no answer. Richard's own voice asks him if he'd like to leave a message after the beep. He hangs up. Plans to call back later.

"I've been looking everywhere for you," Sasha says, when Richard returns to the ballroom. She's standing just inside the door and tugs at his sleeve. "Dance with me."

"Why not?" he smiles.

They step onto the floor. Moving among the others, awkwardly. People bump against them giddily, drunk, light as balloons. Across the room, his mother is seated at the table, nursing a bottle of Vermouth, talking to the other mother, Neil's. The two of them sit alone amid a clutter of dirty dishes, while the others dance. Generals holding their ground. They are always sitting there, it seems to him, the mothers. He's been afraid all these years of getting trapped the way his mother had, the way all the mothers had, her grief a weight he carried with him everywhere, a small but ubiquitous burden, like the nutritious lunches she packed that smelled of peanut butter, over-ripe apples, jelly donuts, a sweet cloying smell that he associates with all her losses, all she's given up for them. All she might have done and didn't. She who would've been a doctor had she not been born a girl. His one clear aim as a boy was to get free and he had. But now he wonders if he really has or will or even wants to.

Dancing with Sasha, his chin leaned against her fragrant hair, Richard feels a sudden tenderness for these people, all of them, for his family moving in circles around the room, the seated moms. It's like seeing them from a very great distance, like terrain glimpsed from a plane, that he can map for miles in every direction. Watching Rachel nuzzle Neil's beard as they dance, Richard can see already how her intense love for him—now that they've married—will mellow in a year, become worn in, smaller, leaving gaps that Rachel will fill with bridge games, a vegetable garden, the children she is already planning to have, an affair. But it doesn't matter. They are here now, in each other's arms, making something lovely that will not last the night.

And, as if his thoughts were an incantation, it begins, the end.

What Richard will remember of the evening after that is a confetti of images, like the colorful piñatas his mother made for him each birthday when he was young, which they slowly tore apart in the course of the day's festivities, leaving Richard inconsolable beside the eviscerated figure of a papier-mâché donkey, sun, or deer—though he should not have been surprised since it happened every year, the same old loss.

What he'll remember of the evening after that is this:

How his father, courtly and maybe still in love with his wife, rose from the table where his mistress sat and walked over and asked Richard's mother to dance. He bowed a little, took Richard's mother's hand in his, and pulled her up from her chair. She was flushed with some sort of strong emotion, but she let him draw her into his arms and for the length of a Sinatra song they held each other. Like old times. Then Uncle Leonard cut in on the couple and Richard's father returned to the table where his mistress sat, dreamily swaying her head to the klezmer version of "Smoke Gets In Your Eyes," and drunk, incautious, she'd clasped his arm, and from there the details blur.

There was a moment when the music, which had buoyed them,

abated, and Rachel shouting into Neil's face, said loud and clear, "Who is that woman with my dad? Is she one of yours?"

And Richard, dancing nearby, said, in a moment of uncharacteristic candor (no longer wanting to pretend things were other than they are), "That is our father's mistress."

Then a general confusion ensued.

Rachel stood beside the table where Richard's father sat, and screamed, "I can't believe you'd do this to me," before running out. Her bouquet dropped to the floor.

At a signal from someone, the band resumed its work and valiantly played on, though only a few diehards danced. Most were getting their coats, when Richard heard her. "A toast," Richard's mother screamed into the roiling music, "a toast to Rachel and Neil." The dancers didn't seem to hear at first, until, like brushing snow from a windshield, Richard's mother swept aside a clutter of dishes from the table and stepped onto it. The music stopped then, or rather fractured, like ice falling off a roof—a few pieces crashing, the rest following in a heap, then silence. Richard's mother loomed above them, the way the bride and groom should have been held aloft on chairs, a kerchief between them like love. But Richard's mother stood alone, holding her glass of Vermouth aloft; she weaved, unsupported, in stocking feet. Everyone turned to watch as she struggled to remember what it was she needed to tell them, the thing she wanted to remind them of.

Her face folded in confusion as she looked over the crowd, as if she didn't recognize them, could not place herself, here among strangers. For a moment, she wavered, towering, as if she couldn't remember why they were gathered here, and maybe at that moment she did not.

"To . . ." she said, sadly. Richard wanted to help her. He wanted to call out "Neil and Rachel," he wanted to call out "Love." But he didn't want to unsteady her, could not stand to see her fall. So he watched in a dreamlike paralysis as she teetered on the table, saying, over and over, "To. To."

Till Richard's father detached himself from his mistress and moved toward his wife, with a certitude and fluidity of motion that made it seem he was inevitably drawn.

"Lydia," he said gently, "Come down, hon." His father had never sounded so gentle, except maybe that one night they'd struck the deer.

But seeing her husband approach, Richard's mother straightened, grew definitive and bold.

"To," she told them grandly, lifting her glass, "To—"

And then she fell.

It was miraculous that she only broke a wrist and ankle, shattering one kneecap; at her age, a broken hip could be decisive, the first step in a steady decline. But these smaller injuries would prove decisive as well, if in a different way. Or so it will seem later that night, when the mistress is dispatched in a cab with Uncle Leonard, while Richard and his parents are reunited in the ambulance. His father appears to have forgotten the mistress, refuses to leave his wife's side. In the eerie light of the ambulance, the men crouch together beside the gurney, an EMT checking vital signs, while Richard's father holds his mother's hand, tears in his eyes. He leans close and says something quietly, into her ear. Richard can see his mother nod slightly and press his father's hand, in reply.

Richard has never known his parents to hold hands before, had not imagined what might be between them, till now—when his mother is vulnerable, his father clearly afraid of losing the woman he clearly loves. Richard can see that his father will never leave her, and had never meant to. As he holds onto the gurney rail, bracing himself against the stops and turns, Richard glimpses the simple thing that had been obscure till now—what a lifetime together might mean: someone there beside you when you fall.

It is late even on the West Coast and Richard knows that Brian will be sleepy and grumpy, he knows the rumpled vanilla smell of him, the tone of his annoyance (Brian never likes staying up late, never enjoys the night as Richard does, preferring the clear optimism of morning, which Richard loathes). It's two hours earlier on the coast and if he calls now, he'll wake Brian at midnight. But he misses him, and so he calls.

"Hell-o," says Brian, jauntily, wide awake.

"Brian?" Richard says. Why the hell is he wide awake?

"Richard?"

There is a sound of music in the background, Miles Davis, loud.

"You were expecting someone else?" Richard asks. He means this to sound like a joke, but it doesn't. "Is someone there with you?"

"No. There is no one here with me," Brian says, repeating each word carefully.

There is a muffled sound, and Richard knows that Brian has covered the receiver. When it clears, the music's lower.

"What's that music?"

"Oh, just the TV."

Richard thinks he hears someone laugh.

Richard does not hear the rest. He hangs up.

It occurs to him that he's just worn out from the wedding, that his own infidelity is what haunts him, not Brian's. He reaches for the phone to call back and apologize (Richard's always the one to apologize, Brian never does), setting his hand on the receiver, when it rings. Before he reads the number in the caller ID box, he knows it is Brian. *It's two in the fucking morning, who else would be calling but Brian?* When the phone rings a second time, it has the insistent anxious ring of someone caught in deception, someone ready with an excuse and an apology. Someone who's about to leave but is having a hard time saying goodbye. It rings once, rings twice, rings three times. So Richard picks up the phone and depresses the button to disconnect the call, then sets the receiver beside the phone to keep the line engaged, and he prepares to sleep.

His skin feels clammy as he lies in bed; it prickles with the static-electrified feeling of fear. The room cradles, rocking back and forth gently, and Richard feels the lightness of knowing that nothing holds him down now, the sense of having slipped free of gravity. He imagines this is how the astronauts must feel, nostalgic for the pull of something larger than themselves, longing to be drawn into the orbit of a greater force and held there. It is the heart they have to worry about in space, his aunt Elizabeth has told him. In zero gravity, the heart will grow too large and slack. Without the pull of a greater force, it fails us.

THEORY OF THE
LEISURE CLASS

I.

CONSPICUOUS LEISURE

The Scottish Brewer and his wife have not joined us this afternoon for our trek through the forest of Tapantí. They are protesting the mud. Boycotting the birds. Outraged by the sloppiness, the untidiness of nature. How they conceived of an ornithological tour that did not require hiking through muck, I cannot conceive, but the Scottish Brewer seems to have imagined that the birds would come to us. Regrettably, the Duck Man and his wife are undeterred; they come up the path behind us, talking loudly. Manuel, our guide, has shushed them repeatedly but to no effect. Our only hope now is to outdistance them, but every so often, through the canopy of green, from amidst the vines and leaves, I hear a distant quack and know that they are out there still, the Duck Man and his wife, somewhere in the jungle, gaining on us.

We are fourteen: six married couples, the General, who has come alone, and Manuel. There are the wealthy Scottish Brewer and his wife, serious birders who seem to feel they are lowering themselves to be traveling in the company of Americans. There are the Sandersons, the very nice couple from Illinois (he was a state legislator for many years and a professor of political science; his wife, Geneen, heads up her local League). There is the Duck Man and his young wife. I call him the Duck Man because he quacks when he wants to screw (pardon my French). These are the things you learn about people on a tour such as this: all the phobias and quirks come out, as if inhibition were taking a vacation too.

In the course of our ten-day tour, we have slogged through mud, mosquitoes, wet, and rain; where possible we have stayed in good hotels. Ours is a domesticated adventure, organized by the American Museum of Natural History. Our guides have been very knowledgeable, very good, and we've traveled a great deal to remote wildlife preserves for which Costa Rica is known.

Most days I've made it a policy to walk at the front of the group with Manuel, where the bird watching is best, but on this, our last day, my husband, Milt, and I have remained back with the General, who lags behind, watching the path for snakes and roots. I point out liana and bromeliads for him to see, but he is too upset to notice. He's been sullen ever since we saw the spiders copulating.

The General was the first to spot them on the philodendron leaf, a mile or so back. He has keen eyes—he was a pilot in the war—and he enjoys holding forth on entomology. He takes pleasure in pointing out a butterfly or spider that the rest of us have missed. He seemed particularly excited by his discovery today. He pulled out his thick British pocket guide to identify the pair. Then he called me over to watch, and then the others came, and together we watched as the male courted then mounted the female. We were all quite moved by the tiny drama—the miracle of creation taking place before our eyes—right up until the moment the female turned and began to eat her mate. His tiny legs quivered, kicking air.

It was not a surprise, of course. We all know about the birds and the bees and that spiders devour their mates. But we are aging—most of us are in our seventies, the General must be eighty, at least—and we are a little sentimental about sex.

Only the Duck Man—who is in his forties (his wife is younger still)—seemed unperturbed. He leaned over the quivering pair on the leaf, shook his head, and said, "Dying for a fuck. Now that's the way to go." Then he laughed and clapped the General on the back.

The General was quiet for a long time after that. He is recently divorced, the General is. His third, I think, though I wouldn't dream of asking.

II.

FORMS OF SACRIFICE

This trip was my idea and Milton is being patient in a way that makes it clear that it was my idea. That he is being a good sport. That he is a good and loving husband, evidence to the contrary. He is always doing things like that—making me look foolish and demanding by pretending he is neither.

Milton would have preferred to lie on a beach somewhere in Florida or the Caribbean, but his doctor recommended moderate exercise after his bypass surgery a year ago. The heart is a muscle after all. And so, because it has always been an ambition of mine to see the Resplendent Quetzal of Costa Rica, and because he owes me now that I know the truth about him, about her, we came here.

"It is possibly inauthentic," Manuel says of the Temple of Quetzal by which we now stand, in a small clearing. He holds a flashlight in one hand and points it into the darkness and raps on the stone wall with his knuckles. "Possibly," he says, "it is a fraud."

This temple is not mentioned in my little yellow guide book, *Inside Costa Rica*, a fact that does not surprise me. Costa Rica is not known for its archaeology. We have come here to look at birds, not ruins, but ruins, it seems, are everywhere. Ruin appears to be inescapable.

The temple, Manuel explains, is likely of Olmec origin, if authentic.

"Despite the practice of human sacrifice," Manuel says, "the pre-Columbian peoples of this region were highly sophisticated. They were arguably no more barbarous than we."

Perhaps Manuel expects to shock us, his post-Columbian tour group, but James Sanderson, the dapper gentleman from Illinois, says, "It's not so very different from the sacrament, is it? The old wafer and wine."

Judging by his comment, Sanderson isn't Catholic.

Judging by his expression, Manuel is.

"The pope might disagree," I say.

"Indeed," says Sanderson's wife, Geneen, "he would."

She and I exchange a complicit smile and ascend into the cool musty interior of what might once have been a temple. Milton waits with the General on the steps. In truth, I think we have not changed that much in five hundred years. We still pluck the heart from the body. Only now we call it a procedure not a ceremony. There are no prayers. The only difference is that we haven't a prayer.

Manuel leads us toward the back of the low, dank room, and shows us with his flashlight the points and pot sherds they have discovered, the bones and seeds. I have heard that one can sometimes feel the presence of the past lingering in a place like this. But I feel nothing—only the cool dead still air, laid against my face like a cloth. The past haunts me these days, but not here.

We stand in darkness, smelling age.

A friend of Milt's and mine, a psychologist who leads trips into the wilderness, says that when she hikes the canyons of Grand Gulch,

Utah, where the Anasazi lived a thousand years ago and where their ruins still stand, she sometimes feels someone walking behind her on the path. And once, sleeping amid Anasazi ruins, she dreamed of tea cups and woke to find she was lying on pot sherds.

Recalling this, I feel a presence close behind me, the sense of breath on my neck, a faint heat, and then hands on my waist. I jump and suck in air.

"Quack, quack."

There is some laughter around us. Brief and uncomfortable.

"I'm over here, honey," a woman's voice says from across the room.

"Oops," the Duck Man breathes into my ear. "Wrong bird."

"Pity it's not duck season," James Sanderson says.

When I step out into the light after the others, Milton is surrounded by the group. He has his arms spread wide, like a vaudeville comedian concluding his act. He shoots his eyes right, then left, in a comic imitation of a search for danger, and says, "It's a *jungle* out here."

Everyone else laughs.

III.
SURVIVALS OF THE
NON-INVIDIOUS INTERESTS

Ahead of me, Milton puffs, each step a pant. His chest canted forward, he takes slow steps. Stops. His hands braced on his hips, he tilts his chin up, his face to the jungle canopy, and squints into the uneven light and the leaves. As if this were the reason for his stopping, to look closer, when really it is merely that he is tired. Fat. But he doesn't fool me. His heart is not strong. Better since the operation, but not strong.

There is a purple scar across his sternum where they went in to fix his heart. It looks like a zipper into the body. I imagine opening it, separating the sides, peeling back the keloidal skin, and lifting out the heart to examine it. I once saw a peasant farmer do this in a film on PBS; the man tethered his goat to a post and, cradling the animal's neck in his arms, his cheek pressed to the goat's foreflank, he drew the sharp tip of his knife in a line from the goat's clavicle to its groin, reached his hand in through the slit to hold the heart, and stopped it. I believe this footage was filmed in Greece. Though it could, I suppose, have been Turkey. What I remember is the worn-out citron of the hills. The startled goat. The beating heart. Stopped.

Funny what you remember, what you forget.

Milton doesn't remember the details. He says it was all a long time ago. But I remember vividly that day in the hospital, the yellow elm leaves scattered like coins across the sidewalk outside, how I cried thinking I might lose him, and how he told me about the woman he almost left me for. I've thought of leaving. Our children are settled in their own lives; they're no reason to stay. But I do.

Ahead of me, Milt waits, his lower lip thrust out as if in contemplation, his habitual sensual frown. His mouth was the first thing that caught my attention that day on campus fifty-two years ago, his mouth and his pink pants, his white cotton T-shirt, his canvas shoes; I took him for Italian. This was just after the war and there were many foreign scholars at the university then; American universities were like tiny European cities in those days. Milton looked exotic; he looked like a movie star; he looked like that actor in *Love Affair*. Charles Boyer, was it? I studied his mouth as we played chess by the lake on our first date that spring in Milwaukee. I loved that frown, his handsome suntanned face, his deliberation, how he watched me when it was my turn to move. I was winning and was about to take his queen, when he first kissed me. I used to joke that he kissed me just so that he wouldn't have to lose.

As we walk back to the bus, mud squashing beneath my tennis shoes, I worry about the camera that dangles from the nylon strap around my neck. There is a fungus that can get inside and fog the lens. Manuel has warned us of this, as he has warned us to watch for the fer-de-lance, but today we have seen no snakes in this Edenic forest.

At times the branches and ropey vines above us obtain a human aspect, in the half-light filtered through the leaves, and I cannot help but see them as limbs of that other sort, dangling above us as we slog this muddied track, their dissevered arms providing an amputated audience to our travail. I used to know the names by heart, the names of the bones and the muscles, like our children's names, which Milton, not I, mistakes; once upon a time—when I was a medical student before I married and gave it up—I could name those structures of the body as if we were on intimate terms: the long muscles that embrace the tibia, the fibula. But I am getting old. Now I have to look them up in *Gray's Anatomy*. The tiny bones of the hand.

IV.

MODERN SURVIVALS

OF PROWESS

At two, we board our tour bus to return to the hacienda for a siesta before the final evening's dinner and festivities. We have spent a good deal of time getting from here to there—on planes and buses—and to pass the time, to keep my mind occupied, I read about what it is we're seeing. It's important to me to know these things; Milton prefers to rely on intuition and impressions, to feel his way through a place, but I like to know the details. It seems all we have, sometimes.

On the bus, we are packed in like sardines and jostle. I read aloud from the guidebook, hoping to cheer the General, who mopes across the aisle, hoping to amuse the Sandersons, and to drown out the Duck, who moans about his aching feet. Milton dozes and wakes, dozes and wakes. But I read on.

"Snakes make up half the nation's reptiles," I say.

The Sandersons murmur admiringly.

"Tourism has replaced coffee and banana exports as Costa Rica's primary source of foreign currency."

Milton opens his eyes wide with mock alarm. "Y'mean," he says, "we're the latest cash crop?" He is mugging for the others. Several of them laugh. Milt squeezes my knee. I move it.

When the bus stops in Orosi, Milton leans out the window and jokes with the locals who try to sell us trinkets. They hold up woven baskets, rattle gourds. He asks if they'll wrap it, or if he can eat it here. They do not understand, they miss the joke, but he laughs, so they laugh. The roads are dusty, sun bleached, empty. Sometimes I feel a terrible fear that they lead nowhere.

As we drive on, trucks pass us on their way to San José, huge semis loaded with tree trunks stripped of branches, stacked six high, held in place by heavy chains. Their fronds wave like hands, hair. Manuel identifies the different species: yolillo, palmetto. "Palmitero," he says, speaking of the local woodsmen, "cut out the hearts of palm, a delicacy."

The bark of the guanacaste trees we pass is covered with yellow flowers. It's the same bright yellow of elm leaves in autumn, the yellow of the leaves I saw on the sidewalk outside the hospital the day they took out Milton's heart. I had read up on the procedure. But some things you cannot prepare for. A man cooled to the point of death. His heart stopped. Then they warm him again, bring him back to life. But is it the same man? The same man I married forty-seven years ago? The same man who pressed my hand, looked at me, his eyes wet with fear, before they wheeled him into the operating theater. I watched from above with the medical students. "Amazing," one young man kept saying, tapping his pen on a clipboard.

When we reach the lodge, our group lingers in the air-conditioned bus to discuss the evening's plans. Only the General retires directly to his room. The Duck Man lies supine across two seats, still moaning about his sunburn and his feet, while his wife murmurs consolation.

Manuel stands in the aisle and explains the schedule: there will be a two-hour siesta before dinner and, as this is our last night, dinner will be a traditional banquet followed by a *grupo folclorico*.

"Put on your dancing shoes," Manuel says smiling, clearly pleased to have mastered cliché.

At the mention of shoes, the Duck Man moans. "My feet are killing me," he says. "God damn. Why did you let me get these shoes?" he says to his wife.

"Honey, I wasn't there," she says.

"Of course, you were there. You're always there. I can't get a goddamn minute alone."

The rest of us fall silent. But Manuel presses on: He tells us that the folkloric group is famous in the region, that the bus for the airport tomorrow will arrive early, so it is best if we pack tonight.

"Goddamn corns," the Duck Man says.

There is a rush of questions as we try to pretend we aren't listening to the Duck.

"Do you want a pad?" the Duck Wife asks. "I'll get you a pad, hon."

"Unnnhhh," the Duck Man groans, as if he might die of a corn. "Unnnhhh."

"Oh, honey," she says. "I'll get you a pad, okay? You just stay put." She steps out into the aisle and we stare.

"Excuse me," she says, then hurries off the bus. We linger in the air-conditioned bus, making small talk, making plans for the evening and the next day, loathe to leave the cooled air.

When the Duck Wife returns a few minutes later, she is flushed. Her dress is damp and clings.

"Hang on, honey," she says. "Let me help you." She is sweaty and her dress has slipped off her shoulder, revealing a beige bra strap, a fleshy, freckled, sunburned curve of shoulder. She bends over and takes hold of his shoe in the aisle. Her dress gaps. The sheen of perspiration across her chest makes her skin look swollen, puffy.

We look, then look away.

From the corner of my eye, I see her struggle to peel off the backing from a moleskin pad with her long shellacked nails. The Duck Man grabs it from her, strips the adhesive, and slaps the pad on.

He gives a deep appreciative groan, a guttural moan.

Relieved, we begin to discuss tonight's cocktails, tomorrow's final sunrise walk.

The Duck Man sits up. His feet drop to the floor with a slap. He puts a palm on his wife's plump shoulder and steps out into the aisle. He stands, leaning on her a moment, testing his feet, then he turns to us and winks.

"See you at dinner," he says. Then he gives his wife a firm slap on the rump. "Quack quack."

The Duck Wife giggles and flushes deeper pink.

He follows her off the bus, quacking as he goes.

V.

THE HIGHER LEARNING
AS AN EXPRESSION
OF THE PECUNIARY CULTURE

While Milt naps before dinner, I sit in the library, French doors open to the veranda, looking out onto the garden of this hacienda, and write in a little notebook I've bought for the trip. The library adjoins the dining room and one can relax here in the late afternoons and read or hear lectures on botany and natural history. Large Zapotec rugs in red and black spread across its floor.

I am keeping a list of what we see. Not like the life list that the

Scottish Brewer keeps or the nice couple from Illinois, the Sandersons. I am not a serious birder, as they say. I make lists to keep things straight—lists of what we see and eat—to help me remember these details, to keep things in their place, past separate from present, to keep unbidden memory out.

We have seen the plumes of smoke from Arenal. We have seen the yellow-bibbed toucan with its florid beak. We have seen the Blue Morpho, the iguanas and the basilisk, the world-weary heron, its long neck thrust forward and held, the image of patient, unrewarded hope. We have seen the Nikon and the Nikes and the bared and hairy legs, the sunglasses and embarrassed tippers.

Nine degrees above the equator, summer and winter are not much different and it's easy to lose track of days. The way, in age, one's days begin to blur. One's memories bleed like watercolor, staining the present, leaving me confused. At the kitchen counter, in the house we've shared for forty years in Iowa, I can be making coffee when suddenly I'll be flooded by a memory of Milton in the hospital, confessing as if forgiveness were mine to give.

Since Milt retired ten years ago, we have been taking classes together at the local university. Milt was a law professor before he turned to business, and learning is a thing we love. Last term we took one in Women Writing Life: Woolf, Duras, McCarthy, Nin, Hong Kingston, and Kincaid. The instructor encouraged each of us to keep a journal, and I have kept one ever since. Milt always wants to know what's in mine, to read over my shoulder. Cheating even in autobiography.

This semester we are taking a course in the sociology of the middle class. We are missing three lectures to come here, but it's worth it. In class we have talked about the construction of taste as a means of distinguishing the emergent middle classes in eighteenth-century England. We have discussed the American myth of classlessness. We have debated whether the derision heaped on liberals these days is a proxy for a corporate assault on the middle class. We are the accused. We, the beleaguered, much-mocked, middle classes.

Our professor claims that we have outlived our glory. The disdain heaped on liberals is a stand-in—he maintains—for a general disdain of the bourgeoisie. The League of Women Voters. The PTA. The Rotarians. Members of NPR, PBS, the ACLU—the names alone sound like a punchline to a joke.

But in our defense I say that we are the ones who are neither so poor nor so rich as to be indifferent. We have the leisure to sympathize and mourn, and the good sense to be ashamed of ourselves. My psychotherapist friend maintains that shame differs from guilt. Guilt, she says, is the consequence of a disruption of the social order, while shame results from a disruption of the natural order, the order of things. Guilt can be made right by an apology, a bread-and-butter note, but shame requires penance, the righting of a wrong; it requires sacrifice.

The professor says we are a dying breed, the middle classes. Even in this country that gave rise to Veblen's theory of the leisure class. Even here, we are going the way of the dodo. Our professor has documented our decline. The United States is, he says, coming more and more to resemble a Latin American country, with the mass of underpaid workers serving a small, self-perpetuating oligarchic class. You see it everywhere, in the cuts to public education, the shift to temporary workers, the lay-offs, the assaults on unions and workers' rights. His thesis is essentially that the culture wars are a distraction from the corporate assault on the citizenry. As the middle class is squeezed out by downsizing and globalization, we have no one to hate but ourselves: Jews against blacks, blacks against Koreans, everyone against the feminists and the intellectuals and the young and the homosexuals, a free-for-all of loathing.

Those of us who believed in the Great Society are dying out. I can hardly stand to go to the opera any more. All the heads are gray. And what will happen when we are gone?

Après nous, le déluge. Après nous, la canard.

It is too depressing to contemplate, so I put aside my journal and pull out Veblen, to read for class; reading before dinner has always felt like a great luxury, a private vice.

"What are you reading?"

It is Sanderson. I am startled by a voice outside my head, but glad to see him.

"*The Theory of the Leisure Class.*"

"Veblen. It's been years."

I tell him about our class and how we're missing three lectures to come on this tour.

"It's worth it," Sanderson says.

"Yes," I say, "it is."

Sanderson is on the board of a local museum and symphony, as I recall.

"What's it about?" the Duck Man asks, appearing in the doorway.

"Us," says Sanderson, expansively, and laughs.

I explain that Veblen was a nineteenth-century economist and sociologist who applied Darwin's theories to the American bourgeoisie to examine which traits survived in the modern industrial age.

"He coined the term 'conspicuous consumption,'" I say.

"I've heard of that," the Duck Man says, then he wanders over to look at a vase.

"Your son's a political scientist, isn't he?" Geneen Sanderson asks.

"Our daughter, yes. She's finishing her PhD at Chicago."

The Sandersons nod and smile. They are from Oak Park. Nice people.

"That's a good school," James Sanderson says.

"You must be very proud of her," says Geneen.

"We are."

When Milt arrives, we four go in, leaving the Duck Man to wait for his wife. Often we take a table for four to avoid the Duck Man and the Scottish Brewer, but tonight it is banquet style. There is no helping it. The Duck Man lands across the table. He leans toward me and says, "Gee, you clean up nice."

VI.

PECUNIARY CANONS

OF TASTE

This is not a proper hotel restaurant or night club. We are too far out in the countryside for that. It is an old converted hacienda. I wonder if the smooth dirt floors are mixed with goat blood, the old way. They are dark brown, solid as stone. Flecked with bits of hay. Flecks of straw can be seen in the thick walls where the white wash has chipped away. Each spring they plaster the exterior with micaceous clay against the year's rains, shoring up against the relentless process of erosion. This afternoon, it rained and the dining room smells of dust, moist earth.

The table where we dine is covered with a heavy linen cloth, the former owner's table perhaps. It has the length and general dimensions of the table you see in paintings of the Last Supper.

I take the liberty of rapping discreetly on its surface to test the density of the wood and find the tops are plastic, metal fold-out tables set end to end. They wobble slightly when the large ceramic platters are placed on them, heaped with stewed beef in chili sauce, rice, chicken fried in oil and spices, cooked pumpkin, potato, carrots, onion, with a small glass bottle of oil, limes, peppers, fried plantains, a platter of limp lettuce leaves smelling of chlorine, sliced tomatoes, cilantro, hearts of palm, cold beer.

I am pleased to know the names in Spanish; my accent, Manuel tells me, is quite good. Milton, however, insists on speaking to the waiters in Italian, which he learned in the army during the war, as if any foreign tongue would do. He likes this pretense of ignorance, likes pretending he does not know what he does. But he does, I know. As if he were an innocent abroad, a charming bungler, but I know better.

Marion, the Duck Man's wife, holds an ice cube in her plump fingers, which are pink and swollen as tropical slugs. There is perspiration on her upper lip, glistening above her coral lipstick. She runs the tip of her tongue over her lips, darts at the sweat, glancing around the table to see if anyone has noticed. I pretend not to. When she catches my eye, I do not smile. Earlier, she wedged three fingers into her water glass to extract the ice she holds in her hand. She'd glanced up midway through her procedure and smiled deprecatingly, as she extracted the chunk of ice and palmed it in an effort at discretion. She rubs the ice cube along the sides of her long, plump throat.

"Failure is the family business," the Duck Man said on our first day out, flashing a broad salesman's smile. But he didn't need to tell us. Milt had already heard of him from men he knows in Omaha. The Duck Man has a reputation: Like the smell of a slaughter house, it carries distances. He is known for buying scrap metal that was once the basis of a productive business. He has made a fortune in scrap, in destroying what others built.

At dinner, his wife holds forth on the eating habits of parrots. They have not been able to have children. She keeps one as a pet in Detroit, where they live, and dotes on it.

When Geneen points out that the exotic animal trade is ruthless and often cruel, that parrots are usually tortured during capture, illegally transported in trunks, often dying en route, the Duck Wife looks uncomfortable, then distressed. She tears her napkin, shreds it.

"I never heard that," she said. "Honey, d'you think it's true?"

The Duck Man shrugs and chews.

They talk about the ballroom-dancing lessons they take each week, about their boat; they seem to signify some unhappy truth about the dying century. Perhaps it is unfair to judge them, but they seem to be all that is tawdry and sad and commercial. They confirm my worst fears, that we are slipping in some significant way, that we are losing ground, *après nous, la canard.*

"Failure is the family business," he says proudly, repeating what is clearly his motto.

"Oh, you," the Duck Wife says. "He's always saying that. You can just ignore him if you want."

Would it were true.

They remind me of our neighbors in Iowa, who are in a state of perpetual tan. The Herberts smile hugely at us from across the hedge. They stopped inviting us to dinner years ago, but they continue to wave at us from the driveway as if it were a great and remarkable pleasure to see us again. They always look as if they were about to set sail, when the fact of the matter is they are going up the street to the Olive Garden at the mall for a bite to eat. It is worst in summer. Then they are in tennis whites, baring their aggressively good teeth. Huge, athletic, unreflective people. Even in winter they are tanned. As if they could defy the season we are in.

VII.

THE BELIEF IN GRACE

After dinner, young women collect the plates and ask if we would like coffee. Milton excuses himself and retires to the room, too tired to wait for the folkloric dancers. Since his operation, he is careful not to overexert himself. Procedures that would have killed us twenty years ago now are routine. Like Darwin's creatures on the Galapagos, we are still evolving. The phrases sound so innocuous—bypass, double bypass, triple bypass, quadruple bypass—more like highway construction, like urban planning, than a matter of the human heart.

The young women bring out bouquets of flowers to fill the empty places at the centers of the tables. One of the dancers invites the General out onto the floor. Soon, the others, even Manuel, even the Sandersons, go watch.

I am alone at the table, when I see the bird of paradise and re-member the hospital room. The bouquet by the bed. It was after the operation. We were holding hands and I asked Milt how he was feel-ing and he said, "I had an affair." For a moment I thought he meant that he was having a ball, a fair, a riot, in the hospital, that he was be-ing ironic. "It ended ten years ago," he said.

That was the first I heard about the woman he had almost left me for years ago. The hospital room reminded him; she'd died in one, he said. If she hadn't died, he would have left me. He was sixty at the time; she was forty-four. He'd been involved with her for twenty years, half our marriage. Those are the numbers, the details I cannot get out of my head. Specifics I do not want to know.

The hospital room was private, thank God. There was no one else to hear his confession. An ugly room. Blank as the heart of God, with all the charm of a dentist's office. White linens. White walls. The only color came from the flowers I'd brought. A vase of orange ti-ger lilies, a sunflower, a bird of paradise, a spray of greens, a branch of yellow elm. I don't know why he had to mention it, after all these years, after three mortgages and seven cars and all the loneliness and compromises.

He reached for my hand and I jerked away and knocked over the vase.

"Damn it," I said. "Goddamn it." I crouched to get the pieces. The bird of paradise had snapped its stem. Water seeped across the lino-leum tiles.

"I'll tell you whatever you want to know," he said.

"I didn't want to know."

"I want things to be clean between us."

"How dare you," I said. "How dare you tell me this now."

Later, I will say, we have done worse things to each other, we have survived much worse, but I'm not sure. Is there worse than this: to make of someone's life a lie?

I don't ask for details. I don't want to know. But Milt tells me when he feels like it. What he remembers. Which isn't much. An amnesiac about his own indiscretions.

Leaves. That is what I remember. Funny the things you remember and don't. Yellow elm leaves. The shadows left on the sidewalk after the leaves had been swept away, their silhouettes like shadows of bodies after a nuclear detonation. The aura remains. Even after the body is gone.

I cannot see what all the commotion is about. The others have formed a ragged circle at the far edge of the room, and they stand together on the dance floor, smiling and clapping to the music. I finish my coffee and stand to leave, and then I see them: the ridiculous couple, waltzing. The Duck Man and his wife. The music is all wrong for a waltz, but they are undeterred. The folkloric dancers have cleared the floor, and, like the others, they watch the Duck Man and his wife, moving around the room in one another's arms. I stop and stare. The couple bobs and glides and turns; they bob and glide and turn. And all the while between them there is a gap—between their thighs and hips and chests. And I understand suddenly that this is how waltzing works, this is what gives it grace, what creates the tension and the poignant beauty of the dance. This empty space. What moves us is not the dancers' proximity but the careful distance they maintain: it is amazing that two people can be so close and still not touch.

And despite myself, I have to say it, they are lovely.

When I get back to the room, the moon is up and bright enough to see by. I make my way to the bed, undress, and slip beneath the covers. Lying there, I am filled with what I'd felt that day in the hospital, just after the moment when I knew that Milton wouldn't live, when they started the dead man's heart again: the unexpected relief that I'd been wrong. And I think of the couple on the dance floor, moving around the room in one another's arms and of that empty space between them. You'd never have guessed they had it in them, that couple, so unlike what I had imagined we'd become. And I cannot help but ask myself, Who'd have believed they had beauty in them, who would have guessed they were capable of grace?

THEORY OF
DRAMATIC ACTION

ACT I

In the last three months, your cat has died, your car has died, your marriage ended. In the last three months, you have lost ten pounds, a job, a city, a state. Now as you drive a U-Haul across the vast stretch-marked belly of the continent, on your way from Colorado to start film school in Ohio, you try to locate a feeling to go with these events. But your life feels like a silent movie, the strange weight of absence heavy in the air around you. What comes instead of grief is blankness, the late-night-TV fuzz of the brain, as if you had simply tuned in at an inopportune moment and must now wait out the morning when regular programming will resume. You narrate your way across the country, imagining yourself the heroine of some B-grade movie or a road-trip flick. *Faster, Faster, Pussycat, Kill, Kill,* you say as you floor it to pass a semi on your left. You think of yourself in the second person, in the present always tense.

You want to be a screenwriter, maybe work in Hollywood. You

admire the films of Billy Wilder and Preston Sturges, Bergman and Godard, and you imagine that your appreciation for the work of others qualifies you for something, mistaking taste for chops. You flatter yourself that you have an eye. An eye for an eye. You can spot talent, which maybe means you have some.

But as you drive toward the storm-strained horizon of Nebraska, you wonder if all you really want is a more dramatic life. Something other than this ordinary pain you've felt for months, that constant dull ache, like a pulled muscle in the heart.

Your first quarter in graduate school, sign up for Screenwriting, Eng 625. The teacher will be a redhead, tall and gaunt, she will be fashionable, she will be glam, she will be pretty and talk fast. She will have dated many of the new directors you admire. She will have worked in what she calls "The Industry" for years. When you mention Hollywood, she will stop you. "No one calls it Hollywood," she says. "Don't ever call it that. And never call a secretary a secretary, they are Executive Assistants. Next month they will be Agents. They are your Best Friend. Without them, no one will ever read your script." She is twenty-eight, an age at which one speaks in capital letters, with certitude. (You are thirty now and were never twenty-eight. You were never twenty-nine. You were never sure.) Take notes on everything she says.

Your first day you will learn about the structure of dramatic action, or what your instructor calls the Three Acts. When you first step in the door, however, it will appear you are going to learn about New Math. On the board is written a sequence of numbers that do not appear to add up. Note them down anyway, in case you need them later.

6	17	10	8	4	3	2	1	9
6	13	10	8	5	7	4	9	2
6	19	2	7	4	5	10	8	3

What makes for dramatic action, your instructor tells the class, is a powerful need meeting an equally powerful obstacle. That, she says, is drama. Dutifully copy down into your notebook the diagram of dramatic action she scrawls across the chalkboard. It will have a Hook, a Plot Twist (I), a False Resolution, a Plot Twist (II), a Climax, a Denouement. Act I, Act II, Act III.

As you write down the heading False Resolution, you think of the life you have left behind, the life you shared with your now ex-lover. The house you built together in the mountains outside Boulder, the vows you made, the hopes you had, your resolution to see this relationship through, to have kids, a steady salary, a life you think now you could not possibly have led. Still, you long for it sometimes. For love. Stability. For resolution in the midst of these irresolute days.

Domesticity is something that you crave from time to time, like McDonald's, but it does not suit you. Does not go down well. Like the McDonald's you ate on your way to class, it makes your throat dry, you find it hard to swallow, which is why you left your ex after four years together, after building a house, left a woman you loved but could not live with. The ordinariness of your life together depressed you, the laundry bin domesticity of it, the day-in-day-out canned corn and peas kind of love you shared. You found yourself wondering if this was all there is; you found yourself looking for options like stocks.

You are not without options. You are a lesbian, but men mistake you all the time, and lately you mistake yourself. Lately you consider dating men; partly for the shock value, partly because you are tired; partly because men are like turtles, they need less attention than a woman requires, demand less; partly because you are tired of being told that you are "just like a man, you cannot commit," tired of hearing this from women you are committed to.

You consider dating a man as you might consider buying another car. You consider your options: models, design, year of manufacture, dents and damage and mileage, comfort of the ride. It seems a practical matter now. Cars and marriage and love. These vehicles that move us through our lives, from the continent of youth into what seems to you now the compromised and embattled territory of middle age.

As you drive home from class, read the signs you pass as if you were practiced in the ancient art of divination. YIELD. STOP. MERGE. DO NOT ENTER. ONE WAY. WRONG WAY. BIG BEAR. TARGET. DIVORCE $99. Think: If the price is right, people will buy anything.

Begin to carry a little notebook with you everywhere you go. Take to heart all signs. The end of the century is here and you know that it is always at the end that people look for signs, the way your lover began to search your dresser drawers, check your throat for marks of sucking while she thought you slept, this before you left her. Signs, you believe, are everywhere. Waiting for us to notice. We're just not looking, not seeing what is there, as your lover looked, all those years, in her fantastic jealousy for proof of certain infidelity, and so missed seeing that you were faithful all along, in love with only her.

Your ex was convinced that you were in love with your friend Erin, to whom (you often said) all the B-words apply: Beautiful, Brilliant, Buxom (Bitch, your ex often said). The two of you met in an art history class in college, and though you rarely meet you talk a lot by phone.

Ten years ago, Erin was a Nebraska beauty queen; now she is a dominatrix in New York. For awhile she was a temp, but sex, she says, pays better and is less of a drain. "Besides," she has told you, "my clients now are way more polite. Submissives have the best manners." By day, she is a painter. Her current work features portraits of vegetables, massive canvases featuring zucchini, pumpkins, Brussels sprouts rising out of loamy fields, alive with insects, portraits of what she calls the unregarded vegetable realm. She reviles the sanitized towers of produce in D'Agostino's, those waxed and dewy stacks. She terms them "veg porn." Artificial, airbrushed, all gloss. "Real vegetables," she insists, "are dirty. Everything real is." New York is a dramatic city and you think sometimes of living there with Erin. There among the dirty vegetables. A real and dramatic life.

In your second week in graduate school, you will discover that you need an elective. You have always wanted to learn ancient Greek, the language that was the source of drama. Because you sign up late, you will need special permission from the instructor. When you go to his office, he will not be not there. Instead he has tacked a note to his door, in what you take to be ancient Greek. He probably thinks this is witty. You do not. This is Ohio. This is the year 2000. Who in the hell reads ancient Greek?

Show up for his class. Sit in the back. The professor is young and handsome. Watch the way his black hair curls over his brow in rings. The hook of his nose. His dark eyes. You have heard he is unorthodox. Greek Unorthodox, you think. Most first-year Greek commences with rote exercises, memorization, but he insists on translating poetry, though none of you know the words. He says you must learn a language through the voices of those who speak it best. Since no one speaks ancient Greek anymore, you read dead people. Today it is Sappho on the subject of beauty. He reads a fragment of her poem, in which some say that ships are beautiful, others say men in battle are, to which Sappho replies, "I say, what you love, is."

The professor, saying this, inadvertently catches your eye. After class you talk. He says you're welcome to join the class. He'd be delighted, he says, smilingly, to have you.

ACT II

Your screenwriting instructor does not like to use the terms antagonist, protagonist, because, she says, she is no longer sure what they mean. The Good Guy, the Bad Guy. She is not sure who is who.

"I used to think there was a 'Good Guy' and a 'Bad Guy,'" she says, making little quotation marks with her fingers in the air. Now she is not so sure. She has read Egri's *Art of Dramatic Writing* in which he claims that Iago is the protagonist in *Othello* because he is the guy who makes stuff happen. He drives the action. "Now," she says, "I just avoid the terms. I say Main Character because anyone can pick That Person out." That person is the person who has a need that may or may not be met. A story, your instructor scrawls across the board, quoting Ken Kesey, is about someone who needs something and what he/she is willing to go through to get it.

You wonder what it is you need now, whether drama is really the ticket. You wonder what you are willing to do, to go through, for a more dramatic life.

As you cross the campus green on your way home, hear your name called out. Look up and see a hand wave. Squint to see who it is, jogging toward you, here where you know no one.

When the professor of Greek reaches you, he is out of breath. He bends over bracing his hands on his thighs; he hangs out his tongue in mock exhaustion like a dog. He tilts his face up toward yours, smiling. His face sparkling a little with sweat.

"Sara, right?" he says, remembering your name.

"Right," you say. His polo shirt gaps away from his chest a little and you see the tangle of black hairs below his clavicle, a few are silver.

"How is it going?" he says, straightening up. He speaks with the precise enunciation of American slang that foreign speakers have.

You tell him Akron reminds you of Venice.

"Really," he says, arching a single lovely eyebrow.

"It reeks of raw sewage," you say.

He has a nice laugh.

"You're not from here," he says. "I didn't think so. Students like you never are."

You wonder what students like you are, but do not ask. Instead you let him ask the questions as together you walk across the quad. He asks how you're finding class, if you're finding your way around. He asks if your boyfriend moved here with you. You know full well what he is asking.

"My girlfriend and I broke up last month," you say, emphasizing girl over friend.

"That's tough," he says, without missing a beat.

You appreciate his equanimity and you relax a little. You tell him, a little wistfully, that in the last two months, your cat has died, your car has died, your marriage ended.

"Sorry," he says, "about the cat."

You appreciate that he does not pity you, that he knows what to take seriously, what not. You feel you could learn a lot from him.

In front of the building where his office is, you stop, his hand on the door handle. People stream out from the doors on either side; you are blocking traffic, but he seems unconcerned.

"Will you be lonely here?" he asks.

"I don't know," you say, and know that this is true. "Is it easy to meet women in Ohio?" You feel a need to remind him that you're a dyke; you feel the need to remind yourself.

He doesn't say whether it is or isn't. He says only, "Sappho was a great poet."

You will learn a lot of things in the coming weeks.

You will learn that the word for "home" shares a root in ancient Greek with the word for "cemetery." Do not be surprised by this. Domesticity, you already suspect, is a dead end.

You will learn that you have no facility at all with ancient Greek. You will learn that French, which you studied in high school for four years, is a snap compared with Greek. Practical as math. What good is a language no one speaks anymore? What good are words if not to communicate with the living? French, you think now, prepared you for the world; it prepared you to order in nice restaurants. So what if the only words you recalled from year to year were *confiture* and *maintenant*, an all purpose *je voudrais, s'il vous plaît?* You will remember tenses, nostalgically. It was while you were studying French that you first realized tense was not just a response to the question, How are you feeling today? but a choice. You developed a special fondness for the future perfect. It sounded so promising then. Your future perfect.

You can still say, *Je ne trouve pas mon chapeau,* and feel yourself linked by language to greatness: Godard, Truffaut, Renoir. Like them you can say: *Robert est là-bas, Où est la piscine?*

Despite your dismal performance in Greek, the prof is encouraging. In the campus cafeteria, when you pass his table, he invites you to join him. He pulls out a chair, clears aside the papers he is reading. He says it's not often that he has bright and beautiful students in class.

"When I do," he says, "I like to take advantage of them."

"Just how literally do you mean that," you ask, taking a seat.

He looks confused for a moment, then he laughs. "You're witty," he says. "I like that."

He doesn't answer your question and you don't ask again.

Instead you talk about the classes you're taking, the director Theo Angelopoulos, whom his family knows. He tells you that he once considered becoming an actor. He has the voice for it, the face, you think. He knows a surprising amount about film. You like the same directors and talk Ts: admiring Tarkovsky, reviling Tarantino. Talking to him, you laugh, and you laugh, and make yourself late for screenwriting.

As you gather up your stuff to go, he suggests you have a drink sometime.

"Sure," you say. "Delighted." And you are, by him.

Ignore his wedding ring.

At night, studying the Greek alphabet, find yourself thinking about the prof. You see his brown face, hear the lovely lilting cadence of his voice. Call friends in faraway places and tell them about your crush, hoping that they will talk you out of it. Tell them that you are afraid that you may be a closet heterosexual. "How," you ask, "will I explain this to my parents?" They laugh and tell you not to worry, it is only hormones, it will pass. "Only hormones?" you ask. "Wars have been declared over hormones." "It's probably the accent," they say. "It's probably the tan." "Wait till winter," they say. "He'll look like mold, a mushroom, when he loses that tan." In a fit of misguided sympathy, a few encourage you in your ardor. They tell you about marriages they've successfully broken up; they tell you that love conquers all. "Yeah," you say, "but what does adultery conquer?"

"Ah, adultery," one friend quips, "that stage between adolescence and senility."

They make an affair with a married man sound like an Armani suit—never out of style.

Still, you will have your doubts and qualms; still you side with the wives and with the moms, women you don't ever want to be. You wonder, idly, if the appeal of the love triangle can be traced back to the Trinity or if it is more archaic, more biological than that, if it has been there from the start, from the moment we entered the world: a mother, a father, a child.

Your first term, you are lonely and spend a lot of time on the phone talking to people in other area codes. You think of these distances that stand between you and the people you love as inconvenient, not a matter of choice. It seems to you a trick of fate, a sleight of hand, a bad joke, bad luck, an unfortunate coincidence that everyone you love lives at least two states away in any given direction. You share no common boundaries or borders. You love these people from a distance, which is how you prefer to love, though you do not realize that yet.

Call your good friend Erin and invite her for a visit, hoping secretly for sex. Hoping to take your mind off him. Meet her at the airport bearing a bouquet of yellow roses when she arrives on a Wednesday before a long weekend. She is unmistakable in the airport crowd: tall and leggy and slender, dressed in leather, a six-foot Amazon with short black hair and bright green eyes.

Take her to a Chinese restaurant straight away to dine. Stuff your mouths with mussels in black bean sauce, broccoli in garlic, moo shu pork. Smile and talk through stringy meat and sauce. She tells you, over dinner, about her job clerking in a queer bookstore in the Village, a part-time thing she's doing once a week to help out a friend who's a manager there. She regales you with tales from the weird world of retail. Her coworkers include a radical faerie and a guy with a bone through his nose and green hair. "It is always the truly frightening looking ones who are the gentlest," she insists. "The more punctures, the sweeter the personality."

Your ex was convinced you were in love with Erin; now, as you watch her pretty mouth, as you laugh and chew, now wonder if you are. Wonder—as you watch her crack the skull of a fortune cookie and read smiling its message meant only for her—wonder if this buzz you feel is desire, or love, or MSG. BEWARE WHAT YOU HOPE FOR, your fortune says.

From across the table, Erin takes your hand and holds it a moment, before turning it palm up. She stares into your palm like it's a book.

"You will live long," she says, "and have many lovers."

"Are you sure it doesn't say, 'I'll love long and have many livers?'"

"I'm sure," she says, releasing your hand and a smile. "Trust me on this."

Outside, on the street, she takes your arm as you walk home. She tells you casually that she's been attracted to you for years, that your ex was an idiot to have ever let you go. She tells you that she'd love to fuck you sometime, when you're ready, if you ever are.

The following day, when you get home from class, Erin is clad in a kimono that clings deliciously to her. She smiles up at you from the couch where she is stretched out with a book. A Bossa Nova plays on the boom box she has brought. She has lit candles, broken open a bottle of red wine. She holds out her glass for you to drink.

For awhile, you sit on the futon and talk, then she opens a canvas satchel beside the couch and pulls out the tricks of her trade. She has brought a leather harness, sheep-skin-lined cuffs, straps and metal-studded collars, a lavender dildo, a whip, and lube. You feel like a sexual hick.

She asks, cheerfully, if you're ready to fuck. She says this as others might ask if you'd like to take a walk.

You are not, as a general rule, into leather, but who are you to decline? She is beautiful and you want her to have a nice time. She has come all the way from Brooklyn. She is your guest. She is your friend. She is a professional. You do not want to be impolite (subs are always polite). So you play it cool. You play it so cool as to appear cold, indifferent to her and this. You coolly watch her strip off her kimono and cinch over her lovely hips a leather harness and a big dildo. You coolly let her strap you to the futon frame. When she asks if she can fuck you, say, politely, coolly, "Sure." Though you'd rather have her hand inside you, her round breasts against your chest, mouth to mouth, cheek to cheek, you're embarrassed by such preferences, feel old-fashioned craving contact, ashamed to discover suddenly that what you really want is simple human touch.

In the face of disappointment, become clinical. In the absence of love, opt for autopsy. Though you know better, imagine talk will help. Talk about why your sex was not great. Wonder aloud if friends make poor lovers. For awhile, Erin will listen to you, her lovely body warm against your side, her limbs entwined in yours as you two lie stretched out across the futon. Then, abruptly, she will say, "I can't take this. I'm going to take a bath."

Join her. In the bath, she will cry. She will say, "You are untender," that having sex with you is like watching a Hal Hartley film. (Feel, fleetingly, complimented by the comparison to Hartley, who is your fave, though you know she doesn't mean this as a compliment.) In Hartley's films, she says, everyone is always talking about love like it's an idea rather than a feeling that they feel. She means you are unfeeling. She means you are cold. An idea with legs. A talking head.

Sit quietly in the tub and let her words pummel you like a rough massage. She waits for you to say something, but you don't know what to say. You have, at last, a more dramatic life but you do not know your lines; you failed to memorize this part, cannot ad lib. She waits and waits and then she gives up waiting. Watch her rise from the water like Botticelli's Venus, watch her dry her long and beautiful body with a towel, watch her open the door, step out into the hall. Hear her pack, hear her call a cab. Sit quietly while the water grows cold around you, like a moat. Watch your toes wrinkle, your fingertips. Even your palms will wrinkle, their lines at last unreadable. Your future, in your hands, inscrutable now.

For your midterm in screenwriting, you have to outline the dramatic arc of your story and then read this aloud to your classmates so they can criticize you to your face. This, you imagine, is as close as people of your generation will ever come to EST. To the encounter groups that defined the sixties. No wonder people took so many drugs back then. You wish, as you enter class, that you'd had the foresight to get stoned.

The guy next to you is shaking ever so slightly as he reads his work aloud. You feel a blush rise along your neck. You are next. The instructor stops him midsentence, says, "Wait. That won't work. You can't just have a character 'Realize Something.'" She makes her fingers into little quotes, scratches the air. "You can't just say, 'And then she realized . . .' This is the year 2000. People don't *have* epiphanies anymore; they have problems. What they do about those problems, how they confront and try to overcome them, is dramatic action."

"Events," your instructor tells the class, "arise from character. Things simply happening to a character do not interest us. We want cause. We want effect." We want, in effect, people to get what is coming to them. Old Testament to the core. An eye for an eye.

Wonder if you are getting what is coming to you. Wonder if the thrill you still feel in the presence of your Greek professor is just a plot twist. Wonder if recent events in your life arise from your character or if they are simply happening to you, like the gentle radiation that rains down from the universe, infiltrating the atmosphere, entering your body from the stars on high. Just passing through.

Be grateful that your midterm in Greek will be multiple choice.

Realize, too late, that it is not and that you have no answers.

Drive to a nearby mall to buy stuff to fill the empty places in your apartment. Buy thick towels and fluffy pillows and bubble bath and comforters. Trawl the aisles in search of missing things, all the things you need and do not have. It will occur to you that you are looking for tenderness in all the wrong places. In the bath aisle at Target, at the meat counter of your local grocery store, among the packaged

beef and lamb. In mangoes, plums, the soles of shoes. Your relationships, meanwhile, are tough as shoe leather, oddly unenduring.

Lie awake in bed at night and listen to the unfamiliar creaks and
cars, the helicopters that patrol your neighborhood, flashing search
lights in your window like a peeping Tom.

Wait for the days to pass, to drop away like the acorns that fall
from the trees as you walk to campus, nuts that sometimes hit you as
you pass beneath the oaks, making you wonder if squirrels have it in
for you.

Miss her.

The professor of Greek ends the term with a sex joke. He says, on the
last day of class, "It was good for me, was it good for you?"

Everyone else laughs.

You don't. You are failing Greek. Ever since Erin's visit your mind
has gone on the blink.

After class, your professor asks if you'd like to have that drink.
"You seem to be having trouble," he says. "I'd like to help if I can."

You tell him you'll stop by for office hours.

He says he'd be happy to be of service.

You know how this will end. This, your screenwriting instructor
has told you, makes for bad drama, bad art, knowing the end before
it's over. You want to tell her it makes for a lousy love affair as well,
which—like art—should be an exploration of your material. If you
know how it will turn out from the beginning, you're probably not
going to be honest as you proceed, she says. You know she is right
about this.

As you prepare for your final in screenwriting, come across the numbers you took down from the board. Try, for a moment, to discern a
pattern. As a child, you loved math, raced ahead in class, tore through
each book of equations, delighted by their beautiful symmetry, their

neat and predictable solutions. Your sister had run away from home. Your brother, in a fit of suburban Buddhism, was bowing to bushes, ruining any hope you ever had of popularity. Your parents, when they spoke at all, fought. Numbers possessed a lovely order.

In college, you studied economics, but you loathed the graphs of supply and demand, the theory of marginal utility with its disturbingly accurate claim that availability diminishes desire and the pleasure one takes in its satisfaction. So you dropped econ and took up film, graduating with a degree in cinema studies, which you realized too late qualifies you for just three things: graduate school, work in video stores, and to feel an unsociable contempt for movies your friends all like.

Now, looking at the quilt of numbers on the page before you, feel nostalgic for the order they present. The hope of order. The rumor of it. Numbers are such a lie. They always promise more than they can deliver, a world in which things add up, in which one plus one equals two, in which there is a predictable sequence, the way infatuation is supposed to lead to romance to vows, maybe kids. But it does not happen this way, you find. In the world, in love. Awkward threes are everywhere: a couple and their best friend; a professor, his wife, and a student.

Looking at these numbers, you think of all the things in your life that do not add up; your life is a set of random variables, figures out of sequence, waiting for an equation to give them shape and purpose, a point, a meaningful relationship to one another, a connection. The plus sign, the minus, the equal, multiplication, division (always long and always painful) are really marks of connection and relationship, and it occurs to you that without these symbols to link 6 to 17 to 10 to 8 to 4, there is no meaning here, nothing worth jotting down: the relationship is all. All or nothing.

ACT III

In the climax, which should come in Act III, Good and Evil meet. Ultimate right and ultimate wrong. You will think of these as Mrs. Right and Mr. Wrong.

In your life, these never meet. Right and Wrong. The categories do not even apply. Instead, you have hard and soft. Tender and untender are the operative terms. Your life, you realize, is undramatic. Painful, without coming to a point. There is no climax except on futons. And, just maybe, with the professor of Greek, on a desk after hours on a Thursday night. You agreed to come for office hours, but he requested you come at the end of the day instead, for a tutorial, a one-on-one.

On the way out the door to meet him, you get a call from Erin, whom you have not spoken to in weeks. When you hear her voice on your machine, pick up. She says she was just calling to say hi, see how you are. She tells you more about the bookstore where she works. "It has a section on polyamory," she says. "Couples come in in threes." Like some haywire Noah's ark. She laughs and then she cries, and when you ask her why she tells you that she's just come in from walking in the park where she felt lonely. Listening to her you feel lonely too, the blue fuzz in your brain giving way to some other feeling, the shape of longing.

She tells you how she walks each afternoon in Prospect Park and feels lonely, wanting so much to have someone to love.

"I never knew you wanted that," you say. "I thought you just wanted to fuck."

"No," she says, her voice sad. "I wanted you."

"I have to go," you say, though you don't want to. "I have an appointment, with a prof."

"At this hour?"

"He's unorthodox," you say. "Greek Unorthodox."

She doesn't laugh. She says, "Call me sometime. I mean, if you want to. I mean, I don't know what I mean." Then she hangs up.

As you walk to campus, acorns pelting you like hail, realize that you are less afraid of desire's attendant domesticity, than of losing what you love, which is your friend. Wonder if perhaps you can arrange something together, some love affair that does not involve a U-Haul, Hers and Hers towels. Think that perhaps the inherited forms of love need not apply to the two of you, as the structure of dramatic action fails to fit your life, that perhaps together you can invent some other form of love, something tender and spacious at one time, a love large as that Colorado sky you left behind, with its fulsome blue, its poignant promising emptiness that hangs like a wedding veil, stretches even now like a chuppah, over your ex's bared and lovely head.

The prof is waiting for you in his office, reclining in his wooden swivel chair. Handsome and at ease, he smiles when you arrive and waves you gently in. Before him on the desk, a book is open. He offers you a chair, and then a drink. He pulls open a drawer of his file cabinet which contains a tiny well-stocked bar: bourbon, scotch, port, Armagnac, vodka. He seems amused by your shock. Accept a glass of port. Cough as it goes down, hot and smoky as a cigar.

Begin by translating from the Greek. The first words of a poem. You're at a loss, so he helps you with the terms you've not yet mastered, which is all of them. His hand gently falls over yours as you follow the words on the page. When his palm moves to your shoulder, then your cheek, you're not surprised. His touch is practiced. You are clearly not the first. He lifts you gently from your chair into an embrace, and as you slip your ass onto the desk, you knock over a framed photo of his wife. You like the bourbon-inflected taste of his mouth. You like his ease, his unembarrassed desire. You like him. But you do not want to fuck. You are not interested in drama anymore.

You don't want to cheat on his wife; you've cheated enough already, cheated yourself, your friend, your ex by thinking that love was ordinary, that domesticity equals death. You realize suddenly that the bonds of love—restrictive as they seem—are like celluloid and silver, a medium necessary to give shape to light, making possible the beautiful image on that big screen in the dark.

It is a bad time to realize this. It is socially awkward, this little epiphany that people, according to your screenwriting instructor, are not supposed to have anymore. Try to bow gracefully out. Knowing there is no hope of that. Knowing that you have come too far for grace. Opt for jokes instead. Say, Sleeping with your professor you worry your performance will be graded; say, You hope that this material will not show up on the final exam; say, I am not joking, when you tell him to take his hands off you or you'll scream. He tells you to grow up. You think you have. Perhaps a tiny bit, a mere increment, just now.

Walk home alone under street lamps, the sidewalk spattered with the shadows of leaves, the sky above you black but full of promise. Take comfort in the knowledge that once upon a time people charted their course by nothing more than this, by these faint but still discernible stars.

On an impulse that night, fly to Erin. First, by commuter jet to Chicago, then by proper plane. There will be stopovers. No delays. You will make all the necessary connections. There will be people to direct you to your gate. You will not need to read the signs. You will be full of hope, will take it on faith that she will be there, waiting for you, with open arms, believing briefly, fervently, though you know it only happens in the movies, that yours will be a Happy Ending.

THE FLANNERY O'CONNOR AWARD
FOR SHORT FICTION